# THE MALTESE ORPHANS

Paul Vincent Lee

**The Maltese Orphans**

First published in Great Britain by Weeryan Ltd
2014

Printed and bound in Great Britain by Lightning Source UK.

Visit: www.paulvincentlee.com
Paul Vincent Lee asserts the moral right to be identified as the author of this work.

A catalogue record for this book is available from the British Library.
ISBN: 978-0-9572399-2-0

*For Ann Marie: For being there, when no-one else cared; and for helping me kennel the Black Dogs.*

# ACKNOWLEDGMENTS

As usual, I don't know either where to start, or where to finish, when it comes to acknowledging all the people who have helped in getting this book "out there."

My family: I know for a fact that without them I would not have survived the darkness. Thank you all. I would, however, like to give a special mention to my son, Paul. He was 21 this year, and I missed his birthday by being away researching / writing this book. Sometimes the price of being a writer is high.

\*\*\*

Practical Mob:

Superintendant Antonella Grech: for her insights into the workings of the Pulizija, and life on Malta.

Shane Watts – photographer par excellence at shanepwatts.com: for supplying the photos for the book cover and my website.

Jes Darmanin from Storm Design: for website development and Social Media work.

My editor......Susan Gottfried......for tireless and informative editing work

My cover designer: Jeanine Henning......what can I say.....fantastic.

My layout and formatting guru......Katie Salidas.......again, what can I say.

\*\*\*

Personal Mob:

Kevin Spiteri, top man at EC Language School in St Julians.....for giving me work teaching English.....even though I don't speak it ....not the inspiration for Thea though!

Madeline Hobbs, for helping a lost Scotsman settle-in initially, on Malta and Gozo, and for driving me around as required without complaint! Thanks, Maddie.......you never did collect your cup.

Marie Grech for being a great landlady – I love this house, Marie!

All the staff of The Crows Nest Bar, St Julians: Joe, Anna and Marisol: especially for putting up with the ever increasing volume; the longer the evening goes on, of my opinionated ranting and rav-ings,.....and, as I stole the: "it started with a Cisk" line for the book from Crow's Nest devotee, Iain Gardner....I must thank him....as well as Hot Chocolate.

The people of Gozo: what a beautiful island you have let me share with you. Thank you.

***

Finally, the harrowing passages in this story surrounding The Home, Tuan and the despicable goings-on there, are not, unfortunately, fiction. There are numerous sources you can look at to verify the story, but my advice would be not to. Tragic does not begin to describe it.

If you would like to contribute to the fund that has been set up to raise money for a permanent memorial on the site: please contact – catherinecorless@hotmail.com

Thank you.

# EARLIER TIMES

Scotland 1964

She was supposed to be her friend forever. But on this day, this stinky winky, smelly welly day, she was not her friend. She would never be her friend again. She decided she even liked some boys more than she liked her.

How could she say that her doll was prettier than hers? Anyone could see that her doll had the prettiest dress, and the shiniest shoes, and a diamond necklace, and…

*Who cares about her and her rubbish doll now, anyway? No one, that's who. Serves her right for being a liar. Mum says no one likes a liar. No one will ever care about her again. Serves her right for getting on Dad's bus, even though she saw me on the bus. She knew it was my turn for a ride and special game. Serves her right for ignoring me. Serves her right for sitting at the front of the bus when we always, always sit at the back. On the long seat. Sometimes, we even lie down on them. Sometimes playing Dad's special game. Sometimes not. She knew it was my turn. Serves her right.*

\*\*\*

Greek Islands 1986

Someone was watching the blond-haired boy playing on the sand. They had watched him every day for a week. On the Tuesday, they had smiled at the boy, and the boy had waved. His mother lay sleeping on a blue and white striped towel a few feet away. On the Wednesday, they had said hello to the boy. On the Thursday, they had eaten Magnums together as they sat and chatted about the best WWF fighters on TV, the boy's mother by now concentrating fully on an all-over tan. On the Friday, they agreed about how horrible vegetables were.

On the Saturday, the boy was gone. His mother contacted the police four hours later. The boy was never seen again.

\*\*\*

Malta 1994

*Pulizija* Constable Thea Spiteri stood in a corner. The sandstone walls of the room were cold and damp. The room was completely bare of any trappings, other than a wooden table and three wooden chairs.

On one side of the table sat a young boy, beside him a priest sent by the Vatican "to oversee proceedings."

On the other side of the table sat Spiteri's superior officer, Inspector Muscat. Spiteri had only been in the *Pulizija* for three months. She had been brought along as reassurance for the child. The boy, with tears in his eyes, had just finished recounting what he knew of the games his friend, Father Ignacio Thomas, liked to play with some of the boys in his care.

Muscat looked at the Pope's envoy. 'Where is this priest now?'

'The church will deal with this matter in its own way, Inspector. As you know, priests cannot be charged with any crime in Malta. That is the law.'

'A five-year-old child has been abducted, probably killed... Surely...'

'And the perpetrator will be punished. You have my word, Inspector.'

Spiteri and Muscat left the orphanage soon after. Spiteri never heard the case mentioned again.

\*\*\*

Kelb boy was sure his eyes were open, but he couldn't see anything. The dirt and mud that was making him choke was also stinging his eyes, and the smell of the dirt reminded him of the toilets he shared with the other boys in hell. He wondered for a moment if that was where he now was: Hell. He knew he had been bad. He didn't understand what it was he had done to be bad, only that he was. Kelb boy felt air on one side of his face. His arms were stuck by his side in the dirt, but his feet were resting on something hard. Kelb boy pushed down as hard as he could. His face was being cut by the rubble scraping his face and one of his shoes came off but a few seconds later, Kelb boy's head pushed through the earth. He could see.

\*\*\*

Scotland 1994

May Hooper was sad her dad was dead. She really was. But he was, and in truth, he hadn't been a good father anyway. She knew that now. Being a bus driver and an alcoholic had always meant that there was little spare money in the house. May Hooper was determined to live a more bountiful life. Her dad could help her now, more than when he was alive. Her mother had died five years previously *so no one will be hurt*. It was the '90s; childhood trauma was *In*. Z List celebrities queuing up to tell their sordid tales of abuse, true or not, desperate for media coverage. May Hooper was in the right place at the right time. And there were Government Grants aplenty to plunder and her vocation to fulfill.

# CHAPTER 1

Winter 2013 Spain

As places for dying go, Malta seemed as good a place as any. Matt Healy looked through the haze of his life at the tiny dot on the map. It had been ringed by a beer stain from one of the many bottles of Estrella he had consumed the night before with Jim Frame, his once-upon-a-time work colleague from the now-defunct Strathclyde Police.

Healy was slumped at the kitchen table in the small pension in Lloret de Mar that he now called home. He had smiled to himself when he first heard his flat referred to as a pension. *True, that's what I am. A pensioner. Someone who lives on, and now in, a pension. God bless Strathclyde Police.* He and Frame weren't really friends, more a case of two guys with an unbreakable bond of depression. Healy vaguely recalled their conversation from the previous night before Frame collapsed on the couch.

'There's only one thing you need to know about Lloret de Mar, Jim.'

'What's that?'

'It's a shit hole.'

'Why do you live here then?'

'I'm shit.'

Healy had known for a while that if he didn't change his life, he was a dead man. He also knew he had to leave Spain. He couldn't stay where he was and stay alive at the same time. He stared again at the map. 'Malta it is, then.'

Even for Matt Healy and Jim Frame, the copious amounts of alcohol consumed over the previous few days were beginning to take their toll, and with Frame due to fly back the next day, they had agreed to moderate their intake for the day and even to cheat: they would go for a proper meal as well.

'What do you know about Malta, Jim?'

'Not a lot, why?'

'I'm moving there.'

'What, when?'

'Soon as.'

'Why?'

'I'll die if I stay here, that's why.'

'What, and you'll live forever if you move to Malta?'

'No, but I might live for a day, really live, and that's got to be better than this.'

The relatively little Healy had to drink that day made no difference to his nightly torment. Healy didn't think of them as dreams. Dreams were jumbled, incoherent, unreal. These were memories: real, painful and unceasing. *Mother, never satisfied, often critical. No father to speak of, but a presence nevertheless. Years of dealing with the dregs of Glasgow. But, most of all, Dornan, Susan Dornan. Friend, colleague, boss, lover, bitch, corpse. Why Susan, why? Always, why?*

The following morning, Healy poured Jim Frame into a taxi bound for Barcelona airport, as he didn't trust Frame's ability to get on the right bus from Lloret's busy bus terminal. He then walked to the little local bodega he had discovered on first moving into his pension, and which he had adopted as his local. No words were exchanged initially as Healy sat on his stool, positioned near the entrance so he could get some breeze, as Pedro's charms did not stretch to air conditioning. Pedro himself placed a black coffee and a Cutty Sark whisky on the bar and went back to reading the sports pages of *El Periodico*. Healy concentrated hard on the offerings. After a few minutes, his shaking hand reached for the coffee. He drank it slowly, smarting slightly at its bitterness.

'Pedro.'

'Si, Senor Matt.'

'*Un café con leche, por favour.*'

'*Que?*'

'A white coffee, Pedro. A white coffee. My Spanish is shit I know, but not that shit.'

'No, no Senior Matt, it's just… another Cutty Sark though… yes?'

' No Pedro, no Cutty Sark, not ever. I don't drink anymore.'

'*Que?*'

'Will you stop saying *que* all the time, Pedro? You sound like the guy from Fawlty Towers, look a bit like him too, now I come to think of it. You heard me okay. From now on, I do not drink alcohol. Comprende?'

'*Que?*'

'Oh very funny, Pedro.'

'But why, Senor Matt?'

'Because, Pedro, up until today, I have been an arsehole, but no more. I'm going to sell the pension and move to a new life.'

'In Scotland?'

Healy pondered the question although he already knew the answer. He loved Scotland in a way but knew he couldn't go back. He kept up to date with the football scores—gloating always good for the soul—and listened to Lori McTear on his iPad for pleasure, but that was it.

'No Pedro, in Malta. Being in Spain has shown me I like the sun, the Mediterranean lifestyle, the whole bit.'

'Why not just stay here then?'

'I can't. Too many demons. I need to start again.'

'How much do you want for the pension? Don't forget, the Spanish property market is terrible, Senor Matt. It might take you a very long time to sell it.'

'Would you be interested in it?'

'Depends, Senor Matt. I am not a rich man.'

'My heart bleeds for you, Pedro. How much?'

'Maybe…. thirty-thousand euro?'

'Scottish *que*.'

'*Que?*

'Scottish *que*; it means fuck off.'

\*\*\*

Winter 2013 Malta

The now-Inspector Thea Spiteri of the Maltese *Pulizija*, CID branch, had just finished playing a vital part in the investigation, the politically sensitive and serious crime investigation into the bribery case against the former chief justice of Malta, Noel Borg. Spiteri didn't attend court every day of the trial but she had made an effort to be there on this day, as she knew that Borg had decided to take the stand in a last-ditch attempt to save his skin. Spiteri was also uneasy about an issue related to the case concerning her own ultimate boss, the police commissioner Chris Debono.

Daphne Arrigo was approximately the same age as Thea Spiteri and, like Spiteri, she was single, good looking, no kids, and loved her job as an investigator. But unlike Spiteri, Daphne Arrigo was an investigative journalist with the *Malta Times* and not a *Pulizija* officer.

Arrigo and Spiteri had never actually met, but they both knew who each other were, and both knew exactly why they were sitting in a Valetta court listening to the trial.

Arrigo was there because her investigations had helped put Borg in prison and because she felt there was still more to come out surrounding this story. Spiteri was there because she felt the same.

Borg had taken the stand a few moments earlier; Anthony Demajo, the Prosecutor, had just asked Borg how he actually came into possession of the money used as the bribe.

'Patrick Rizzo came into my office and just left it on my table,' replied Borg.

'And what was your reaction to this happening?' asked Demajo.

'I told Rizzo I didn't want it.'

'And what did he say?'

'He just said, "Too late, my job is to give it to you. I've done that. I wish I'd never gotten involved with these people but it's your problem now."'

'What did you do then?'

'I tried calling some trusted colleagues, but I couldn't get a hold of any of them.'

'Was one of the people you called Police Commissioner Debono?'

'Yes.'

'Why did you call him?'

'I told you, I wanted advice about what to do with the money from someone I trusted.'

'What did you do with the money?'

'I took it home and put it in a drawer.'

'Why didn't you go straight to the police? Tell them, hand the money over.'

'I thought about it, but I couldn't.'

'Why not?'

'Because I'd already told some people what a judgement in a drugs case was going to be before the judgement was official. I hadn't acted as a Chief Justice should have. I was scared.'

'Why had you done that?'

'Friendship had led me to divulge information that, as I said, I shouldn't have divulged.'

'What was the information that you divulged?'

'The length of sentence an accused was going to be given.'

'And?'

'And... that I thought the sentence was harsh and that if he appealed on certain grounds, his appeal would come to me, and I would be inclined to reduce it.'

'Who did you divulge this information to?'

'I can't remember.'

'Was one of the people Nicola Tizian?'

'As I said, I can't remember.'

'But Mr Tizian is a friend of yours, is he not?'

'I wouldn't say friend necessarily. More an acquaintance.'

'Was one of the people you gave the information to Commissioner Debono?'

'Look, how many times do I need to tell you? I can't remember.'

'So Dr Borg, you get up the next day. What do you do?'

'I went to my office.'

'Was anyone there?'

'Rizzo was waiting for me outside.'

'What did he want?'

'He just said, "You'll get the rest of the money over the next couple of months.'

'What did you think he meant by that?'

'I didn't know.'

'You didn't know! Shall I tell you then? Obviously, at some point you had agreed an amount for doing what you could regarding this drugs trial you mentioned. You weren't given all the money the previous day, so you were just being informed that everything was okay, you would get the rest. Is that not so, Dr?'

'No amount of money was ever mentioned.'

'So you admit that you did have discussions about what you could do to help?'

'Conversations, yes. There is nothing wrong with that. I did not interfere in the judgement. My mistake was telling friends the verdict, but the verdict had already been decided.'

'What did you do with the money?'

'I phoned a priest I know and asked his advice.'

'And what did he say?'

'He suggested I give it to charity.'

'And did you?'

'No.'

'Why not?'

'I was too scared to leave the house; these were not nice people that I had mistakenly become involved with.'

'I repeat, what did you do with the money?'

'I gave it to a priest and asked him to give it to Commissioner Debono.'

'And the priest's name?'

'Father Francesco Marandon.'

'And did he?'

'I assume so.'

'Do you? Well, you assume wrongly, Dr Borg. Both Father Marandon and Commissioner Debono deny having any knowledge of what you are talking about.'

The following week, both women were happy to hear that the former chief justice had been sentenced to two years in prison.

# CHAPTER 2

Spring Malta 2014

The cat was probably dead when it was nailed to the cross. Sometimes they were, sometimes they weren't. It made no difference: this was God's work. The poor street lighting helped the hooded apparition go about its holy work unnoticed. It knew it would never be caught. The shadows were its guardian angels; people had to learn the true meaning of loss.

***

Six months had passed since Matt Healy made the decision to move from Spain to Malta. Pedro had been right about the property market, but he had eventually sold the pension to a Russian company who appeared to be buying the whole resort. Healy had seen that development as particularly alarming but accepted with a degree of relief that it wasn't his concern. He had decided not to buy a property in Malta until he knew for sure whether he liked the island or not, so instead, he had rented a flat in Pembroke, which was close enough to St Julians Bay to walk in twenty minutes if he felt like experiencing the buzz of the busy tourist town, but far enough away to be isolated from the late night madness.

Every morning, he walked to Madliena Tower; passing through the heritage site that seperates Pembroke from the sea. The tower was one of a number that had been built in the 1700s by the Knights of St John to help with communication and to warn of invasion. Healy then dived off the rocks and swam for a while before heading back home for breakfast. Most importantly of all, Matt Healy had not drunk ince his epiphany morning in Pedro's bodega six months previously.

It was March, and the vast array of colours in the fields heralding the imminent arrival of the spring fruits added to Healy's feelings of well-being. He felt fit, healthy… and lonely. He had no problem going into bars or sitting at a meal while others drank wine. It was more difficult than he had expected to strike up and maintain conversations when you were drinking fruit juice and everyone else was on the road to Happyville, USA. But, overall, he was content with his life and was glad he had made the move. Like most visitors to the island, Healy was taken aback by the number of churches there were; three-hundred sixty, he had read in a guide, built to service a population that was ninety-seven-percent Catholic. The sheer proliferation of churches sometimes made Healy pause to consider his own background. In Glasgow, being a Catholic took on a completely different set of conditions than being one in Malta, and Healy had gone through a lot of the associated crap in his school and teen years before *coming to his senses* and giving up on religion all together. His experiences of having now lived in two Catholic countries, Spain and Malta, weren't going to change that. *You bring your mind with you, Matt.* Unfortunately for Matt Healy, that meant the demons came, too.

***

Jamie Smart was driving his mother to distraction. Mary Smart liked to live by the rules, and if the recommendation was to be in the airport at least two hours before a flight, then she would be there three hours before *just to be on the safe side*. But even Mary Smart was questioning her own diligence when challenged with how to entertain a boisterous five year old for three hours at Prestwick Airport. Even two large vodkas and Coke at the bar that was All Things Elvis—except cool—weren't helping.

'Jamie, will you just sit at peace for ten minutes, for God's sake.'

'Will we see God when we're up in the sky, Mum?'

'You might see him before then if you drop any more of those crisps. I'm warning you.'

'How's Dad no' coming wi' us on holiday?'

''Cause he's an arsehole, Jamie. You'll see that when you're older.'

'Father Rodgers says saying *arsehole* is a sin.'

'Did he? He should have tried being married to your dad then.'

'I heard Dad shouting at the telly the other night. The wummin on there said men can get married to each other in Scotland noo. Dad said the world was full o' faggots. What are faggots, Mum?'

'Ask Father Rodgers. He's bound to know a few.'

May Hooper, on the other hand, was just irritated by the idea of going to Malta full stop. Five days earlier, she had listened to her agent's frantic call and had grudgingly had to accept that he was right, as he had been on most decisions regarding her books up until this point.

'Malta, Sam? Really? How many people live there? It's hardly a big market.'

'I know May, but the point is there's a three-day convention there next week: Protecting Our Children. There will be a lot of delegates from Italy and Spain there, as well as the UK. Even some from the USA, I hear. It's a no brainer, you have to be there; think of the potential contacts! Anyway, hark at you, a week's free holiday in the sun, five-star hotel… and you're complaining!'

'Right okay. I know you're right, but I'm not a sunbathing, beach-type person, Sam. You know that.'

'Stay in the hotel bar then! You've survived Greece, Portugal, Spain… Malta will be a dawdle!'

'Sod off.'

'Just one thing. Eh, as it's all a bit last minute… I had to book you on a Ryanair flight.'

'For fuck's sake, Sam. Are you kidding?'

'Just on the way out. BA to Heathrow on way back. Sorry.'

'You're lucky I like you, Sam!'

'Play it again, Sam?'

'You know that line was never said in the movie, don't you?'

'I'll be back?'

'See you in St Louis. Bye.'

*\*\**

David Decelis, like many Maltese, had immigrated to Australia when he was young. Again, like many of those people, he often longed to return to his homeland. He had a good life in Melbourne, but his parents had both died the previous year and Decelis had a feeling that now was the right time, and in David Decelis' case, he felt he had a God-given mission to complete. David Decelis was unaware at that time how right he would turn out to be.

*\*\**

"The archipelago of Malta is made up of three populated islands—Malta, Gozo, and Comino—and three other islands populated only by birds. Malta, the largest of the islands by far, is 320 sq km, and crime is still relatively low, although appearing to be on the increase." Matt Healy was sitting in a café reading an article in *The Independent* newspaper on Malta's latest crime figures and trying miserably to equate the physical size of Malta and its crime rate with that of Glasgow. "The population of Malta is approximately 450,000; with another 35,000 living on Gozo." *Christ, I wish I still drank.* He glanced up and saw a plane begin its descent into Malta's airport, twenty odd kilometres to the southwest. *That'll be the flight from Prestwick. Crime won't be non-existent now.*

"Criminologist Jose Cuneo told our crime reporter that the recent spate of violent crime was almost all centred on Paceville, but that closing down the area was not the answer; the violence would not stop, merely move somewhere else."

Healy glanced over at the table showing the crime statistics for the previous year, 2013. "Drugs 24, Bodily Harm 184."

'In a year... bloody hell, that's a quiet weekend in Glasgow!'

"Most crimes occur between 3.00 a.m. and 6.00 a.m…"

'You don't say. Fucking four years at university to come up with that.' Healy tossed the paper to the side and ordered another coffee.


Unknown to Healy, a few streets away, two officers from the Maltese Police, the *Pulizija*, were also enjoying a coffee, The younger officer, Sergeant Jason Attard, also studied the approaching plane.

'More fodder for Paceville I suppose, Inspector,' he said to his boss, Inspector Thea Spiteri.

'The island depends on tourism, Jason. Don't be so bloody negative. You were young yourself once, remember,' replied Thea Spiteri. Although Attard wasn't old—thirty six—Spiteri just couldn't imagine her colleague ever being young. It was true that an area of St Julians, Paceville, had become in recent years a bit of an area of concern in terms of young tourists and the inevitable accompanying problems that they bring. But, in reality, the area only covered a few streets and hadn't been allowed to get out of hand like parts of the Spanish holiday islands. Besides, Inspector Thea Spiteri of the island's CID had more to worry about. The reasonably recent removal of Gaddafi from power in Libya had opened up potential trading opportunities for the island, which the government was keen to exploit, but it had also opened the island up to serious potential problems with drugs and gun running. A few days earlier, a motorcycle policeman had told her about stopping a car for a minor traffic violation. Inside the car were four Libyan students. In the course of their conversation, one of the students had almost casually remarked that in twenty years' time, most Maltese people will have left the island. When asked why he thought that, the young medical student—in Malta to improve his English at one of the many language schools on the island—had casually replied that it was inevitable, as thousands of Libyans had decided to settle in Malta, that Malta would become a Muslim country and the present population would move away.

On top of that, rumours of long-standing links between high-ranking *Pulizija* officers, politicians of both main parties in Malta, and the Corsican Mafia were starting to be voiced openly.

There was talk within the force of setting up a specialist unit to tackle, or at the very least monitor the situation. Spiteri's work on the Borg case the previous year had been noted, and she had been sounded out if she would be interested, but she was uncertain about what she should do. Her rise through the ranks of the *Pulizija* had been steady and hard won. There was a certain appeal about becoming involved in an international major crime unit but, at the same time, she felt drawn to sticking with crime that touched the ordinary people of Malta, her people.

\*\*\*

Thea Spiteri did not consider herself to be an outsider, but deep down, she knew she was. Spiteri was born in 1976,but she did not know on what exact date or exactly where. She just knew that she had been born in a field, where her mother, who was no more than a child herself, was a fruit picker. The young mother was the only one who knew who the father was and would never say. Distraught and bewildered, and with parents who would never accept the situation, the young girl stayed in the field nursing the child until darkness fell. Around 8.00 p.m., she wrapped the baby in a bed sheet she had smuggled out of her house that morning, and walked into the village.

Fortunately for new mother and baby, the aged and devout Thea Muscat, considered her job of closing up St Martin's Chapel each evening at 9.00 p.m. as an honour. These days, she seldom had to ask anyone to leave. That evening was no different until she saw a yellow bundle of cloth lying under the baptismal font, a bundle of cloth that was whimpering.

An hour later, the Mother Superior from a nearby convent was cradling the baby and laughing as the baby appeared to be sticking her tongue out at her. 'There's gratitude for you!'

As the nun prepared to take the baby away, she looked up at the smiling old lady who had discovered her. 'What is your first name?'

'Thea.'

'Then Thea it is… Thea Spiteri… Thea the orphan child.'

\*\*\*

Mary Smart was no less harassed at Malta Airport than she was at Prestwick. Jamie had slept on the three-and-a-half hour flight from Scotland, and although she was grateful in a way—*some peace is better than none at all*—she knew there would be a price to pay later, and 'later' had arrived, as as Jamie charged around the baggage reclaim area in Luqa Airport like some dervish on speed while she tried to retrieve two suitcases from a moving belt that she was sure speeded up whenever she approached. She was eventually helped by a fellow passenger who grabbed her cases for her, and convinced Jamie it would be a good idea to sit on top of them on the trolley, and "act as a pilot" through the crowds of people. Mary Smart thanked the man profusely and accepted the knowing nod from his wife.

'Who are you with?' the woman asked.

'Just me and the boy,' replied Mary.

'No. I mean what holiday company? Where are you staying?'

Mary beamed with joy. She had saved especially hard this year, *despite her useless shit of a husband, Peter.*

'The Hotel Juliani. It's four stars actually, but you only live once.'

'Quite right.'

'Has your holiday company arranged a bus to the hotel?'

'Oh no. I did it all myself online. I booked a taxi. Only twenty euros.'

'Good for you. Have a lovely holiday and Jamie, don't you be getting into any mischief.'

Someone standing unobtrusively, mingling with the queues at the Hertz Car Hire booth, someone who had rehearsed this occasion in their head a hundred times, watched and waited.

# CHAPTER 3

"Father and son murdered!"

'No way, no bloody way!' Matt Healy stared at the headlines blaring out from the front page of the *Malta Times*. *Please don't tell me this is some fucking Scottish nutter off his head on drink.*

Healy read on, an unexplainable tension lowly draining from his body. The article explained that the father and son in question were well known to police for their drug activities. Both had been executed gangland style, and both, Healy surmised, wouldn't be much of a loss to Malta. An Inspector Thea Spiteri had been assigned to the case. *Start with the relatives, love, then move to friends; guarantee the killer is in there somewhere.*

Healy looked out at the glimmering Mediterranean. He thought back to his time in the police, a time where murder was his thing and people listened when he spoke. He had never really signed up to the notion of serial killers around every corner—"Hannibal Lector, my arse"—but his final case had ended in complete failure and utter personal devastation due to a serial killer. His obsession with one suspect had allowed him to miss what was staring him in the face. And it had cost him the love of his life: his boss, Susan Dornan. *Why Susan, why?*

Thea Spiteri and Jason Attard looked down at the two rotting corpses, dumped in a field at Quajjenza. Spiteri felt some degree of sympathy for the boy; nothing for the father. The father had been as odious an individual as it was possible to be in her eyes, a man who had been hell bent on bringing the evils of mass drug importing onto her beloved island. The son was just a kid who had no chance. *The sins of the fathers.*

'What do you think?' Attard asked.

'Not much, to be perfectly honest, Jason.'

'What do you mean?'

'What do you mean? Do I feel sympathy? Maybe, a little, for the boy. Do I care that much? No, not really. Will I try my best to get the killers and put them away? Of course.'

She had barely gotten the words out of her mouth when the police commissioner arrive at the scene. The double killing was big news in Malta, with a lot of public interest, but it was unusual for the commissioner to appear in person.

'What do you think, Thea?' asked Debono.

'Well, unless I'm very much mistaken, this is the body of Joe Galizia and his son, Tom; so-called drug lords.'

'You're not mistaken. It's him alright.'

'Isn't he the one whose brother was tied in to the Borg bribery trial last year?'

'Who wasn't?' replied Debono rather drolly.

'Right. Make sure I'm kept right up to date on this, Thea. How are you, Jason?'

'Fine, Commissioner; I'll make sure you get everything.'

Debono nodded and headed back to his car.

'"Oh, how are you, Jason? Fine… I'll make sure you get everything,"' taunted Spiteri. 'Who's a popular boy then!'

'He's a great spotter of potential, that's all!'

'Yea, okay, Inspector Potential. Where do we start?'

'Known drug dealers?'

'Relatives.'

'It's a closed community, Thea. They won't talk.'

'They'll talk.'

'What makes you think that?'

'A mother has just lost her son. Stabbed over thirty times, shot, and thrown into a hole full of manure. She'll talk.'

\*\*\*

Mary Smart was in heaven. Her hotel had a kids play area and a happy hour. She knew that Jamie wouldn't be content to spend the whole day in the kids area, but they had reached a compromise: play area in the morning, beach in the afternoon. The evenings were still to be agreed, but most British families were staying in the hotel to gorge on the two-for-one offers, so Jamie was usually able to pal up with some other bored kid whose parents were on a mission to see who could become unconscious first.

The observer from the airport had to be careful. They couldn't let either the mother or child see them; not at the moment.

\*\*\*

Mary Smart may have been in heaven, but a man who had devoted his life to ensuring his place in eternal happiness, Father Francesco Marandon, was distraught. A murder on his beloved island was practically unthinkable. Two murders, and one just a boy, was more than his aging body could take. He had known Thea Spiteri for many years and knew that she would be affected greatly by this outrage, but he also knew that she would do her job diligently and, more importantly, discreetly. He also had a feeling that she would receive very little help from the commissioner. *Malta cannot have this kind of evil permeating its walls; the ancient walls that have seen a thousand invasions. From before even the Crusades to the scourge of fascism, Malta had stood firm. Drugs would not be her downfall. He would see to that. He would leave it a few days, give her time, and then he would call her.*

# CHAPTER 4

Jason Attard was impressed, perhaps even in awe. Less than forty-eight hours had elapsed since the double killing, and the case was closed. Thea Spiteri had been right: the grieving mother had revealed all, and the boy's uncle had been arrested for the killing. Moreover, he had confessed and said that the killing had been the 'honourable thing to do.' Attard looked across the room at Spiteri. She seemed neither pleased nor content.

She wasn't. Spiteri herself was still agonising over whether to leave her role in CID and move to the new unit. Although the two recent murders were drug related, the victims were low-end players and she couldn't help having a feeling that the investigation was too easy; she maintained a feeling that the uncle had been somehow 'given up, sacrificed' in order to stop any further digging into the families and organizations involved. She glanced around the CID office. In her opinion, none of them were ready to take over her role. This meant that if she left, a new person would be brought in and, although that was part of life in the police, she felt a certain reluctance to let that happen just yet. She felt a responsibility to her colleagues.

Spiteri rose and walked over to the coffee machine. Attard caught her eye, raised his coffee mug, smiled. Spiteri liked Jason; she occasionally got the feeling that she had met Attard before he joined the police, but she knew that that wasn't really possible, given their age difference. As she waited for the machine to deposit what passed for coffee, she examined herself in a mirror that hung beside the coffee machine. She had often thought it was an odd place for a mirror  but decided it was, in fact, a clever place; it allowed for self-reflection in every way. Spiteri had once been described by a former boyfriend as sultry, she liked that. In fact, it was the only contribution the ex had made that she did like. *Unmarried, no kids, self sufficient, healthy, sultry ! I'm a bloody catch. How come no one's bothered catching me then?*

'Everything okay, Kap?' asked Jason, who had wandered over to the coffee machine.

'Yes, everything's fine. Do you think I'm sultry, Jason?'

Attard's face went crimson; he looked down at the floor. 'I'm not sure.'

Thea laughed. 'Don't worry, I'm only joking. Your chastity is safe!'

Attard's belief in no sex before marriage caused him to be the butt of some fairly fierce ridicule at times, but he handled it well, and Spiteri secretly admired him for it. Like nearly everyone on the island, Thea Spiteri had been raised Catholic, but also like nearly everyone else on the island, she only saw the inside of a church on family occasions, where the after-church activities were the real attraction. Jason Attard's embarrassment had subsided. He looked back over at Spiteri and wondered if she knew who he was, when they had first met, and that he was saving himself for her. That no one else would have her.

***

There aren't a lot of beaches on Malta and, although St George's Bay beach was man-made, it suited Mary Smart perfectly. True, it was busy, packed at times, and there wasn't anything for Jamie to do except potter about the water's edge and pester her for ice cream but, for lying sleeping and getting a suntan the neighbours would be talking about for weeks, it fitted the bill.

The airport observer walked around the bay about once every hour, taking breaks in different bars and coffee shops, not inviting attention, not losing track of the boy's movements. On the third day, and assured that Mary Smart was sleeping, through having studied her body movement well, even in sleep, a decision was made.

*Now is the time.*

The boy wandered over to the ice cream kiosk, stared at the mind-numbing choice.

'Why don't you get strawberry and I'll have vanilla? We better go round the corner to eat these eh? Don't want to get caught.'

The boy skipped with glee. He loved tricking his mum; Jamie Smart could not talk for joy.

Matt Healy was shouting at his newspaper. 'Bloody told you! The uncle, bloody knew it.' Healy put his paper down. *It's always someone they know.* His mind wandered back to Glasgow. *No, Matt, it's gone. She's gone. For fuck's sake, move on.* Healy looked back down at his paper. He was impressed. Less than two days and it was done and dusted, a double murder put to bed. He looked again for the name of the Officer in charge. *Thea Spiteri. Bet she's a right battle axe, face like a Rottweiler. Still... impressive.*

Healy had had his morning swim and was looking forward to the day ahead. He hadn't any specific plans but had gotten into a routine of just jumping on a bus in Pembroke, and seeing where his day took him. The day before, he had gotten off in Sliema and wandered around the harbour area there. He felt an attraction somehow to being near water and felt that he could while away the day in places like Sliema without noticing his loneliness. Jim Frame had called him from Glasgow the night before and regaled him with a catalogue of complaints about the new Scottish police force and the apparent self-destruction of his favourite football team. He had dropped a hint about maybe coming over to see Healy soon, but Healy had managed to stall him by confirming that he was teetotal and wouldn't be making any exceptions, and that everywhere shut at 10.00 p.m. in Malta.

'Really?' asked Frame.

'Really.'

'What, even the whorehouses?'

'None.'

'Aye right.'

'Tell you what then, Jim. Get a flight out here and see, or go to Benidorm as per usual, and go home with sore balls and partial memory loss.'


Mary Smart was awake, but not fully focused. Well, not on where Jamie might be. *Some of these young guys are gorgeous. Wish I'd known this kind of world existed when I was being courted with a Carlsberg and kneetrembler by that pig, Peter. Jamie? Where's he got to now?*

Mary Smart wasn't the most perceptive of people but she knew something was wrong. She just didn't know what. The sea was calm and blue; people were laughing. The sun was still shining and the scent of coconut oil was still in the air. Young lovers were kissing and older couples were watching and remembering. Children were walking down from the ice cream kiosks with cones and smiles in abundance. Children? That was it. Children. But no Jamie.

'Jamie? Jamie, where are you?'

Mary Smart was on her feet now, walking with apparent purpose, but in reality wandering blindly in ever more manic strides.

'Jamie! Jamie! Oh God, please no.'

Relief. A blue and white car was parked at a coffee stall on the curve of the bay. "*Pulizija.*" She ran to the car.

'My son is missing. He wouldn't just have gone off. Help me. Please help me.'

'Don't worry. I'm sure he's just wandered to a shop, maybe even a toilet. We'll find him,' said Con Benetto.

They didn't.

*It's troubling, upsetting. Of course it is. A child's death was a tragedy, endless, never-ending pain. I've known it, others needed to be shown. I wonder sometimes why I feel compelled to do this work. Time is passing, I have been given a path, and I must take it. Jamie, be happy now, you are at peace. I hope I didn't hurt you, little one.*

There were no tears as Jamie Smart's broken body was laid to rest.

# CHAPTER 5

In Scotland, Jim Frame studied the story spread all over the front pages of the *Daily Record* and the *Sun* newspapers. The abduction of Jamie Smart was being covered as luridly as possible by both, with disparaging remarks about the efforts of the Maltese police to the fore. Similarities to the Madeline McCann case, where another Scottish child had been abducted—on that occasion in Portugal—were being made. There were also references in later editions to the Ben Needham case, where a young blonde child, similar in size and age to Jamie, had gone missing on the Greek island of Kos. *That will cheer Jamie's parents up no end, considering neither of those poor kids were ever found.*

Before the story had broken, Jim Frame had pondered his most recent conversation with Matt Healy. He knew he was serious about staying off the drink, but something else had changed in his old colleague. He wasn't quite sure how to describe it, or even if he was right, but Frame had decided that Healy had lost a bit of purpose in his life. He had always felt that Matt was running away from the Azrael case, a case that had caused so much despondency in the squad at the time, but especially so in Healy's case. The squad had been disbanded and Healy had disappeared to Spain, riding on a fog of despair and alcohol.

Frame wondered if he was being callous, opportunistic, unfeeling; but this abduction, right on Matt Healy's doorstep, might just be the thing to pull him back into a place Frame felt Healy really belonged. He was going to phone him.

'I know this is very difficult for you, Mary, but is there anything more, anything at all, you can tell us about the time leading up to you realising Jamie was missing?' Thea Spiteri gently asked Mary Smart. They were sitting in a room in the police station in St Julians Bay. The station was situated right on the sea front, wedged incongruously between hotels, and a restaurant that had a list of former customers proudly displayed beside its menu: Brad Pitt, Daniel Craig…

'No.'

'Is Jamie's dad coming over?'

'Yes. I called him. For all the good that useless bastard will be. Pretending he cares. If he cared, where's he been most of Jamie's life?' Mary Smart started to cry. She realised she was already talking as if Jamie's life was over.

'When did you separate?'

'Officially? This year. But I finally told him never to come back last year.'

'Any reason in particular?'

'Yea. No, just the drink. You know.'

'Did you tell him to let you know when he was arriving, that I would arrange to have him picked up?'

'Yea, but he said no. Sorry, but he disnae like cops. Said he would make his own way. Meet me in the hotel. He's no staying in ma room though, I'll fucking tell you that.'

'We'll get him a room. Maybe in a hotel close by. Okay?'

'Yes. Thanks. Sorry. Will you find Jamie?'

'We'll try our best, I promise.'

'I know, but will you find him? Even if, you know…'

'Let's not think that way. Okay, so you're sure you can't think of anything else?'

'No, sorry.'

'Okay, I'll get you taken back to your hotel.'

Thea Spiteri watched out the window as Mary Smart slumped into the back of the police car. *How would I stand up if it were me? Could I cope? Remain positive?*

Like Jim Frame, Matt Healy had read the almost blanket coverage of the child abduction in the *Malta Times*. *Scottish, too. Terrible.* He felt a pang of guilt over his thoughts about the flight coming in from Prestwick. *Poor kid was probably on that flight. Jesus.* He pondered for a long time on how the Maltese police would conduct this type of investigation. He wondered if abductions had taken place before on the island. He thought back to his own experiences of missing child cases. Thankfully, in his time, nearly all the children had been found: some alive, some dead. He did think about a case that he was too young to actually have been involved in but that received a lot of press coverage years later, when a young woman claimed, in fact wrote a book, naming her own father as the killer.

A young girl had been sent to the local shops to buy milk. She never came back and was never seen again. The case eventually went cold, although was never closed. Twenty years later, the young girl's friend, May Hooper, brought out a book accusing her own father of being the killer. He was dead by the time the book came out but had a history of child abuse and was driving a bus the night the child went missing, driving along the same route the child would have taken to get to the shops. The book caused quite a stir, the case was re-opened, but no real progress was made. May Hooper, though, went on to form a charity to help young people and was subsequently awarded an OBE. The last Healy had heard of her was that she devoted her time to speaking at seminars and the like on child welfare issues and helping police in child abduction cases. *Good on her.*

Healy's phone ringing brought him back to the present. 'Hello.'

'Matt, it's Jim.'

'No, I'm not going back on the drink for old time's sake!'"

'Ha bloody ha. Your loss, if you ask me.'

'I'm not asking.'

'Fine. What about the abduction over there?'

'What about it?'

'Don't pretend you're not interested.'

'Interested? Yes, I'm interested. What are you getting at?'

'Go to the police. Tell them who you are, offer to help.'

'Okay. Right. I'll do that, Jim. Let me see. Okay. "Officers, my name is Matt Healy. I'm a washed-up former cop, and I'm here to tell you what to do."'

'Okay, mock. But I'm telling you they could do with your help, what with the kid being Scottish and all.'

'What's that got to do with anything?'

'Victim empathy.'

'Victim empathy! You on the drink this morning?'

'You know what I mean. Look, they'll be talking to the mum, right? Probably won't understand her accent for a start. You could be a great help, Matt.'

'What? As an interpreter?'

'Why don't you want to help? You that busy or something?'

'I didn't say I didn't want to help. What I'm saying is they don't need my help. What would we have said, back in the day, if someone has strolled into Pitt Street and announced that they were "here to help?" Do me a favour, Jim.'

'I think you're wrong. The police in these foreign countries are hopeless.'

'Hopeless? What makes you say that?'

'In today's *Sun*, they list twenty, twenty, cases of crimes abroad involving Brits, and not one solved.'

'Bye, Jim.'

Healy shook his head as he slammed the phone down. He knew Frame was a bit of a dinosaur, but at the same time, he did wonder if he could help. He looked out of his kitchen window. He could see Madliena Tower shimmering. *I'm going for a run.*

David Decelis stood at his bedroom window in the Dragonnara Hotel. The page of the child abduction story in the Malta Times was spread across his bed. He looked out over St George's Bay. He smiled. *And so it begins.*

'What is happening to our island, Thea?' Father Marandon gently enquired. He didn't need to say who was calling.

'I know. But I think it's just an unfortunate thing, Francesco. Nothing more.'

'Do you think the two murders and the abduction are related?'

'I don't think so. There's nothing obvious linking them at least. No, definitely not.'

'Evil takes many forms, Thea. Do not dismiss it.'

'I won't. How are you?'

'I'm well. Considering. When are you coming to see me?'

'Soon, Francesco, soon.'

'Make sure you do. I've given up looking for you at Mass!'

'Prayers won't stop crimes being committed, Francesco.'

'No, but they give the good people the strength to catch the wrongdoers.'

'You think so?'

'I know so. Goodbye, Thea.'

'Bye, Father.'

Thea Spiteri loved Father Francesco, took comfort from his calls, but just couldn't believe, truly believe, in his God. She looked over at Sergeant Claudia Sansome. She was a believer despite the fact that her only child, Catherine, aged five, had been killed when she ran out onto a street in her home village, Haz-Zeebug, and was hit by a speeding car driven by a German tourist. She and Spiteri had never been close, but Spiteri had tried imagine Sansome's pain. Spiteri had once asked her, "How can you still believe, Claudia?"

Claudia had merely replied, "Google Arthur Ashe, the tennis player."

Spiteri had been thrown by the response, but wasted no time when she got home to look up Ashe. The former Wimbledon champion had contracted AIDS through a faulty blood transfusion and was close to death when he was asked if, as a devout Christian, he never asked God, 'Why Me?'

He had replied, 'The world over, 50 million children start playing tennis, 5 million learn to play tennis, 500,000 learn pro tennis, 50,000 come to the circuit, 5,000 reach the Grand Slam, 50 reach Wimbledon, 4 reach the semi-finals, 2 the finals. When I was holding the trophy, I never asked, "Why Me?" Today, in pain, I should not be asking God, "Why me?"'

Thea remembered lying awake most of the night, thinking of the words of a tennis player she had never heard of until that day. By the morning, she was still not a believer.

***

Miriam Calder hated her description. Not her description in terms of looks—she wasn't interested in that kind of inanity—her description in terms of her work: Child Abduction Expert. *Bloody child abduction expert, how?* She didn't know how to abduct a child, just how others went about doing it. And even then, she didn't always get that right. More importantly than that, she had no idea why they did what they did. *Motive? Bloody motive for these kinds of people? Forget it. Could X be the killer? Yes. Go from there.* She was an exponent of the criminology school of thought that children were just unfortunate that they fell into one of the five groups always targeted by serial killers: children, women, gay men, prostitutes, and the elderly; in other words, the vulnerable. *Why do they never target footballers? I wouldn't bloody object to that.* What comes first? Wanting to just kill? Or realising you have the opportunity to kill within a certain group. In Miriam Calder's view, it was clear: access and opportunity were the key. Motivation was a different issue. This secondary issue often led her into conflict with her peers. She considered profiling, the darling of the FBI and Hollywood to be, in her opinion after careful consideration, shite. She once had a discussion with a student who saw profiling as the only value in keeping killers alive: 'allows us to study them.' Calder had sat her down and gently broke the news: 'Serial killers fall into two groups. Ones who talk and ones who don't. The ones that don't talk, we'll that's that. The ones that do talk talk crap, so what sort of basis is that to work on? Get Inside the mind of a psycho? Tony Hill? Get real.'

She had read about the latest high-profile abduction that had taken place the day before in Malta. *Red tops in their usual frenzy regarding foreign police forces.* Like all abductions, it intrigued her, but she had no contacts in Malta and she never volunteered her services; she always waited to be invited.

Her invite would come. Unfortunately for Miriam Calder, it would be her last case.

# CHAPTER 6

Peter Smart arrived in a maelstrom of anger, despair, and apparent duty free lubrication. Mary Smart had received a call from the hotel reception requesting she come down as her husband had arrived and was "upset." She came out of the lift and saw her soon-to-be-ex husband leaning against a marble pillar in the foyer.

'Ma boy, Mary. Ma boy, whit's happened to ma boy?'

'Bit late for tears, Peter. You'd been any sort of father, he might still be alive.' Mary Smart grimaced at the realisation of what she had just said.

'He's no deid, Mary. Diynae say that. He's no deid.'

'No. Look at the state of you. Could you not have stayed sober, just for once?'

'Diynae start, Mary. I'm grieving, for fuck's sake. Anyway, where the fuck were you when he was taken? Eh, answer me that. Away shagging, no doubt.'

'You're pathetic. The police have got you a room across the road. Go and sober up; they'll want to talk to you.'

'Whit aboot?'

'Oh, I can't guess. Your son, maybe?'

Mary Smart watched as Peter Smart staggered towards the nearby hotel. Something niggled at the back of her mind, but she just couldn't pin down what it was.

\*\*\*

Jim Frame agonised over what he was about to do. He knew Matt Healy would be livid, but he also knew it was just what Healy needed. The *Sun* newspaper was still running the story as front page news and humbly mentioning that they were paying for Mary Smart to stay on in Malta "for as long as she needed." Frame picked up his phone, paused, stared out of a window for a moment, then called his media contact.

\*\*\*

*Noel Borg Walks Free*

Daphne Arrigo read the headline in *The Independent* with a mixture of disgust and anger. The former Chief Justice had only served thirteen months of what was already a lenient sentence of two years in prison, and he hadn't actually spent any days in prison at all. He had managed to do his time in the Mount Carmel Hospital Forensic Unit after persuading his medical team that he was depressed. The unit had none of the austerity of Corradino Correctional Facility and was more a hospital type regime, as the unit was ostensibly for inmates who were sick or trying to overcome drug addiction.

'You're depressed? I'm fucking depressed!' shouted Arrigo to her empty bedroom. *I'm not letting this go. The whole thing stinks.* Arrigo jumped up from her bed and headed for the shower.

\*\*\*

Matt Healy was surprised that there was someone knocking at his door that early in the morning; he didn't get many visitors. None, as a matter of fact.

'Thank you so much for helping me?' said Mary Smart.

'Sorry?'

'You're Matt Healy aren't you?'

'Yes, but… Look, I'm sorry but I don't know what you are talking about.'

Mary Smart held up a copy of that day's *Sun* newspaper: *UK Cop Brought In.* Healy was bemused but managed a 'you had better come in.'

He guided Mary Smart into the kitchen, flicked on the kettle, motioned for her to sit down, and took the proffered paper from her—all without speaking. He read the story twice, certain he had misunderstood it the first time. "Former UK cop Matt Healy, now resident in Malta, is being drafted in by the Maltese Police in order to help them solve the mystery disappearance of Scottish youngster Jamie Smart."

'Fucking Jim Frame! I'm going to kill him.' Healy turned to Mary Smart. 'Mrs Smart, there's been a misunderstanding. The Maltese Police haven't contacted me, and even if they did, I couldn't help. I'm a washed-up former cop with next to no experience in abductions. Sorry. I can't help you.'

'But they're going to contact you.'

'Who is?'

'The Maltese Police. They told me.'

'They told you? When? How?'

'This morning. A reporter from the *Sun* had been on to them. Asked them why they weren't utilising an expert right on their doorstep.'

'Jesus. Look, I'm not an expert! Nowhere near it, unless you count drinking. Sorry, you'll need to go.'

'Maybe you can help my ex as well, then?'

'What?'

'He's a drunk. Maybe you can show him how to stop?'

'Look, Mary isn't it, I'm sorry, but I'm not the man you think I am. I appreciate you're in torment over your son, but the Maltese Police are the best people to deal with this. I'm sure of that.'

'So you won't help me?'

'I can't help you.'

Healy watched as Mary Smart walked slowly away down Triq San Filipe towards St George's Bay. *Frame, I am going to fucking kill you.*

Jason Attard sat staring at his coffee, almost as if he was studying it. Father Francesco Marandon was sitting opposite and was studying him. 'Is something troubling you, Jason? Having to deal with this abduction case, maybe?'

'No, Francesco, it's not that.'

'Then, what? Can I help?'

'Can I confide in you, Father?'

'Do you really need to ask that, Jason?'

'I love her.'

'Ah. I take it you mean, Thea?'

'Yes. Who else?'

'Who else indeed? Jason, I have known you both a long time; I love you both. You just have to let life take its course. If it's meant to be, it will happen.'

'She doesn't even know I exist.'

'Now you are talking rubbish, Jason. I happen to know she has the highest regard for you.'

'The highest regard! Hardly passionate.'

'Passion can come later, Jason. If it comes at the beginning, and then dies...'

'You know Thea well, Francesco. Do you think I should tell her?'

'What do you think?'

'If I tell her and she is not interested, then I would have to leave the police. Maybe even the island.'

'Don't be foolish, Jason. Why would you have to leave? Do you think you would be the first young man to have lost out in love?'

'No, but...'

'But nothing. Wait and see. Just wait and see.'

'What about a person's destiny?'

'Destiny may lead you to a path; you have free choice to walk that path or not.'

\*\*\*

Peter Smart lay on top of the bed in his hotel room. The air conditioning was on at full blast, yet he was still sweating. *How does anyone stand this fucking heat?* But Peter Smart knew it was not the heat that was making him sweat. He hated the police at the best of times, but he knew this was a whole different level. He wondered if they would interview Mary separately, what she would say. His mind turned to Jamie. He buried his head in his pillow and wept uncontrollably.

\*\*\*

Spiteri hardly heard the gentle knock on her office door. She knew it must be Claudia Sansome. *It's almost as if she doesn't exist anymore, a spirit.*

'Come in.'

'There's a man at the front desk asking for you. He says he's a former cop from the UK. Says he would "like to speak to you about the missing child,"' said Claudia Sansome.

'What's his name?'

'Healy.'

Thea Spiteri checked the name against a copy of that morning's *Sun* newspaper. *Yes, it is him. I thought so. Arrogant arsehole. I'll soon put him straight.*

'Show him in.'

Sansome nodded and left the room.

'Thanks for agreeing to meet me, Inspector Spiteri.'

Thea Spiteri was slightly taken aback, both by the appearance and manner of the man who had just entered. She had been expecting an older man, a man with attitude.

'Please, call me Susan.'

'Shit.'

'Pardon?'

'God. Sorry. Memories.'

'Not good ones, I take it?'

'Not all.' *Some though, definitely some.* Spiteri had not been the only one thrown by appearances. Based on his experiences in Scotland—and senior policewomen—Healy had been expecting an almost man-like creature to confront him when he entered Spiteri's office. He could not have been more wrong. *My God, she's beautiful.*

'Please, call me Thea, then. That is my real name. For some reason, English people prefer using my middle name, Susan. I'm not really sure why.'

'Well I'm Scottish, so it's definitely Thea. First of all, I want to apologise for a story you may have seen in a British newspaper this morning. I knew nothing about this. I suspect a former colleague of mine back in the UK may have thought he was doing a good thing, but he never consulted me, and the bloody *Sun* newspaper definitely didn't speak to me.'

'So what are you doing here, Mr Healy?'

'Matt, please. Well, only to apologise, really, about the story.'

'So you aren't here to show us how it's done?'

'No. Again, sorry. None of that crap came from me. Anyway, good luck with the investigation. I hope you find the boy. Thanks for your time.' Healy got up to leave.

'You're not prepared to help, then?'

Healy turned. He thought he could detect a slight smile on Spiteri's face.

'Eh.'

'Sit down, Matt. I'm interested in your views on the case. Forget about the thing in the paper. I had the pleasure of actually speaking to the guy who wrote that stuff; the word *moron* springs to mind.'

'I don't have any views.'

'Would you like to hear what we know?'

'I'm not sure.'

'Why's that?'

'I'll start thinking about it. Before you know it, I'll have commandeered an office!'

'No... you won't.'

Healy got the message: this was Spiteri's case.

'Well, if you want to give me a brief summary, I'll tell you what I think.'

'Fine. Well, we know... zilch.'

'Zilch?'

'That's a word, isn't it?'

'Sure. Just not a very good one in this context. You've got absolutely no clues, leads, nothing?'

'Nothing. Oh, we've brought in known weirdos. Asked for any photos taken on the beach that day, etc... nothing.'

'So what do you think?'

'If the child is still alive, they must be off the island by now. Malta is very small. Close communities; someone would notice something, report it.'

'So...'

'He's dead.'

'How many similar cases have there been on the island?'

'None. This is the first.'

'Won't be helping your tourism image. I bet your bosses are pleased.'

'Ecstatic. I'm going to interview the parents tomorrow morning. Would you like to sit in—for translation purposes, if nothing else?'

Healy smiled. 'If you're sure.'

'Fine. But Matt, you're only there to listen. You understand that?'

'Yes, of course.'

That night, Matt Healy dreamt of two Susans: Spiteri introducing herself as Susan but with another Susan's face. His Scottish Susan was smiling at him, waving at him from the sea as he sat on the Pembroke rocks, then disappearing under the waves… only to re-emerge as Spiteri for an instant before she, too, submerged under the waves. This time, like a candle melting in a flame.

# CHAPTER 7

Thea Spiteri had decided to interview Peter Smart in his hotel room rather than in a police station, as she wanted the atmosphere to be as relaxed as possible, given the circumstances. On entering the room, she had immediately regretted her decision. The smell of stale sweat, even more stale alcohol, and discarded food, made the atmosphere in the room almost unbearable.

'Perhaps we could sit out on the terrace, Peter?' ventured Spiteri, drawing back the glass door without waiting for an answer.

'You the guy in the paper?' asked Smart. His question was aimed at Healy, but his gaze was on the floor.

'He is, but he's just here to observe. Okay?' 'What do you want to know?' asked Peter Smart.

'Just a little bit of background, Peter. I know this can't be easy for you, especially given the circumstances between you and Mary, but what can you tell us about the kind of boy Jamie was… sorry, is?'

'What circumstances? What has that cow been saying?'

Spiteri was taken slightly aback. 'Nothing. I just meant you being separated.'

'Right. Sorry, it's just that I don't trust her.'

'In what way?'

'Any fucking way! Sorry.'

'So, what can you tell us about Jamie?'

'Great kid, loved him to bits.'

'I'm sure, but was he a curious child? Did he tend to wander off?'

'Naw. Stranger danger, all that shit. I told him about weirdos.'

'So you don't think he would have gone off with someone he didn't know?'

'Naw. Whit was she doin, by the way, when he disappeared?'

Spiteri glanced over at Healy. She clearly hadn't picked up Smart's meaning. Healy just shook his head gently.

'How did you hear about Jamie, Peter?'

'Papers. Nothing from you lot.'

'We assumed Mary would contact you. Didn't she?'

'Naw.'

'She told us she'd called you.'

'Well, she didnae.'

'Why's that, do you think?'

'Told you: she's a bitch.'

'Anything you want to tell us, Peter. Anything at all you think might help?'

Peter Smart just shook his head.

Spiteri and Healy headed for the door.

'If he's dead, do you think you'll find his body?'

Spiteri turned and stared at Smart. 'We're not thinking along those lines, Mr Smart. Not at the moment.' Healy stared at Smart too, but said nothing. They walked out into the midday heat.

'What do you make of that, Matt? Am I missing something, a culture thing or whatever?'

'*Culture's* not a word I'd use concerning him. Fancy a drink? Coffee, I mean. I don't drink. Well, I mean, you have what you like. I'm having coffee.'

'Okay. On me; the Maltese *Pulizija* has huge expense accounts.'

'I'll bet.'

They found a table in a nearby bar dinner and spent a few moments deciding on two coffees. 'You don't have to, you know. Not for my sake,' said Healy.

'I'm not. So, what do you make of that? Could be grief, I suppose.'

'Did he look grief-stricken to you, Thea?'

'Affects people in different ways.'

'Suppose. When are you next talking to the mother?'

'I call her every day, but no real point in a face to face every day. What am I supposed to say?'

Healy thought for a moment. 'The next time you go to see her, can I sit in?'

'Okay, but why?'

'Not sure.'

'Right. Glad you cleared that up then.'

Healy looked at Spiteri and wondered. They both smiled. *God, you are beautiful.*

'Anyway. What about the missing boy? I know you said you had nothing, but is there anything, anything at all, I can help you with?'

'What about the mother?'

'What about her?'

'Do you think she could be involved?'

'Seriously?'

'She likes a drink apparently. She was pretty much out of her head most nights. Slept it off during the day. Could have killed him by accident one night. Paniced. Shouted "abduction" the next day.'

'What about the body?'

'Dumped it,' Spiteri said with a shrug.

'Where?'

'Don't know.'

'No, it's just not feasible. A dead body, even a child's, is not easy to make just disappear. Plus there would have been signs in the room. No, it doesn't add up. I think she's genuine, but remind me never to fall out with you. God, Mary Smart never crossed my mind.'

'Really? A lot of people think Madeline McCann's mother killed her.'

'A lot of sickos, maybe. No chance.'

'But as a policeman, you have to look at it. Most murdered children are killed by a parent or relative, Matt.'

'Yes. I know. But believe me, not in this case. Or the McCann case.' Healy looked at Spiteri, wondered. 'Mind you, both cases involve Scots; that could be significant.'

'Really, why?

'Well, we've been known to eat our young!'

Spiteri laughed. She liked this guy. She, too, started to wonder.


Miriam Calder had never been to Malta. She was still desperately seeking a way to get to the island, as she knew time was of the essence. Calder was becoming more and more irritated by the ridiculous asides that seemed obligatory when newspapers covered sensational stories, especially ones where foreigners' inadequacies could be highlighted. Nevertheless, she was taking a keen interest in the case developing in Malta. *Matt Healy? I think I know him. Shouldn't be too hard to track down where he used to work, pull some strings.*

*** 

Jason Attard was beside himself with rage. Spiteri had called to say she was going for lunch with Matt Healy and was only to be disturbed if anything significant came up.

*Anything significant!* In all the time Attard had known Spiteri, she had never let her personal life interfere with her work. *Who exactly was this*

*Healy, anyway? No one really knows anything about him, he just appeared. Fucking, Batman, to the rescue! Well, I'll find out. Thea is mine.*

Jason Attard had never really contemplated having a partner or being married. He had been happy enough living in a family after he had been permanently adopted at the age of ten; in the years leading up to then, he had been fostered by a few families but had always been sent back as he was "not a very loving child, distant." Mr and Mrs Demicoli were slightly older than the normal age of couples who wanted to adopt children, and they wanted a slightly older child than normal as well, a child "past the baby stage." Jason, too, seemed to settle into the routine of the Demicoli household and, on the whole, all three family members were happy. The couple lived quiet lives. The only major drama Jason could remember was the disappearance of Mrs Demicoli's much-loved cat. The couple encouraged Jason in everything, and he wanted for nothing. Mr and Mrs Demicoli passed away within a month of each other when Jason was twenty years old. Jason wasn't left any substantial amount of money, but he was left the apartment, and so, for a young man who had had the start in life he had, things had turned out well in the end. Jason had never attempted to find out who his real parents were, but when he was eighteen, Father Francesco Marandon had called at the Demicoli house and suggested that he and Jason go for a walk. As they walked, Father Marandon revealed Jason's history. At first, he did not know what to make of it, but Francesco Marandon had pointed out the good fortune that Jason had in his life compared to some: 'You know that that is true, Jason,' and Attard had agreed. It was also around this time that Jason Attard decided to join the *Pulizija*. When he was accepted, he was overjoyed. He was going to be doing the job he was born to do.

Walking back after their coffee, Spiteri probed Healy. 'Are you religious, Matt?'

'No. Why?'

'I just wondered.'

'Are you?'

'Yes, and no.' Spiteri laughed at herself.

'Okay, can I change my answer? I'm a yes-no as well!'

'Really? Catholic?'

'Unfortunately.'

'Why do you say that?'

'Well, you can never quite rid yourself of it.'

'Maybe that's a good thing?'

'You?'

'The same.'

'And do you still carry the guilt thing?'

'Yea, I suppose I do.'

'I'd like you to meet someone. A friend of mine. Maybe have dinner together.'

'Sounds good.'

'He's a priest.'

'Oh.'

'Is that a problem?'

'Not if he isn't a Jesuit! '

'He's Dominican. Lives in the monastery at Ir-Rabat. What's wrong with Jesuits though?'

'I'd rather discuss religion with the Taliban than a Jesuit. Nut cases, every one.'

'No, he's great. He's helped me many times over the years. Sometimes I'm not sure he's even Catholic!'

'Really?'

'Well, no, not really. But you know what I mean. He's never going to be Pope. Put it that way.'

'That's strange.'

'What is?'

'Neither am I.'

*\*\*\**

Mary Smart wasn't exactly impressed, but she was at least grateful that her estranged husband had turned up sober. As Peter Smart walked into the Black Bear in St Julians, the strange feeling that she had experienced a couple of days earlier, when he had first arrived, returned. She was even more taken aback when he ordered tea for himself.

'You look tired, love,' he said once the waiter had gone.

'Get away. Can't think why.'

'Look, Mary, can't we just concentrate on Jamie for now?'

'Okay. Let's do that, Peter. When was the last time you saw him? When was the last time you paid a penny towards his keep? When…' Mary Smart shook her head slowly, and looked away.

'I'm sorry, Mary. I know I've not been, well, the best of fathers or husbands, but I'm working on something now. I'll see you all right.'

'You? Working? Is that a joke?'

'It's no a job as such, more a business opportunity. It will work, and like I say, I'll see you right.'

'Can't wait. Why have you asked me here, Peter? What do you want?'

'We need to show the cops a united front, Mary. Can we drop the bad feelings, name calling and that, at least till this is all over?'

'This? You mean Jamie?'

Peter Smart looked over the road. He watched as various families sat around enjoying their lunch. *I'll maybe try there tonight. Looks promising.*

'Mary, I know cops. They'll bend things. Next thing you know, they'll be blaming you. Us.'

'What are you saying? You think I'm to blame for this!'

The waiting staff in the bar were beginning to become uneasy. The middle-aged blonde British holiday maker was beginning to get too loud. Other customers were beginning to leave. Peter Smart was in a sweat. This was not how he'd planned things. *Why does she have to be like this?*

Mary Smart considered throwing her vodka and Coke over her ex; instead, she turned and walked away. Peter Smart looked back over the road. *Aye, definitely tonight.*

***

Nicola Tizian sat at the bar in the Black Bear sipping an espresso. He was looking over at the pathetic couple from *somewhere in the UK, judging by their cheap clothes,* but not with any sense of apprehension. Nicola Tizian had killed many men and ordered the killings of many more. Now, at the age of fifty-two, he was in charge of all the interests of his family in Malta and Corsica. His family being the Neapolitan Camorra.

For years, the Cosa Nostra and Camorra clans had seen Malta as an ideal place to launder the vast amounts of monies that they were extorting in Sicily and the south of Italy. They invested heavily in the tourist-focused entertainment spots of Malta, with restaurants, clubs, casinos, and bars all acting as fronts for providing apparently legal income. Even better, as far as the Camorra were concerned, they had been able to establish themselves on the island, not in the usual way of unfettered violence, but by forming close relationships with local top businessmen, political patrons, and tapping into the financial and legal know-how of the Maltese legal firms.

*If only Corsica was so malleable. What are the politicians thinking about? Their intransigence has made Corsica have the highest per capita murder rate in Europe! Fools. One hundred fifty needless killings in seven years. For what? We still run things. Corsica, the birth place of Napoleon! It's in our blood to take over, to rule.*

The previous year, Nicola Tizian had ordered the killing of Corsica's best-known lawyer, Paolo Sollacaro, but was sure that such extreme measures would not be needed in the pliable approach of the Maltese power brokers. *Why can't they be realistic like here in Malta?*

This ideal environment in Malta for doing business with the authorities quietly and discreetly, making his order for the shooting of the two idiots who thought they were big-time capos, a few weeks previously, all the more annoying. But, fortunately, he had control over the police investigation and the whole story had seeped out of the consciousness of the island soon enough.

# CHAPTER 8

Matt Healy was pleasantly surprised at Spiteri's choice of restaurant. Meet, overlooking St Julians Bay, was an Argentinean Steak House, which suited Healy; he was just surprised that it would be Spiteri's choice.

'Normally it wouldn't be, but I don't think Father Francesco eats enough, so I bring him here, order for him, and then watch over him till he eats it!'

'Is there a sort of Mother-Father thing going on there, Thea?'

Spiteri wavered only for a second. 'Sharp, Matt. Very quick.'

'Not in all things.'

Spiteri decided not to look for any double meaning. 'What do you think you'll have? Francesco is always late.'

Healy was still examining the menu when Spiteri rose and gave a rather stooped man a hug. 'Francesco, this is the sinner from Scotland I was telling you about.'

Healy started to protest, but Father Marandon raised a wrinkled hand. 'Ignore her, Matt, we are all sinners. Especially her!'

Spiteri blushed slightly. 'Now, Francesco, the confessional is still sacrosanct, as far as I recall. Or is that out the window as well, along with limbo, St Patrick, and fish on a Friday?'

'Glad you mentioned St Patrick there, Thea. Is that a touch of the Irish I hear in your voice, Father?' asked Healy.

'Ah, to be sure, to be sure. Me shillelagh's in me pocket; and please, Matt, call me Francesco.'

'How does that come about, then?'

'Well, I was born in County Galway. But came to Malta when I was sixteen or seventeen.'

'Right, any brothers or sisters?'

'Well now, there are two ways to answer that! I've either got none or hundreds.'

'Meaning?'

'I was an orphan or, to be strictly accurate, the child of a fallen woman. I was born and brought up in a place called The Home in a village named Tuam. It was run by nuns; some say it was a terrible place, but I didn't really think so. It closed in the early 60's, when I was sixteen... the oldest child there. I'm not sure why, but I was never picked for adoption as hundreds of my peers were and, unfortunately, a few others died there over the years.

'I didn't mind though, as I got on well with the nuns and priests who visited and became a sort of helper around the place. Anyway, like I said, it closed and I had to go somewhere. A priest I was close to felt that I should move away from Ireland, start a new life. He suggested I study for the priesthood and that he could get me a place in The Sacred Heart seminary up in Rabat, in Gozo, if I liked the idea. Obviously, I'd never heard of Gozo, but that just added to the adventure. So I came here and the rest, as they say, is history.'

'The seminary wasn't run by Jesuits was it?'

'It was up until 1909... then handed over to the local diocese.'

'Good.'

'Why do you say that?'

'Let's just say they're not my favourite people.'

'Nor mine!'

'You've always lived here then. You've never been back to Ireland?'

'Oh yes, I've been. It's a bit like Malta: full of Catholics and empty churches. I've been all over, really; you go where you're told in this game; but, yes, I was based in Malta. '

'And you never traced your parents, I take it?'

'No, I never tried, to be honest. They'll be with the angels by now.'

'Do you believe that, really?'

'Well, put it this way: its better than oblivion, wouldn't you say?'

'Don't know, never met any angels.'

'Thea's not far short, don't you think?'

Both Healy and Spiteri blushed.

'You're a very bad man, Francesco' said Spiteri.

'Don't listen to her, Matt. What if I'm right?'

'I'll take my chances, Father. I will definitely take my chances.'

Spiteri interrupted, 'This conversation is getting much too intimate. At least wait till we're drunk!' She regretted her words as quickly as she said them. 'God, sorry, Matt.'

'Hey, I told you, no problem. You and Francesco get as sozzled as you like. Might be interesting to watch!'

'Problems with the demon drink in the past, Matt?'

'Yea, but I'm okay now. I just take cocaine instead.'

A slight breeze blew in from the bay and the awning above them flapped a little, but the noise was drowned out by the sound of laughter from three new friends rising into the warm evening.

Matt Healy had really enjoyed the previous evening's dinner, and enjoyed it even more without any worries over a hangover. He had taken the one-hour time difference between Malta and the UK, waited for 9.00 a.m. Malta time, and called Jim Frame.

'Nice to see you're still getting into work early.'

'Matt, look, I thought I was doing the right thing…'

'Forget it, but since you got me into this, you can help me out. What was the name of that woman, the one who specialised in child abductions?'

'Are you psychic?'

'Eh, what do you mean?'

'Her name is Miriam Calder, and she's been enquiring about you. How she might get in touch.'

'Really? Interesting. Do you think she'd be willing to come over here, give us a hand?'

'Us?'

'Aye, very good, Jim. Don't push your luck, mate. Give me her number.'

Healy's conversation with Calder went so smoothly, he was kicking himself for not having thought to call her sooner. He picked up the phone again and called Thea Spiteri.

***

Thea Spiteri thought she detected a hint of anger in Jason Attard's voice.

'When was this agreed?' he had asked.

'Last night. Why? You seem to have a problem with it?'

'Last night? How did that come about?'

'Jason, sorry, but I'm not being cross examined by you. What is the issue here?'

'I just think I should have been consulted. Healy's not even a policeman anymore. A drunk, yes. Policeman, no.'

'Sit down, Sergeant Attard. Now! What is this about? Really about?'

'How do you know you can trust him?'

'How did you know he had had a problem with alcohol?'

'I looked him up.'

'Looked him up?'

'On the Internet.'

'Why?'

'Research. Has it ever crossed your mind he could be a suspect?'

'Don't be ridiculous.'

'Why ridiculous? As I say, what do you really know about him? He was a suspect once before, or did he forget to mention that?'

'What are you talking about?'

'There were a number of killings a few years back in Scotland. Healy was a suspect.'

'And?'

'Someone else was arrested.'

'And?'

'And what… he was still a suspect.'

'But I'm assuming since he's here, wrongly suspected.'

'Maybe.'

'Oh, for Christ's sake, Jason. What have you got against him?'

'Nothing. I just think you ought to be careful.'

'Thank you for your concern, but I'm a big girl now—and your superior officer, I might add.'

'Still…'

'Enough, Jason. Father Francesco liked him.'

'What?'

'Father Francesco liked him; he was with us at dinner last night.'

'Oh well, that's that then.' Attard got up and left the room. *A double betrayal. I will not let all my sacrifices go to waste now. They will both suffer for this.*

\*\*\*

That evening, Miriam Calder came off the Edinburgh flight looking harassed Thea Spiteri, although impressed by the speed at which she had answered the request for her help, was slightly put off by the woman's appearance.

Matt Healy sensed Spiteri's awkwardness. 'Don't be fooled, Thea. She's all there, and more.'

'All there?'

'Focused, knows what she's doing. She just looks eccentric. Maybe she is a little, but if anyone can help us, it's her.'

'Good evening, Ms Calder. I'm Inspector Spiteri. Thank you for coming at such short notice.'

'Not at all, Inspector. The truth is I was desperate to come, so thank you for asking,' replied Miriam Calder, acknowledging Matt Healy with a nod.

'You come very highly recommended.' Spiteri, too, nodded in Healy's direction.

'Yes, I worked with Matt a couple of times, I'm sure; I hope I can live up to my billing.' Calder and Healy shook hands while walking back to the car.

'Shall I take you to the hotel first, allow you to freshen up?'

'Yes, that would be lovely, but bring me up to date with the case on the way.'

'That won't take long,' muttered Healy.

The journey to The Meridian Hotel only took about twenty minutes but, unfortunately for Spiteri, that was more than enough time for her to inform Miriam Calder of everything they had on the abduction.

'Don't worry, Inspector; I didn't really expect much more. All these cases tend to be the same. If the child isn't recovered in forty-eight hours, then…'

'So you think Jamie Smart is dead?'

'No, I try not to think anything per se, I just deal in possibilities and probabilities, try to work out where an investigation should go, not where it's been.'

Neither Healy nor Spiteri were quite sure what Calder meant; but neither challenged her. 'I would like to talk to both the parents, separately, as soon as possible, perhaps tomorrow afternoon? I'll read over the case notes you've kindly given me tonight and visit the abduction scene in the morning; alone if that's okay with you both? I don't like other people's input until I've got things clear in my own mind.'

'Yea, fine,' said Healy. Spiteri gave him a withering look but said nothing. *Slapped wrist for you, Matt.*

'Yes. I'll assign a driver to pick you up at 9.00 a.m?'

'Marvellous.'

'I'll be speaking to the mother, Mary Smart, myself in the morning. It's a thankless task, as I'm sure you'll know, but I feel I have to keep her as informed as I can.'

'Quite. And the father?'

Healy couldn't resist. 'Bit of an arsehole. Heavy drinker, hates the mother.'

'He has lost a child, Matt, when all's said and done,' replied Calder.

'I suppose.' Healy felt rebuked; he caught Spiteri smiling in the rearview mirror. He stuck out his tongue.

'No *suppose* about it.'

Spiteri felt she was going to enjoy Miriam Calder's company after all.

Healy stayed in the car as Spiteri helped Calder into the hotel foyer with her bags. 'Why don't we all meet up tomorrow night for dinner? You can give me an update of your initial thoughts then.'

'Sounds lovely.'

'Good. I'll give the details to the driver.'

Spiteri got back into the car just as Healy was getting out.

'I've decided I'll walk from here.'

'To Pembroke? It's a fair walk.'

'I like walking.'

'Do you want to sit in tomorrow with Mary Smart?'

'No! Well, yes, I suppose so. What about Calder? When are you tying in with her? I'd like to be in on that, if that's okay?'

'Don't worry; we're going to meet for dinner tomorrow evening.'

'We? I'm beginning to think you're dating me, Inspector.'

'I take it you've started drinking again then?' Spiteri ordered her driver to head off, a slight smile crossing her lips.

Healy turned and started walking back towards Pembroke. He, too, was smiling.

Both were blissfully unaware of the traumas about to invade their lives.

# CHAPTER 9

Thea Spiteri had decided to bring Mary Smart into the St Julians police station the following morning. She watched her coming out of the police car and up the stairs to the station, wondering what she could say that would offer even a glimmer of hope to a distraught mother. She felt a degree of guilt for even thinking that Mary Smart could be involved in her own child's disappearance, but it was her job to examine every possibility. *Some mothers do kill their own children, Thea.* Her thoughts didn't bring her much comfort somehow.

'How are you today, Mary?'

Mary Smart didn't answer. She didn't need to. Healy gestured to Spiteri; could he speak? Spiteri nodded.

'Mary, we've brought a missing child expert over from the UK. She's the best. It's good news: the Maltese police are leaving no stone unturned.'

'Has she ever traced a child alive?' There was no malice or anger in Mary Smart's voice, merely resignation.

'Yes, she's solved lots of cases.' Spiteri looked at Healy, eyebrows raised; Healy shrugged.

'Oh well, that's good.'

'She's going to come and talk to you this afternoon, Mary, in your hotel, around 3.00 p.m. Then she's going to talk to Peter, around 4.00 p.m.'

'Oh well, that's good.'

Spiteri intervened, tried to focus on the job. 'Mary, can we just go over a couple of things about the day Jamie went missing?'

'If you like.'

'Did you see anyone strange, anyone who looked out of place?'

'No! Don't you think I would have said, done something if I'd seen some fucking weirdo hanging about Jamie?'

'Of course. I know this is stressful... I just mean anything odd, unusual. It may not have struck you as important at the time but...'

'No. Well.'

'Well, what?'

'It's nothing, daft.'

'Tell us.'

'Well, that morning, the morning Jamie went missing.'

'Yes.'

'As we were walking to the beach, I stopped to look in a shop window and, oh this is stupid.'

'What?'

'Well, in the reflection, I thought for a moment I saw Peter.'

'Peter?'

'Peter! My fucking, useless bastard of a husband. Jamie's Dad. I looked round. He wasn't there. It wasn't him. Strange thing, though.'

'What is?'

'His clothes.'

'What about them?'

'When he turned up at my hotel, the day he flew in, he was wearing exactly the same clothes as I imagined I'd seen him wearing.'

Claudia Sansome led Mary Smart to the waiting car while both Healy and Spiteri watched out of a second floor window.

'What do you make of that?' Spiteri asked.

'Hard to say, but it needs checking. If you get someone to check passenger lists, I'll call Scotland, get some background info on Peter Smart. Probably be tomorrow, though, before I have anything.'

'Same with me. Things move slowly in Malta.'

'Well, it's something. I think we should keep it to ourselves until we've spoken to Miriam Calder tonight. See what she thinks of the father.'

'Okay. I need to get on with other things, Matt. See you in Mono tonight at eight p.m?'

'Right.'

Although Sliema is another town, the lack of space on Malta ostensibly means that areas merge seamlessly into others, with only the Maltese themselves seeming to know where one place starts and another finishes. Mono was a trendier restaurant than Meet, and it was off the tourist trail, its cubicle seating lending itself to conducting more discrete conversations. Healy nodded his approval as he looked around for Spiteri. She obviously hadn't arrived yet, but a waiter pointed Healy towards a table by a side window, opened just enough to allow a cooling breeze in. He didn't have to wait long before Spiteri's familiar ride drew up outside. He watched as the front passenger door opened, disappointment soon surfacing as he saw Jason Attard disembark and open the back door for Spiteri. *Get a grip, Matt. This is work.*

'Hi, You've not been waiting long, I hope?' asked Spiteri.

'No, just got here. Hello again, Jason.'

'Hello.' Mumbled, rather than said.

*What's up with his face?*

'Miriam not arrived yet then?'

'No.'

'Let's order some drinks '

Spiteri and Attard decided to just settle for beers, waiting to see if Calder would want wine. Healy chose water.

Healy glanced out of the window as the waiter placed the drinks on the table. 'Isn't that Francesco?'

'What? Where?' asked Spiteri.

She followed Healy's gaze and saw that it was indeed Father Francesco striding purposefully on the opposite side of the road. Spiteri rose and walked over to the entrance.

'Francesco!'

The old priest looked faintly startled and took a moment to focus. 'Come in, Francesco. Matt and Jason are here. I can't ask you to join us I'm afraid; police work.'

'Oh, no no, I couldn't anyway. I'm on my way to visit an old and very dear friend. The end is near, I fear.'

'Sorry to hear that, Francesco. Is there anything I can do?'

'Pray, Thea, you could always pray. And you, Jason. I'll not include you, Matt. The shock might obliterate heaven! Anyway, I must hurry. Your other guest not arrived yet?'

'No, on her way.'

'Good. Bye. Enjoy your evening.'

Jason Attard turned to Healy after waving the old priest off. 'How long were you a policeman, Matt?'

'Oh, twenty-odd years.'

Attard leaned closer to Healy, his eyes on fire. 'Why did you leave?'

Healy got the sense he was being grilled, that Attard somehow knew the answers already.

'It was just the right time. And I lost someone, someone I cared about. Like I said, it was the right time.'

'How long have you been sober?'

'Jason!' Spiteri interrupted.

'It's okay, Thea. Under a year. Why?'

'No, that's admirable. I was just wondering.'

'No problem.' In truth, something else was picking away at the back of his mind. He just couldn't work out what.

The driver of the car sent to pick up Miriam Calder had been uncertain of the exact location of Mono and had actually driven passed the entrance a few moments earlier. He was now doing his best to perform a three-point turn in a street so narrow, even a ten-point turn would be a feat of driving excellence.

'Driver, sorry, what is your name?' asked Calder.

'Victor Denaro, Ma'am. Do not worry; I will have you there in two minutes.'

'No, Victor, that's the thing. I'm not feeling very well. Could you just take me back to the hotel and let Inspector Spiteri know I will call her in the morning? Give her my apologies.'

'Yes, of course, but are you sure? I will only be a few minutes.'

'Yes, I'm sure. It's perfectly fine. I just need some rest.'

A silence lingered over the table in Mono, and Spiteri was livid at Attard, regretting even inviting him, but she had been persuaded by his obvious displeasure at being, in his eyes, sidelined previously.

'I wonder what is keeping Miriam's car?' asked Spiteri. Her phone rang.

'Yes. I see. Okay, that's fine. Yes, just go home. I'll call you in the morning.' Spiteri's eyes narrowed slightly, as she closed her mobile and put it back in her bag.

'Miriam's not feeling well. She's just going to speak to us in the morning.'

'Right, well if it's okay with you, Inspector, I'll just go. After all, Ms Calder's contribution is all I wanted to hear, not small talk.'

Spiteri glared at Attard. 'Yes, that will be more than fine. And Sergeant, I will see you in the St Julians office at eight a.m. Sharp.'

Attard strode out of the restaurant. He did not say goodbye to Healy.

'Have I done something to offend Attard, Thea?'

'No. I don't really know what has come over him in recent days.'

She watched Attard's back as he walked down towards the Sliema harbour, his mobile phone pressed to his ear. Spiteri wondered momentarily who he could be calling, as he didn't seem to have a social life. She turned to Healy. 'Well, what do you want to do then, Matt?'

'I'm not that hungry now, to be honest. It's a pity about Miriam, but you saw yourself that she looked shattered coming off that plane last night. She's no spring chicken, you know. Fancy a stroll?'

'Why not? I'll show you where the Jewish assassins were!'

'Eh?'

'You'll see.'

Thea Spiteri and Matt Healy wandered along the Sliema seafront. Spiteri showed Healy where the scenes from the Spielberg film *Munich* had been shot. Healy pointed to the paintings of eyes on all the fishing boats and asked for an explanation.

'The Eye of Osiris. The fishermen believe he protects them, wards off the evil spirits that exist out on the sea.'

'Right.'

'Oh, Matt. Bend a little to the spirit world!'

'Right.'

'Osiris is also the god of fertility.' Spiteri smiled and looked away. Healy was happy to let her talk. Healy was just… happy.

They walked for an hour before Spiteri hinted that she would need to call her lift and get home. Healy looked in her eyes, contemplated an attempt at a kiss, resisted. 'Okay. I'll just walk.'

'Are you sure?'

'Yea, I like it.'

'Oh, so it's not my company then, it's the walking.'

'I wouldn't say that, I wouldn't say that at all.'

Even though it was 11.00 p.m. by the time Healy got home, it was still hot, and he was drenched in sweat. He decided on a cool bath and straight to bed. He never noticed the flashing red light on his answering machine.

He was also unaware that Spiteri had forgotten to mention that Osiris was also the god of the dead.

# CHAPTER 10

Matt Healy could only describe it as being startled awake. At first, he thought it was a bird that had flown into his room and was trapped. Then he thought he'd left the radio or television on pause and it had sprung back to life. He tried to focus his eyes, but the room was in darkness.

He slowly pulled himself from the depths of sleep. *Phone, phone, it's the phone.*

'Matt, it's Jim.'

'Jim? Jim! Are you fucking kidding me or what. What time is it?'

'It's eight a.m. here.'

'Seven in the morning here! I repeat; are you fucking kidding me?'

'Matt, you'll want to hear this. I promise.'

Healy was about to burst into another bout of expletives but something in Jim Frame's tone stopped him.

'What is it?'

'Peter Smart.'

'What about him?'

'He's a kiddie fiddler.'

By this point, Healy was sitting up in bed, fully alert.

'You're shitting me?'

'Nope, and there's more.'

'What?'

'Well, no charges have ever been brought, but he's also been reported twice for hitting kids. The last time—wait for it—by Mary Smart herself. But here's the thing: Mary Smart also made a claim for damages for the mental trauma brought on by the assault on Jamie. She got fuck all, but it makes you think.'

'It certainly does. Thanks, Jim. Sorry for jumping down your throat.'

'No problem, got to go. Bye'

Healy lay back on his pillow. He tried to assess just what impact the information he'd just been given had on the case. The truth was that, although of interest, it didn't really have any. *Unless...* Although it was too early to call Spiteri, he toyed with the idea of calling Attard, *just for badness.*

He decided instead to get up, make a coffee, and think. *Think, Matt, think.* His eye was drawn back to the phone. The answering light was flashing. He pressed the play button. There was a lot of static, *probably a mobile phone.* "Ma... it's Miriam... der... I need... it's def... the... father. There's an ea... open... coffee... St Geo... please, meet... eight o'clock... Bye."

'Jesus Christ.' Healy couldn't believe it. What had Calder found out? How did she find it out after one meeting with the Smarts? He and Spiteri had both spoken to them and not really gotten anywhere. He checked his watch. Time for a quick shower, walk down to meet Calder. *Is the boy alive?*

Matt arrived at Anthony's Coffee Shop at two minutes to 8.00 a.m. Even at that time, he wasn't the first customer. Early morning shift workers occupied a couple of tables. Healy sat down at a corner table, away from the others; he would want privacy for his talk with Calder. He ordered a coffee, hoped she wouldn't be long. After a couple of minutes, his attention was drawn to a couple of the workers sitting at a pavement table; they seemed animated and were pointing at the beach. Healy looked over. At first, he couldn't see anything but then, through the early morning heat haze, he could see a number of people standing on the sand at the far end of the bay. People in blue uniforms. Healy's instinct took over; he knew. He dropped a two euro coin on the table, stood up, and started walking. He had only gone a few meters when his mobile rang.

'Matt, it's me,' Spiteri said.

'I know.'

'Matt, its bad news.'

'I know.'

Spiteri was confused. 'What? How do you know?'

'I'm walking towards you right now.'

Spiteri turned, made Healy out walking on the pavement around the bay. He arrived in a couple of minutes. Ashen.

'It's Miriam, isn't it?'

'Yes.'

'Can I see?'

'Matt, it's not really appropriate.'

'For Christ's sake, Thea. I brought her here.'

'Okay.'

Miriam Calder appeared to be sleeping in a foetal position on the beach, apart from the clear stab wound in her back. The word WHY written in the sand, just beyond the ends of her righthand fingers.

'Jesus, Matt, I'm so sorry.'

'Any leads?'

'Matt.'

'Any leads!'

Spiteri ignored Healy's tone, tried to placate him. 'No, too soon. Did you know her well?'

'Hardly at all. Consulted her on a couple of cases back in Scotland. Couldn't even remember her name, to be honest, had to call an old contact to get her details. She was very matter-of-fact, abrupt even. Well, you saw that yourself. She knew her stuff.'

'How come you're here so quickly?'

'That's the thing. She left a message on my phone about midnight last night. Asked me to meet her here for a coffee. I was going to call you, but it was early. She told me it was the father who abducted Jamie... and an earlier call from Scotland kind of confirmed it. I was going to hear what she had found out, then call you. Get Smart in; this will be down to him as well. He must have sussed she knew it was him.'

'What do you make of her writing "Why" in the sand?'

'How do you know she did? Could have been anyone.'

'I don't think so. This was a quick kill. The killer wasn't for hanging about, can't see him wasting time writing things in the sand. She's got sand under her fingernails, but that isn't conclusive either, I know.'

'No question mark.'

'What?'

'No question mark after the *Why*.'

'Well, I don't suppose grammar was top of her agenda at that point, Matt.'

'Maybe not, but why write anything?'

'A cry of despair? You said yourself she was very intense.'

'Suppose.'

Healy turned and walked back the way he had come.

'Matt, where are you going?'

'For a drink.'

Spiteri desperately wanted to follow him, but her duty lay with Miriam Calder.

Jason Attard followed the conversation intently whilst directing the cordoning off of the beach. He smiled silently to himself. *All good things come to those who wait… and act.*

'Language classes!' Claudia Sansome feigned mock shock. 'You?'

'And why not?' replied her husband.

'Why? What language?'

'It will help with the business. I'll be able to talk to the tourists easier. Malta University does lots of evening classes: French, Spanish, Italian, German.'

'So what one are you going to do?'

'I haven't made up my mind. We'll see.'

Joseph Sansome waved at an incredulous Claudia Sansome as he jumped into his Land Rover and drove away. He knew exactly what language he was going to try to pick up. *I only need the basics, Catherine, baby.*

# CHAPTER 11

A couple of hours had passed since Matt Healy bought the whisky. He couldn't get Cutty Sark, so had bought the first bottle he had recognised, J & B. He hadn't answered his phone or even opened his curtains.

Neither had he opened the bottle. He had stared at it, talked to it, put it in a cupboard, and taken it back out again. He had read the label countless times and pondered the processes that had gone into making the golden liquid. But he hadn't opened it, and he knew now that he wouldn't. He rose from the kitchen table, put the glass back in the cupboard, and went outside. He opened the plastic bin at the end of his drive and threw the bottle inside.

As he turned to go back inside, a car drew up. It was a car he recognised. 'Hello, Matt,' said Spiteri as she got out of the driver's side.

'No driver?'

'Wanted a bit of privacy.'

'Right. Come in.'

Spiteri sat at the kitchen table, opposite Healy. 'I called you.'

'I know.'

'Right. What did Calder's message say, Matt. Do you still have it?'

'Yes, it's not that clear, a lot of static, but basically she said Jamie's father was responsible, and that she needed to talk to me. I also got a call from Scotland. Smart has a history of violence and interfering with kids. Nothing actually proved, though. I'll get you the phone. You'll have to take the whole thing, they don't use tapes anymore.'

'Fine. I'll replace it, though. Might need to keep it for a while.'

'Did you check Smart's flight for when he arrived?'

'Yes, the day before Jamie went missing.'

'That should do it, then.'

'We couldn't find him last night, but Attard is picking him up from the hotel now. He's just arrived there; been out all night. I'm going to interview him shortly. You can't sit in, but you can observe if you like.'

'I'll need to freshen up.'

'Yea, I think that would be wise.'

As Healy showered, Spiteri looked around his home. *Nothing. No photos, no mementoes, nothing personal.*

An hour later, Matt Healy watched as Thea Spiteri and a female officer he had never seen before entered the interview room. Peter Smart was already sitting at the lone wooden desk. He looked agitated, but no more so than usual. It was hard to tell if he had been drinking that morning or not.

Spiteri led the interview. 'How are you feeling this morning, Peter?'

'Like shit.'

'How did your chat with Miriam Calder go?'

'Okay, I suppose.'

'She thinks you abducted Jamie.'

'What? What the fuck is this?'

'Is he still alive, Peter? Please tell me he's still alive.'

Smart jumped up. 'I want to speak to my MP.'

'What?'

'Not my MP, the embassy guy. That's it. The embassy guy.'

'Sit down.'

'No.'

'Sit down or I'll arrest you now and you'll be taken straight to prison awaiting a hearing. Could take months.'

Healy didn't think for a minute that what Spiteri had just said was true, but Peter Smart sat down.

'When did you fly in to Malta, Peter?'

Smart's head slumped. 'Alright, alright. I flew in the day before Jamie went missing. No crime in that, though.'

'Why did you do that?'

'I followed her out here.'

'Who?'

'Britney Spears. Who the fuck do you think? That bitch of a wife of mine.'

'Why?'

'I was hoping to catch her out shagging, okay? This fucking divorce is costing a fortune. I'm just trying to get some balance, stop all the blame being put on me.'

'A fortune? Do you have a fortune?'

'Aye okay, but… What? Are you kidding me? Fees, the house, furniture… she's going to get everything.'

'Shame. You being an ideal husband. You got a criminal record, Peter?'

'No.'

Spiteri stared into Smart's eyes but never spoke.

'Well, no really.'

'What does that mean?'

'That bitch.'

'What bitch is that, Peter?'

'The fucking wife, that's who. Reported me a while back, said I was *touching* Jamie. Fucking lies. Police couldn't prove a thing. Just one of her plots to get at me, leave me with nothing.'

'You ever hit Mary, Peter?'

'Only man and wife type stuff. Don't know about here like, but in Glasgow... well, it happens.'

'Nice. Ever hit any other women, Peter, other than your wife, of course?'

'No.'

'Any other kids ever say you had touched them?'

'I'm no putting up with this!'

'Where's Jamie?'

'I don't fucking know.'

'When was the last time you saw Miriam Calder?'

Smart shook his head 'What?'

'Miriam Calder. When did you last see her?'

'You know all this. Yesterday!'

'Why did you kill her?'

'What! Man, this is fucking insane. I want somebody in here. Now.'

'Fine. We'll arrange that. Just so you know, we're going to charge you with two murders. You'll be put before a magistrate tomorrow. You won't get bail, I can assure you of that. Goodbye for now, Mr Smart.'

Spiteri and the other officer left the interview room. They were happy with the way things had gone. They were about to get a lot happier.

'Inspector.' It was Jason Attard who was walking towards them.

'Yes?'

'The knife that killed Miriam Calder. I found it.'

'Great. Where did you find it?'

'In Peter Smart's room at the hotel. I thought if it wasn't on the beach, he had probably taken it back to his room to wash or get rid of in the hotel dumpster. I searched his room. Bloodstained knife under the bedside cabinet. Thank you very much and goodnight.'

Spiteri turned to Healy. 'And that, as they say, is that. Well done, Jason. Great work. Get the knife to forensics.'

'Already done.'

Matt Healy was waiting at the entrance to the police station as Spiteri came out. She was smiling. 'Case closed, I think, Matt.'

'Possibly.'

'Possibly?'

'Why would Smart kill Calder? Okay, she might have accused him, although I doubt she would be that unprofessional. But also, kill your own child?'

'People do, Matt, all the time.'

'I know, it's just…'

'Just what?'

'I don't know.' Healy wrung his hands.

Spiteri could see that Healy was on edge. 'Can I make a suggestion, Matt?'

'Sure, what?'

'Speak to Father Francesco.'

'What? What about?'

'Your demons.'

Healy looked out over the ridiculously blue sea. 'I don't know, Thea. It's been a long time.'

'I'm not suggesting a confession. Just talk to him. I've known him a long time. So have others. He can help you. He helped me.'

Healy didn't want to probe exactly what Spiteri meant by her last comment. He just nodded and said, 'I'll think about it.'


Claudia Sansome was thinking about her husband. Since their daughter's death, he had never spoken about her. He had carried on pursuing his business dream, and now he was talking about going to evening classes. Claudia assumed it was because, like her, he accepted God's will.

It was true that Joseph Sansome had always dreamt of having his own business. He had taken whatever work he could get: construction work, working in a slaughterhouse and, finally, in a pizza parlour in Sliema. A year after taking the job, Joseph learnt that the owners of the parlour, Philip and Eva Attard, Jason Attard's aunt and uncle, intended to emigrate to Canada. Claudia Sansome spoke to Jason, Jason spoke to his relatives, and an honourable deal was struck, Maltese style. Joseph worked hard, the business was successful, but Joseph Sansome was a broken man.

He and Claudia had paid for a statue of St Catherine to be commissioned and erected outside the chapel of the same name in Zejtun, in memory of their daughter. Although everyone in the town felt for the heartbroken couple, it appeared that at least one person did not. A week after their memorial statue was put in place, two dead cats had been nailed to crosses and left at the base of the statue. Investigations by the *Pulizija* came up with nothing, the town got on with its daily activities, and thoughts of Catherine, the cats, and heartbreak evaporated into the subconscious of the island. Joseph went to work each day, he came home in the evening, ate his dinner, and asked his wife about her day. Some days, he listened more intently than others.

On the days she spoke of the abducted child, he listened the most carefully of all.

\*\*\*

'Thank you for agreeing to see me, Francesco.'

'Don't be silly, Matt. I consider you a friend. Have you been to the Dingli Cliffs? I often go there in times of crisis.'

'No, but who says I have a crisis?'

'You wouldn't have phoned me otherwise.'

The drive to the Dingli Cliffs only took about twenty-five minutes, but it was twenty-five minutes Matt Healy wouldn't forget in a hurry. A combination of the state of Father Marandon's car, driving in Malta in general, and the ageing priest's clear ambivalence towards road signs made Matt a relieved man when he finally got out at the cliffs. He had to admit the views were stunning.

'Let's sit. What's troubling you, Matt?'

'I'm not sure about this, Father. I'm a former Catholic. I told you that.'

'No one's a former Catholic, Matt. You are one; you're just resisting it! Anyway, I'm not trying to drag you back. To be honest, sometimes I feel like walking away, myself.'

Healy admired the older man's honesty, his matter-of-fact style. 'Why don't you?'

'Nowhere to go! Ha, no, I'm at peace. But we're here to talk about you. What's wrong?'

'I've been running away for a while now, Francesco. I want to stop, but I can't.'

'Running away from what?'

'Myself. How I was the cause of the death of someone I loved. How I lost everything through jealousy and not doing my job properly. And now, as you know, I'm running away from drink.'

'Matt, you and I live in a world at a time where human beings, as a race, have more than they ever dreamt of. We can write and say what we want. Basically, do whatever we want. We have access to more knowledge than Plato, Michelangelo, Aristotle, and Einstein ever dreamed of. We can easily see more of the world than Alexander the Great, Attila, Napoleon, even Hitler could ever have hoped to see. Yet, we take drugs, we drink to excess, we cheat, and we steal. We worship images on screens bigger than some people's living space. We say we crave reality, yet live in fogs of media images and stage-managed situations which, just to underline our own stupidity, we call reality. Why?'

'I don't know. Tell me.'

'Because Matt, although we have all that, our lives have no real meaning, no real purpose. Oh yes, of course, we go to work, we get our kids what they want, we have a car, we go a package holiday, but why do we do that? We do it to carry on functioning, to pretend we are living. But we are not living. We are existing within a false reality that has been created to make us think we are alive when in fact, we are just creatures who have been reduced to accepting that merely existing is enough.'

'But existing is necessary, surely?'

'No Matt. Living is necessary. No one lies on their death bed wishing they had paid their mortgage off earlier, or that the plasma screen in the living room was eighty inches instead of seventy-two.'

'So…'

'So meaning and purpose, Matt. Find that, and you will have everything you hoped a bottle of whisky could have given you.'

Healy looked out at the distant horizon.

'Did you kill this person you loved?' asked Francesco.

'No, but I may as well have.'

'Was it a woman?'

'Yes.'

'She was murdered?'

'Yes.'

'Was the person truly responsible caught?'

'Yes.'

'Then justice is done. You must move on. You are here now. There are worse places, believe me. And there are people here who care for you.'

'People?'

'Thea, for one.'

Healy strained forward, looked over the edge of the cliff. 'Long way down.'

'Did you hear me?'

'I heard. I can't get involved, not again. For Thea's sake, believe me.'

'Can't she be the judge of that?'

'I need to eliminate the past.'

'Many have tried, Matt. It can't be done, but you can rid yourself of the burden of it.'

'How?'

'Belief. Belief in yourself, in the power within you, to accept where you are on your journey… and to continue that journey, meaning and purpose, Matt, meaning and purpose.'

'What about the guilt? Catholics are big on guilt as I recall.'

'And on forgiveness, Matt. It is the sin that is to be hated, not the sinner.'

Matt Healy looked again over the edge of the cliffs. 'Mind if I drive back, Francesco?'


Mary Smart sat trance-like in her hotel room. Thea Spiteri had called ahead to say she was coming; she had news. It was not the news Mary Smart had hoped for. Even finding Jamie's body would be better than what she had just heard.

'I don't believe it.' Her voice was barely audible.

'I'm sorry, Mary, but it's true.'

'Where's Jamie? Is he alive?'

'Your husband won't say. I'm sorry, but we don't think so.'

The wail started somewhere in Mary Smart's inner core. When it came to the surface, Spiteri motioned for the policewoman in attendance to get a doctor. Half an hour later, Mary Smart was lying on her hotel bed. Her eyes were closed, and Spiteri started for the door.

'Money.' Spiteri turned and looked at the bed, unsure what she had heard.

'Did you speak, Mary?'

'Money. It's all that bastard is interested in. Money must be what's behind what he did to Jamie.'

Spiteri paused. She couldn't see a connection, not at first. A dark realisation came into her mind. 'Mary, did you take out holiday insurance?'

'No, too dear. Didn't think I'd need it for a week in the sun.'

'Did you mention that to Peter, about no insurance?'

'I can't remember. I might have done when I was asking him for a contribution. I don't know.'

Spiteri phoned Sansome before she left the foyer of the hotel and told her to find out if any sort of insurance policy had been taken out on Jamie Smart's life.

Two days later, Healy and Spiteri sat at a roadside café overlooking Baluta Bay. 'Christ, I've heard it all now. Insurance money! Poor kid. And Smart still hasn't said about the body?'

'Nothing. Still says he had nothing to do with any of this.'

'What did he say about the insurance policy?'

'He just said it was a spur of the moment thing. His wife had been screaming about what would happen if Jamie needed to go to hospital, he'd had a win on the horses...'

'Lying bastard.'

'I hear you spoke with Francesco?'

'Oh did you. So much for *in confidence*.'

'It wasn't the confessional, Matt. Did it help?'

Healy shrugged. 'He mentioned you.'

'Oh, did he now? So much for *in confidence*.'

Healy and Spiteri gazed out over the bay. Their fingertips touched. Neither pulled away.

# CHAPTER 12

Mary Smart had been moved from her hotel to the Dean Hamlet Aparthotel. She had a self-contained room, but never cooked. She did drink.

She, and her son, were yesterday's news. The *Sun* newspaper's Crime Reporter had long gone, and the newspaper was hinting, none too gently, that it couldn't be paying for Mary to stay in Malta indefinitely. Mary Smart didn't care; she wasn't leaving the island without her son.

Rita Gatt, the hotel's manageress, felt that she had been more than sympathetic to her devastated guest's plight, but having a desolate, drunk Glaswegian sitting day after day at your pool was definitely not good for business. The story of the abduction alone had resulted in many holiday cancellations on the islands. She stood in the hotel's foyer, waiting for Spiteri and Healy.

'Listen, I've done my best, but this can't go on. Can you speak to her, persuade her to go home, maybe?' she pleaded rather than asked.

'We'll talk to her, but we can't force her to do anything,' replied Spiteri.

Healy and Spiteri walked out to the pool. A bedraggled, but not noticeably drunk, Mary Smart was sitting on a white plastic chair. She was wearing a wool cardigan over a heavy jumper and jeans, despite the heat.

'Hello, Mary,' said Spiteri.

'Any news?'

'Sorry, no.'

'Right.'

'Mary,' It was Healy talking, 'can I make a suggestion?'

'As long as I don't have to pay it any heed.'

'Go home. There is nothing you can do here.' Healy knelt down in front of Mary Smart, took her hand, and looked into her bloodshot eyes. ' Mary, I live on this island, as you know. I promise I will not stop looking for Jamie, and as soon as I've any news, I'll call you.'

'That's it? That's your advice?'

'Yea.' Healy felt deflated.

'Do you have any children?'

'No.'

'Thought not.'

Spiteri decided to interrupt. 'Mary, I don't have any children either. But one of my colleagues lost a child a few years back. It's something that I'm sure haunts her every day, but you have to move on. Matt is right. Go home. I also swear that I will never stop looking for Jamie.'

Mary Smart's gaunt face looked up at Spiteri. 'Is he dead?'

Spiteri felt no need to lie. 'I think so.'

'What will happen to his father?'

'If he's convicted, he'll go to prison for life.'

'No death penalty?'

'No, we are the same as the UK No death penalty.'

'Pity.' Mary Smart rose unsteadily.

'Where are you going, Mary?'

'Home. My life is over. May as well die someplace I know.'

Spiteri and Healy watched as Mary Smart walked down the corridor towards the lifts. They looked at each other, silently acknowledging that she was right. They slowly traipsed after Mary Smart.

'Do you have any idea where the body could be, Thea? After all, Smart doesn't know the island, and he wouldn't have taken the chance of taking it a long way from St George's Bay, surely?'

'Matt, come on, don't you think I've spent every waking hour wondering where the poor child can be, that we haven't searched in every conceivable place?'

'Yes, sorry.'

'It's okay. I understand.'

'I suppose it's even harder with this being the first time it's happened on the island?'

'It's not.'

'Not what?'

'The first time.'

Healy stopped, stared at Spiteri. 'You said it was.'

'I lied.'

'Why?'

'Let's go for a coffee.'

Healy sat opposite Spiteri on the terrace outside the Dean Hamlet Coffee Shop. He thought she looked tired.

'So. Not the first time?' Healy asked once the waiter had served them two espressos.

'A couple of kids went missing before. Maybe more than a couple.'

'And you didn't bother to tell me?'

'Look, Matt, you're not in the police anymore.'

'Thanks, I forgot. I was under the impression I was helping you.'

'Matt, I'm sorry, but you're not Maltese. It's difficult.'

'What is?'

'This kind of society. The previous cases aren't actually on record, even the two we know about.'

'What? Why? What do you mean?'

'It was hushed up.'

'Who by?'

'It was years ago Matt, different times. I was a raw constable at the time.'

'Who by?'

'The church.'

'There's a shock. What about the parents, what did they do?'

'That's the thing, how it was possible. Both the boys were in an orphanage. It was Malta in the '90s. When the second one went missing, we focused on the staff, and a young priest who was acting as a kind of mentor to the boys came to the fore as our man. That's how I first met Francesco; he acted as a kind of conduit between the government, police, and church.'

'A conduit! Nice. What happened?'

'The priest was spirited away, the investigation disappeared.'

'The '90s aren't the dim and distant past, Thea.'

'I know, but things move slowly here. The church is a major power. Priests still cannot be charged with a crime here, even now. The present government is trying to change that, but it's not easy. The Maltese are a simple, God-fearing people, Matt. It's all they know. Sometimes I think it's all they want to know, and it's maybe changing, but very slowly.'

'Were the boys ever found?'

'One was. The road from the coast up towards Naxxar was being widened and the construction work unearthed the body. It was pure chance, really. That's what kick-started the investigation.'

'How do you know it was the priest?'

'Another kid at the orphanage, he was about six at the time I think, had spent all his life there, came forward, admitted to having sex with the priest and being asked to run away with him.'

'Oh well, a homosexual priest, that's that then. I'll alert the media. What happened to that kid?'

'I don't know. Grew up, moved on, who knows.'

'And the other missing kid?'

'Never found.'

'Jesus Christ, Thea. What sort of investigation was that?'

Spiteri appeared to be on the point of tears. 'Why don't you just shut up , Matt. It's all right for you. Besides, there have been no more abductions, so…'

'No more abductions! How do you know? You said yourself it was by chance that the first investigation was instigated.'

'So everything worked out just dandy in Scotland did it, Matt? Nothing swept under the carpet there? Nobody's pension rights preserved by "forgetting" a drink drive charge?'

Healy sat and stared. Took in the implications of what had just been said.

'I'm not saying that.' The sight of Spiteri's slumped shoulders, showed Healy that Spiteri was close to tears.

'Nobody, and no system, is perfect, Matt. You accept what you have to accept and move on.'

Healy looked down the lane at the side of the coffee shop. *If only you knew the whole story, Thea. Why I really am the way I am.*

# CHAPTER 13

Two days had passed since Thea Spiteri had told Healy about the other abductions. He had been angry, but in the end, had had to concede that there was no link to those cases—*or should that be non-cases*—and Jamie Smart's disappearance. Healy had spent the two days tramping around the areas surrounding St Julians: Pembroke, Is-Sweiqi, Il-Meilah, Tal Ibrag, Misrah. Within himself, he knew it was a hopeless task, but he intended keeping the promise he had made to Mary Smart.

*What if that bastard Peter had a car? Did Spiteri check car hire places? What if he had an accomplice? Naw, too selfish and too risky. What if, what if… what, fucking, if.*

Healy walked as far as Mosta and Naxxar. In Hal Ghargur, he saw a beautiful blonde woman getting into a blue car outside the side entrance to the huge church dominating the village. She smiled at Healy before starting the engine. He pondered romance. *Not for you, Matt. Look at how romance always ends for you. Still, Spiteri's beauty is hard to ignore. Ask her out. Use an excuse about wanting to talk about something. Let her know it's not a date.* The blonde woman drove off. *What would she have thought, if someone came up with that approach to her? Guess I'll never know.*

***

Claudia and Joseph Sansome had married in 1988. They were both twenty years old, and very much in love. Claudia had joined the *Pulizija* two months earlier and was keen to make a career in the force. She also wanted children. Joseph was hard working and had the same drive that Claudia had, but in a different direction. He hoped to have his own business one day. He too wanted children. In the meantime, Claudia was happy to make a home of the maisonette they had rented in Haz Zeebug and settle for a couple of cats, even though Joseph obviously didn't like them. They were both happy to let God bless them with children.

In 1989, the Sansomes were indeed blessed: their baby daughter, Catherine, was born. Life for the Sansomes was perfect.

In 1994, the Sansomes attended a funeral Mass in St Nicholas Chapel in Siggiewi, Joseph's home village, and buried their daughter in the tiny graveyard at Ta Bordin, where his family had a plot.

The Sansomes were never happy again. They stayed together, bonded forever by grief. They breathed, walked, talked, worked, ate, and slept. They functioned, but they were dead, and neither had any desire to live. A few months later, even the cats left.

***

'Why don't I cook you a meal? A traditional Maltese dish. No aphrodisiacs, since it's not a date,' said Spiteri.

Healy had plucked up the courage and suggested a meal to Spiteri. He had used his "not a date" line, which he was particularly pleased with. Spiteri's response, though welcome, left him feeling that it might have backfired.

'Well, yes, if you're sure. That would be great.'

'What's your address?'

'I'll get you picked up.'

88

'Is that allowed?'

'This is Malta. We cover things up.'

Healy wasn't quite sure how to take the comment. He settled for 'Okay.'

Spiteri lived in a converted farm house, referred to as a House of Character by the numerous estate agents on the island, on a plot of land surrounded by vineyards and orchards, between Mdina and Madliena. Healy inwardly acknowledged that she had been right to send a driver; otherwise, he would never have found it. The house was the nearest thing to heaven he had ever seen.

'My God, Thea. What a beautiful house.'

'Thank you. It's taken me years to get it like this.'

'Is it a family home?'

Thea smiled. 'I'll tell you at dinner.'

'What are we having?'

'Everything.'

\*\*\*

May Hooper was also settling down to a meal, but she was eating alone, in her hotel room. She had read about the abduction of the Scottish boy and the murder of Miriam Calder, who she knew vaguely through their work in the field of child abuse. She had immediately informed the hotel reception that her plans had changed and that she would be staying on 'for a while.' She was delighted that her agent had booked her into the Corinthian Hotel, as it was close to St George's Bay, where the boy had disappeared and the murder took place, as it would allow her to go down to the bay and see things for herself. She then contacted the *Pulizija*, explained who she was, and asked that Inspector Spiteri be informed that she would like a meeting as she may be able to assist in the investigation.

\*\*\*

Claudia Sansome knew her husband was seeing another woman. She understood. They hadn't had sex in years, and never would again.

She knew he would never leave her, and she would never leave him. Sometimes grief can be stronger than love.

Joseph Sansome did not think his wife was seeing another man. He understood. He understood her need to leave the house, live a different life to the one with him. He knew it wasn't sex she sought. He knew she would never leave him, and he would never leave her. Sometimes grief can be stronger than love.

***

'Bigilla.'

'What?'

'Bigilla. Broad bean pate.'

'Really? It's lovely.'

'Thank you.'

'So, tell me about yourself, Thea.'

'Well, I'm a woman.'

'Yes, I can see that.'

'Do you know where the name Spiteri comes from?'

'Italy?'

'No. I mean, the meaning.'

'No.'

'Spiteri was the name given to children born out of wedlock, or orphans or, basically, children without parents. I'm the classic Disney character,' Spiteri said with a smile. 'Born in a field, poor mother, wrapped in a blanket and left on church stairs.'

'My mother used to shout that at me all the time: "Were you born in a field?" I never realised it actually happened.'

'I was eventually adopted by a couple, obviously since I was such a beautiful child! And was brought up in Hamrun. My parents were nice people, good people, but they were emotionally distant, so I lived quite a solitary life. Oh, I don't mean I was unhappy or anything; I did okay at school, had friends. I could have gone on to college, maybe even university, but I wasn't interested. I'd only ever wanted to join the *Pulizija*, so here I am.'

'Anyway, time passed and my parents passed on. A couple of years later, my father's brother, my Uncle Mathew, who I barely knew, also died. He'd never married and had lived a quiet life as a fruit farmer out here. I was staggered when I was told that he had left everything to me. I sold all the land around the house—farming seemed like too hard work!—and used the money to modernise the house.'

'Right. You've done a fantastic job, Thea. How do you feel now about your childhood?'

'Thank you. It's no stigma now, but it was.'

'I see. And…'

'And, yes, that is why I felt a bond to the children in the orphanage. Francesco sensed it. We kept in touch, became friends. He wasn't here that much but once he came back, we formed a close bond.'

'But I sense you're a non-believer?'

'I see myself as a Don't Know… an agnostic rather than an atheist. You?'

'The same, I suppose.'

'Married?'

'What?'

'Have you ever married?'

'No. You?'

'You'd know if I was.'

'How's that?'

'I don't believe in divorce. Traditionalist. If it's broke, fix it; don't throw it away. All I'd ask of a partner is not to lie to me. I hate lies, Matt.'

'Very profound.'

'Not really. Practical. There aren't many good men around.'

'Or women.'

'I take it you've been hurt'

'Haven't we all?'

'Maybe, but there are degrees of hurt.'

'I'd say death is a pretty serious degree.'

'Ah.' Spiteri walked into the kitchen. 'Do you like fish?'

'Yes.'

'That's a relief. We're having Torta Tal – Lampuki.'

Spiteri didn't wait for the obvious question; she just inwardly smiled and brought two plates to the table, placing one in front of Healy.

'Eat!'

Healy did as he was told.

'Do you like it?'

'Yes, it's really nice, but I like to know what I'm eating!'

'Okay. Fish, onions, tomatoes, cauliflower, olives… in a pie.'

'I don't like cauliflower. Reminds me of school meals!'

'Too late. You've eaten it.'

\*\*\*

This time, it was a dog. It had been hit by a car and was probably going to die anyway. It didn't twitch when the nail went through its paw. The apparition thought the dog's tail may have moved, but, no matter, God's work needed to go on. The square around St James Chapel, on the outskirts of Haz-Zebbug, was deserted. The cross holding the crucified dog was heavy. It would have been better to hoist it up the front of the church tower, but the weight proved too much, even for the apparition. When Father Mark opened the heavy front doors at 6.30 a.m, for the two or three adherents to attend 7.00 a.m. Mass, the cross fell on top of him, pushing him down onto the floor beside the baptismal font. It took Father Mark quite a few moments to comprehend what had happened, what was lying beside him. It took nearly a minute for him to notice the shallow whining of the dog.

\*\*\*

'It's a pity you don't drink,' teased Spiteri.

'Oh, why?'

'I have a lovely white Maltese wine for the fish and an equally lovely red, for the Fenkata.'

'Okay, stop right there. I happen to know that Maltese wine is not highly rated. And what is Fenkata?'

'You're right in a way about the wine. The Maltese farmers are traditionalists, and a lot of them choose grapes for their yield rather than quality. Local whites are usually from Ghirgentina grapes, and the reds from Gellewza. They can be okay, but it's a bit of a hit and miss at times. I like wines from the Meridiana estate. Technically, it's Italian wine I suppose because the grapes were originally imported from Italy in the 80s, but let's not split hairs.'

'And Fenkata?'

'My speciality! Spaghetti with rabbit sauce, then fried rabbit and potato.'

'I don't eat rabbits. I had one when I was a boy, Benji his name was.'

Spiteri's face fell; Healy smiled.

'Bastard!'

Healy's smile turned into shared laughter.

# CHAPTER 14

'It's not my case, Francesco. You know that.'

'I know, but this has been going on for years now, Thea. It's sacrilege, that's what it is. Sacrilege. Whoever is conducting the investigation is incompetent.'

'Well, I wouldn't say that. It's obviously being done by some poor, demented soul. You should have empathy for them!'

'Empathy! Try telling that to Father Mark; he soiled his cassock! I hope that's not laughing I hear, Thea?'

Spiteri sensed Father Francesco himself was trying to suppress a laugh. 'Not at all, bit of a sore throat.'

'Okay, well, please, Thea. See if you can get more effort put into finding this mignun.'

'Mignun? Is that a psychiatric term?'

'Bye, Thea.'

'Hold on, would you like to meet for dinner on Wednesday evening?'

'Just us?'

'No, Matt will be there.'

'You like him, then?'

'Yes, but don't let your imagination run away from you!'

'Are you sleeping with him?'

'Eight p.m. in The Gozitan in St J's. Bye.'

'Bye.' It was Father Francesco's turn to laugh.


May Hooper had phoned the hotel reception and was making some enquiries.

'Is the water park far from here?'

'No, madam, a ten-minute drive.'

'Is it busy at this time of year? Lots of families?'

'I believe so, madam. Mostly Germans, I understand.'

'Fine, thank you.'

She had stayed in the park for about an hour, but decided that it was too busy for her purposes. She left early, and went back to her hotel with the intention of getting changed and walking down to St George's Bay.

'Ms Hooper. I'm a police officer assigned to accompany you. Jason Attard.' He offered his hand. 'Inspector Spiteri is very busy, as I'm sure you can appreciate, but she has asked me to come and escort you anywhere you want to go. She says she hopes to be able to meet with you personally soon.'

'Oh, right. Well, I'm not really sure why I need an escort, but nice to meet you.' She shook his hand. May Hooper thought that Attard was reasonably attractive, but too young for her. Attard had no similar thoughts; he was betrothed; in his mind

'No, I'm not an escort as such. My boss feels it will be good for me to learn from you at the same time as making sure you are safe. A woman has been killed, after all. They hope I'll become an expert in child abuse, abductions, murders, and the like.'

'The like? There is no "the like," Jason. The people who commit these kind of crimes see children as objects, not human beings. Objects. Objects to be used for their purposes in the same way that you and I might use a pen then throw it away when it's done.'

'Christ.'

'I don't think any God can be around much when these kinds of things are happening, Jason.'

'No, I suppose not.'

'Anyway, the abduction here has been solved, thankfully. The kid's own father did it for the insurance money.'

'You think so?'

'What?'

'That the father did it; it wasn't abduction, as such.'

'Yes.'

'I doubt it.'

'Why?'

'It just doesn't ring true.'

'If I'm allowed to speak to the father for half an hour, I'll tell you if you've got the right man.'

'Really? How?'

'I know these people. Has the child ever been found?'

'No.'

'Mmm. Don't you think that's odd?'

'Not really. He's pled not guilty. He's not likely to reveal where the body is, is he?'

'I understand he's also been charged with Miriam Calder's murder? Again, you don't find that odd?'

'No, what do you mean?'

'Well, a guy flies in from Scotland, never been in Malta before. Abducts and kills his own son, buries him so well that no one can find him, and follows that up by killing someone he's only met for the first time a few hours before.'

'Wait and see if you get to meet him; he's, what is it you say in Scotland: "a bampot."'

'So was Timothy Evans, hung under practically the same circumstances, and he never killed anyone.'

\*\*\*

Someone else who was unsure of Peter Smart's guilt, Matt Healy, had other more pressing concerns. He was sitting at his kitchen table in Pembroke, going over his fitful sleep of the night before. He had gone to bed on a high. His meal at Thea Spiteri's home had been wonderful, and to make things even better, she had suggested meeting up again that Wednesday. She told him she was also going to invite Father Francesco, but Healy didn't see that as an issue. On the contrary, he saw the old priest as an ally, even a matchmaker, and Healy knew he needed all the help he could get—as far as relationships with women were concerned But that night, the black dog had come for Healy. He lay on his bed, neither awake nor asleep. He was walking through some sort of netherworld. His bed was wet from his sweat, but he was cold... *Oh, so cold. Why, Susan? Why did you leave me? Why didn't you trust me? Susan Dornan turned, smiled, pointed. Healy looked: Susan Spiteri was walking towards him. Smiling. Holding outstretched hands to him. Healy looked back towards Dornan. She was gone. He turned to Spiteri. She too was gone. Only a patch of sand with the word* Why *remained.*

\*\*\*

'I won't be in till late on Wednesday night, Claudia,' said Joseph Sansome.

'That's okay. I'll be late myself,' said Claudia as she looked out the kitchen window. Joseph considered asking where she was going, what she did on the nights she was out. But the truth was that he didn't care. He had more important things to consider. Joseph had converted Catherine's old room into an office, and he spent most evenings, whether Claudia was home or not, in the room with the door locked.

# CHAPTER 15

Matt Healy made a momentous decision. He was going to buy a hat. And wear it that evening to The Gozitan, where he was meeting Thea and Father Francesco. He had never been a hat man, but he was going a bit thin on top now and knew from life in Spain that getting the top of your head burned was no fun. *Besides, I think I'll look very dapper!*

He strolled into St Julians, giving himself plenty of time to buy the hat and then amble along to the restaurant. He stopped for a moment to enjoy the spectacle of a Maltese Traffic Warden, helpfully trying to explain to two Dutch lads, attempting to fish off a jetty, that "Reserved for Fish Hawkers" was not the same thing as "Fishing Allowed." Just as Healy was about to move on, he noticed Attard walking down the hill from The Corinthian Hotel, accompanied by a woman who looked vaguely familiar. Jason Attard stopped and introduced Healy and Hooper.

'Matt is an ex-policeman from your homeland, May.'

'Really. Are you here on holiday, retired, or bounty hunting?'

'All three.'

Hooper and Healy smiled. Attard looked out across the bay. 'We better be going,' he said.

'Maybe we could meet for a drink, Matt?'

'He doesn't drink.' Attard said it before thinking it through.

'Yes. Thank you, Jason. I can answer for myself. My young friend is right: I don't drink alcohol, but I would be happy to meet you for a coffee tomorrow, say, two p.m?'

'Perfect. Come up to the coffee shop on the hotel's terrace, The Corinthian, up there,' she said, nodding.

'Yes, I know it. See you tomorrow. Bye.'

Attard and Hooper moved off, leaving Healy wondering just what Attard's problem with him was.

After a bit of deliberation, posturing and haggling, Healy settled for an off-white Panama. *Very, Our Man in Havana… ish.*

He sauntered past some trendy wine bars that he had never been in, and walked into The Gozitan. Spiteri and Father Francesco were already there and giving the menu a thorough examination.

'My God, it's James Bond!' said Father Francesco as Healy approached their table.

Spiteri nodded and smiled. Healy was a happy man.

'Lamb from Gozo is on special, Matt. I recommend it. It's what I'm having.'

'Yes, I think I'll copy you, Thea,' said Father Francesco.

'Three lamb it is, then,' said Healy.

'What do you make of people nailing cats to church doors, Matt?'

'Oh, for God's sake, Francesco, let's talk about something nice, at least to start!' said Spiteri.

'Well, I don't think they're in the SPCA,' said Healy.

'No, I suppose not.'

'That's how I made detective!'

Healy turned to Spiteri. *Jesus, you're beautiful.* 'I've just bumped into Attard and a Hooper woman. Jason can't stand me. Why?'

'A Hooper woman? Sounds like a cartoon!' said Father Francesco.

'Oh sorry, Francesco. She's an apparent expert on all things child abuse. Over here for a conference and to plug her book. She contacted me yesterday. Apparently she's staying on in Malta to see if she can help with the Jamie Smart abduction,' said Spiteri.

'Ah.'

'No idea about Jason, Matt,' said Spiteri. 'He's been acting a bit oddly all round lately, to be honest. Anyway, he called me today. Hooper still wants to meet me, discuss the Peter Smart case.'

'Peter Head Case, more like. Did you agree?'

'Why not? It's not as if it can do any harm, and if she could come up with something to help find Jamie…'

'Right.'

'I'm picking her up at nine a.m; I'll brief her on the way to Carradino in Paulo. I've set up a meeting there for her and Smart at ten a.m.'

'Carradino?'

'The prison where Smart's being held.'

'Thea, *correctional facility*, please,' interrupted Francesco.

'Right.'

He wasn't sure why, but Matt Healy did not say, that he too, was meeting May Hooper the next day.

\*\*\*

Jason Attard hadn't asked May Hooper to dinner. She was glad. He was a nice enough young man but always gave her the impression that his mind was elsewhere. She sat in Hugo's and skimmed through a tourist guide. She had always had an interest in churches and had soon realised that if there was one place in the world you wanted to be if you were interested in churches, it was Malta.

"The Citadel in Rabat, Gozo's capital, was constructed in the Eighth century, when Arab rulers built the imposing defensive walls." A car horn blared outside and made Hooper look  An irate driver was lambasting a tour bus driver for stopping on a blind corner. The bus driver didn't appear too perturbed. *Evening Gozo Tour* was the message emblazoned on the side of the bus. *Fate takes a hand. Gozo, here I come.* May Hooper quickly finished her strawberry daiquiri, boarded the bus, sat back, and watched as the other passengers, many of them families, boarded  She smiled as one of the families, with a slight air of entitlement , commandeered the first three rows at the front of the bus.

\*\*\*

Joseph Sansome was not dining a whore, or anyone else. In fact, he had never been unfaithful to Claudia and never intended to be. He didn't look back at the time when he and his wife were close; it only brought back memories of Catherine. And Joseph Sansome was only interested in Catherine's legacy, in ensuring Catherine's name lived on, and that other people got to know the meaning of loss.

\*\*\*

'That was a really lovely meal. Thank you, Thea,' said Father Francesco.

'Oh, you're welcome, I'm sure. Remember this kindness before you ask me any more questions along the lines of those recent ones!'

'What's this? You being un-priestly again, Francesco?' asked Healy.

There was a twinkle in Father Marandon's eyes. He had his response ready but noticed that Thea had become distracted.

Thea Spiteri had noticed a *Pulizija* car drawing up outside the restaurant. The driver,on his radio,  appeared agitated. The passenger door opened, a young officer who Spiteri recognised but did not know by name walked tentatively into the restaurant and looked around. Spiteri knew he was looking for her: she always left word where she was going to be, in this case in the hope that Jamie Smart's body had been found. She waved at the policeman to come over.

'Sorry to disturb you, Inspector…'

'Never mind all that. Something's happened hasn't it? Have you found the missing boy?'

'I'm afraid not, and, well, eh…'

'God, spit it out. What is it?'

'Another child has gone missing.'

Thea Spiteri rose quickly to her feet, Matt Healy shook his head, and Father Marandon blessed himself.

***

Joseph Sansome was already in bed when Claudia returned. He wasn't asleep but pretended he was. He watched, slightly surprised, as Claudia took off all her clothes, including her underwear, and placed them in the washing machine, which was housed in an alcove in the en suite bathroom. She then ran a shower. He continued to watch her silhouette as she dried herself. He was not aroused. He closed his eyes and quickly fell asleep.

Claudia suspected that her husband may have been watching her, but she didn't care. She knew she would not have to ward off any unwanted advances. Those days were long gone; she didn't miss them. She continued to ensure she was spotlessly clean.

# CHAPTER 16

Nicola Tizian wasn't a man who normally worried about what the police or other authorities were doing, but he could tell that the people who were sitting across from him were worried. The Vella family owned the biggest construction company in Malta. The grandfather, one of the two men sitting across from Tizian, had started the company just after the end of WW II, their father had grown the company, and now Tony and Mario Vella were running the conglomerate while their father concentrated on his role as the Environment Minister in the ruling Labour government.

With there being no casinos on Sicily, it was a fact that traffic from Sicily provided nearly fifty percent of the casino trade in Malta, so it made sense that the Vellas wanted to become involved in the building of any new casinos, hotels, or resorts that would be given planning permission by the Maltese Authorities. The lure of vast returns, both legal and through money laundering, meant that criminal organizations had developed a voracious appetite for land. This, in turn, meant that the officials involved in approving planning applications were on the front line. They could make large amounts of money for themselves, either through donations to their party or by having healthy bank accounts in Switzerland. Alternatively, they could resist the apparent unfettered acquisition of land if they were brave enough. A proliferation of Internet Gaming companies—remote gaming—had also been approved by the Lotteries and Gaming Authority, LGA, and to further muddy the waters, the Maltese Financial Services Authority, MFSA, had licensed several companies to provide financial services, which in turn were used to disguise the origin of criminal proceeds through trust funds and investment funds.

The monies for these projects—and the accompanying bribes—made its way into Malta through a web of international wire transfers all over Europe, in effect making the whole European Banking industry a large money launderette. It was, however, these kinds of transfers that were worrying the Vella brothers.

Malta's Financial Intelligence Analysis Unit, FIAU, had summoned the brothers to a meeting at their headquarters, as they wanted to question them on two possibly fraudulent multi-million euro transfers. The Vella brothers had immediately asked Tizian for a meeting.

'You have nothing to worry about,' Tizian assured them.

'But what if this leads to *Pulizija* involvement? We are not criminals. We can't live like that,' said Tony Vella.

Tizian smiled inwardly. *They actually think of themselves as being straight.* He also chose to ignore, but not forget, the implied insult. 'You have nothing to fear from the *Pulizija*. I have told you that before. You are also covered from the financial authorities. Our lawyers in Geneva are, at this very moment, preparing the documents that will show that the funds came from a pension scheme that invests in construction projects all over the world.'

'Are you sure things will be okay?'

'Well, if you don't like that idea, why don't I organise something similar to the unfortunate incident in Naples yesterday morning?' The

Maltese Times of that morning had carried a front page story of the assassination, in broad daylight, of a top official in the Naples Planning Department. He had been shot twice in the head by a man who walked up to the official at 9.00 a.m. as he was buying a newspaper and then walked, not run, walked, away.

'No, no… We are just asking.' Both brothers made themselves clear.

***

May Hooper already knew about the abduction on Gozo when she got the message from the hotel reception letting her know that Inspector Thea Spiteri had called to say that their meeting, scheduled for that morning, was off. She was impressed that, even though she must be under intense pressure, Spiteri had found time to contact her. She was even more impressed to find out that her scheduled interview with Peter Smart was still on, and that a car would pick her up from the hotel foyer shortly. If she was surprised to see Matt Healy in the front passenger seat when the car pulled up, she didn't show it.

'Hi, May.'

'Hello. You riding shotgun?'

'Thea just thought it would be best if Smart recognised a friendly face.'

'And is yours?'

'What?'

'Friendly?'

'Well, Attard told me about your doubts about Smart, and I'll admit that I find the whole thing a bit strange.'

'In what way?'

'Same as you, I guess. Let's just see what he has to say. Don't forget: he probably did kill Miriam Calder.'

'Did he?'

'Well, the knife with her blood on it found hidden in his hotel room is a bit of a giveaway.'

'Would you murder someone on a beach, then carry the blood-stained weapon back to your own hotel room and just leave it there?'

Healy never replied.

*\*\**

Thea Spiteri had been on Gozo all night. The child apparently abducted was a young German girl, Ingrid Lam. She had gone missing from a party visiting Ramla Bay on Gozo. Luckily for Spiteri, the parents spoke perfect English. The girl's father appeared reasonably calm given the circumstances, but his wife gave the impression she was paralysed.

Initially, Spiteri had had more of a problem with the Gozitan *Pulizija* officer, who organised the initial search. 'Look, the similarity here is too marked. It's obviously linked to the case on Malta.'

'Why?'

'Why? What, no abductions on these islands ever, then two in a couple of weeks, and you don't think there may be a link?'

'We do things differently on Gozo.'

'Do you. Good for you, but I have been assigned this case by the Magistrate. Discussion over.'

Over the next few hours, Spiteri found out that the German couple had agreed to go to different places , as the children were fighting over what to do. Some wanted to stay at the beach at Rambla Bay; some wanted to go to see the nearby Roman ruins. The missing girl had stayed with her mother and a friend she had made at the beach. She accepted that the Gozitan *Pulizija* had, after a slow start, conducted a thorough search. But, unlike in Malta, they did have some sort of information about what had happened. The *Pulizija* had established, from talking to Ingrid's holiday friend, that "a man in a Jeep had stopped and asked the two girls for directions. He had spoken in German. Ingrid said that she knew where the hotel the man was asking about was. 'Yes, I stay there!' Ingrid had said. The man had then asked if Ingrid would show him." Ingrid had gotten into the Jeep willingly.

Healy's mobile phone rang, breaking the silence in the car. 'Hello.'

'Matt, it's me, Francesco.'

'Hello.'

'It's happened again.'

Healy was thrown momentarily 'I know. I was with you... in the restaurant.'

'No, not that.'

'What, then.'

'Another church desecrated. Madliena this time. Terrible, terrible.'

'It's pretty gruesome, I agree, but in the bigger scheme of things... well, just ask, Thea.'

'Oh, I know. I'm an old fool, but the world has changed, Matt. People have changed, and not for the better. Any word from Thea?'

'No, nothing. I'm on my way to the prison to talk to Smart with May Hooper.'

'Oh, right. I'd better go. Bye.'

'Man of few words?' May Hooper said from the backseat.

'Not usually, I can assure you. It was Father Marandon. He lives in the Dominican Monastery up near Rabat. Good man. Wise. Easy to talk to, not like some priests.'

'Rabat, do you mean in Gozo?'

'No, there is a Rabat here in Malta, too. Beside Mdina.'

'Oh. I was in the Gozo Rabat yesterday.'

'Yes? Impressive?'

'I thought so.'

'This is the prison now, on the left,' said the same young constable who had come to the restaurant looking for Spiteri, spoiling a good evening.

Healy looked over at the grim building, but his thoughts were on why May Hooper had never said anything about being on Gozo the previous night. *The night of the abduction. Strange.*

# CHAPTER 17

Carradino Correctional Facility was an imposing-enough-looking building, but compared to the ones Healy had been used to in UK, it was distinctly lower league. After a minute or two of name checking and box ticking, Healy and Hooper were admitted into the inner sanctum A plaque on the wall read "*Suavis Aspero*" *Firm but fair.* Healy had no idea of the mottos in Barlinnie and Strangeways prisons, but he was pretty sure that it wasn't firm but fair.

He and Hooper were shown into an interview room just off the main exercise yard. It was clean and bright, and a table and four chairs sat in the middle of the room. A separate individual chair sat in the corner. Peter Smart was lead into the room by two guards and sat down opposite Healy and Hooper. One of the guards left, closing and locking the steel door behind him. The other guard took a seat in the corner.

Peter Smart looked the epitome of the condemned man. His blank gaze shifted slowly between his two visitors. After a moment, he bowed his head.

'Do you remember me, Peter?' asked Healy. 'I saw you at the police station. After Jamie went missing. Matt Healy.'

'Have you found him?'

'No. Sorry.'

'Peter, my name is May Hooper. I'm not a police officer, but I've worked on several mur… eh, abduction cases.'

'Right.'

'Where did you bury Jamie's body, Peter?' barked Healy.

Smart raised his head, ignored Hooper. 'I didn't do any of this, Mr Healy.'

'You took out an insurance policy. A murder weapon was found in your hotel room.'

'Planted.'

'By who, Peter? Nobody knows you here. Who would want to frame you?'

'I didn't even know the dead woman. Why would I want to kill her? She said she believed I was innocent, for Christ's sake!'

'Is that true, Peter, she actually said that?' asked May Hooper.

'I swear she did. I was happy when she left my hotel. I felt she was on my side.'

'What do you think happened to Jamie, Peter?' asked Healy.

Smart paused, stared at the wall behind Healy. 'Someone snatched him.'

'Any ideas who?'

'No, unless it was that tramp of a wife of mine. Got pissed, killed him by mistake somehow, an accident maybe, panicked, hid the body.'

'Do you honestly think that, Peter?'

'No… I don't.'

Healy glanced over at Hooper. She shook her head, nodded to the door.

'Mr Healy?' said Smart.

Healy turned, expectant. 'Yes, Peter.'

'Do you think I'll still get the insurance money?'

\*\*\*

Hooper and Healy got their driver to drop them at Tigne Point and let him know that he could just leave them there; they would walk back along the sea front. They found a small restaurant that didn't look too touristy. Healy ordered *barbuljata* and a bottle of sparkling water, Hooper deciding on *Froga tal-bajd* and a glass of white wine. They spent a few minutes waiting for the food to arrive, admiring the views of the Mediterranean and the sparse remains of the old Tigne Fort that once guarded the entrance to Marsamxett Harbour along with the fort at St Elmo. Healy decided to focus on their visit to the prison.

'So what do you make of Smart, May?'

'Interesting.'

'In what way?'

'Well, he's clearly innocent.'

'Why do you say that?'

'I know the world of abuse, Matt. It wasn't him, believe me.'

'What about Calder's murder? Did he do that, do you think?'

'It's not really my area of expertise, but if he didn't abduct the child, why would he kill Calder?'

'Nutcase?'

'Maybe, but I don't see it.'

'No, to be honest, neither do I. So, how exactly does someone become an expert in abuse and abduction?' Healy asked with a slight smile.

Hooper too smiled. 'Good question! Are you aware of my background?'

'A bit, but that, unfortunately, has happened to a lot of kids. They move on.'

'I know. I can't really explain why, but whenever a story appeared on the TV or in the papers, I just devoured it. And, of course, fate seems to have played a part.'

'Sorry, what do you mean?'

'Matt Healy, are you telling me you haven't read my book!'

'Sorry, no.'

'In 1991, my family went on holiday to Bodrum, in Turkey. We were there for a week. We didn't see TV or read a paper when we were there; it was a good holiday, really. Anyway, when we got back, the papers were full of a child abduction case, Ben Needham. Terrible. He's never been found, although there have been loads of potential sightings.'

'I remember, but didn't that happen in Greece?'

'Yes, a Greek island called Kos. Bodrum is four kilometers by sea from Kos. A ferry runs every hour.'

'And you think your father could have been involved?'

May Hooper shrugged her shoulders, looked out to sea.

'Was he ever questioned about it?'

Hooper laughed. 'Matt, he wasn't even questioned about my friend's murder until I wrote my book. Even then, it was a joke.'

Healy pondered for a moment. He tried to work out if what he had just heard was significant or merely co-incidence. Like most policemen, he didn't believe in coincidence.

'I see what you mean, May, but it's a bit of a stretch, don't you think?'

'Mmm.'

\*\*\*

Father Marandon was beside himself with anxiety and fear. *Another child abduction, another desecration. My island, my world, is being attacked by evil. Why is the Lord allowing this? Why?*

He had called Thea three times, but she, perhaps understandably, hadn't answered or called back. He had thought about calling Healy, but he knew he was most likely with this so-called expert and he didn't want any involvement there. *Abduction expert. Holy mother of God, preserve us.*

\*\*\*

Hooper and Healy declined coffee. Matt Healy wanted to get home as quickly as possible; he had work to do, so he had used tiredness as an excuse and suggested a taxi instead of the walk. Hooper readily agreed but asked to be dropped in St Julians, as she wanted to buy as many papers as possible, to read about the latest abduction. After dropping Hooper off, Healy took the taxi to Pembroke Park and got out there. He wanted to walk the coastal trail back to his house and clear his head. *Am I losing the plot? Can there really be a connection between Hooper's father and the abduction on Kos? Shit, I wish I still drank.* Striding through his front door, Healy checked his watch. *5.00 p.m, 4 back home. That skiver Frame should still be there.* After two rings, Frame's familiar twang answered, 'Aye.'

'What bloody way is that to answer the phone?'

'Ah knew it wis you.'

'No, you didn't. How?'

'Ah could smell the sobriety doon the line!'

'Very funny. Listen, Jim, have you got a lot on? I need you to do a couple of things for me.'

'Matt, this is Glasgow. Remember, there's always a lot on.'

'I know, Jim, but I've got a suspicion about someone, a well kent face in Scotland. Wouldn't do your career any harm if I'm right.'

'Who?'

'Ever heard of May Hooper?'

'Naw. Bye.'

'Jim, come on. May Hooper. Wrote a book blaming her own father for a murder back in the Sixties in Coatbridge.'

'Oh aye, her. I know what you're talking about, just didn't recognise the name.'

'She's over here just now, doing a tour or something. Anyway, she asked to speak to Peter Smart, you know, the arsehole that's charged with abducting his own son. I went with her, and we went for lunch after, got talking.'

'Did you shag her?'

'For fuck's sake, Jim. Listen. At lunch, she mentions that her and her dad just happened to be staying four kilometers away from that place, Kos, the island that Needham boy was abducted from in 1991.'

'So?'

'So? Fucking, so! Are you winding me up? Don't you see a link?'

'No really.'

'Jim, as a favour to me, will you contact the Greek police, see if it was ever suspected that Hooper's father was involved? Can you also try and find out if any of the officers involved in the Coatbridge murder are still alive?'

'Whit? Greek police, twenty odd years ago… don't think you've got much chance.'

'Okay, but will you try?'

'Okay, since it's you.'

'How are the Rangers getting on these days?'

'Fuck off.'

Healy and Frame were both smiling as Frame slammed the phone down. Jim Frame was a big fan of Rangers Football Club, a club whose disintegration into being a lower league team caused him many a sleepless night. Even though Healy supported their bitter rivals, Celtic Football Club, Frame knew there was no malice in his remark. He walked to the coffee machine in the corner of the squad room; a young, attractive policewoman was standing stirring a cup-a-soup. "I might need to go to the Greek islands on a case soon, all a bit hush-hush. Fancy coming?"

'In your dreams, Grandpa.'

They both walked away laughing.

# CHAPTER 18

Jason Attard was a happy man. Thae Spiteri had called him the previous night and told him to meet her at 10.00 a.m. in her office in the *Pulizija* Valetta building 'to discuss both abductions.' He took it as sign of her trust in his judgement. He wasn't at all happy when he knocked and entered Spiteri's office to find Healy and Hooper already sitting there.

'Sit down, Jason. I want to review everything we have concerning these abductions. The deputy commissioner has phoned me twice today already. I can't keep telling him we've nothing. Did you chase up forensics?'

'Yes. They said they'll have word to us today.'

'Good. Okay. Next thing. Matt and May went to interview Peter Smart yesterday. They...'

'Why?' interrupted Attard.

'Why, what?' replied Spiteri.

'Why did they do that? What's it got to do with them?'

Spiteri stared for a moment at Attard, then said, 'Well, first of all, I asked them to, and secondly, they are trying to help find two children that we have patently failed to find. Do you have a problem with that, Jason?'

'No.'

'Fine. Right, the bottom line. Neither Matt nor May think Smart abducted his son. If they're right, whoever did do it is still out there and may well now have abducted another child.'

'If they're right.' Attard looked over at Healy and Hooper. 'What are you basing your view on, a hunch?'

'It doesn't add up,' said Hooper. 'I studied his body language, his breathing pattern, his eye movement. Believe me, he didn't do it.'

'Yea? What about the knife?' said Attard.

'We're talking about the abduction here.' Healy interrupted. 'But since you ask, what possible motive would Smart have for killing Calder?'

'How about he's bloody mad?'

'How about he didn't do it? How about the two things aren't even linked? How about you start acting like a policeman?'

'Fuck you. What the fuck are you even doing here?' Attard turned to Spiteri. 'The police in his own country didn't want him. Why do we?'

'Outside. Now, Sergeant,' said Spiteri as she rose from her chair.

'Where did that come from, Matt?' asked Hooper.

'No idea, but I intend to find out.'

Spiteri re-entered her office. 'Sorry about that, Matt. I think the abductions are getting to him.'

'Forget it. What are you going to do about Smart?'

'Do? Nothing. He'll still go to trial, of course.'

A gentle knock on the door stopped Healy from replying.

'Yes, come in!' shouted Spiteri.

Herbert, a vetern policeman from the front reception, came in. 'I thought you'd want to see this straight away, Thea. It's from forensics.'

'Thanks, Herbert.' Spiteri smiled as Herbert left. She looked at her guests. 'Not keen on deference, our Herbert!'

'Quite right,' said Healy.

'Oh my God.'

'What is it?'

'The report on the knife. Blood is Calder's alright; but the knife wasn't the one used to kill her. The wound pattern is all wrong, apparently. Shit shit shit.'

'How can that be? Are they sure?'

'Apparently. They've even made a note that they've double checked their results.'

'What about Smart now? I promised Mary I'd keep her informed, Thea.'

'That's up to the Magistrate, not me. I assume he'll still be charged with the abduction. I don't know, to be honest.'

Healy turned to Hooper. 'May, I'm going to stay on for a few minutes, something I want to discuss with Thea.'

'Sure, no problem. I need to call my agent anyway, see what's happening, where I need to be.'

'That's right. I forgot, aren't you supposed to be away by now?'

'Yea, I was, but I decided to stay on, as you know. Then the Gozo abduction happened. I hoped I could help.'

'We appreciate it, May,' said Healy.

'If there's nothing urgent on, I'll maybe stay on a few more days. I love the island, so much history.'

May Hooper headed off and left Healy and Spiteri to their chat.

'I quite like her, Matt. You?' said Spiteri after Hooper had gone.

'Mmm. Awkward.'

'Why?'

'I want you to check something for me, if that's okay?'

'What?'

'The flight May Hooper was on. Was it the same flight as the Smarts?'

'Why do you want to know that?'

'Nothing, just curious. If anything comes up you need to know, I promise you'll be the first to know.'

'Right. Well. Anyway, do you fancy dinner tomorrow night, my place?'

'Yea, great.'

'I'll ask Francesco, too.'

'Great.' There being an extra guest slightly dissapponted Healy this time.


Father Maradon sat looking at Jason Attard. He had watched Jason grow, watched him become a fine young man, had been grateful for his friendship. But he was now concerned about the changes he saw in him.

'Jason, where is this anger coming from?'

'He must have some hold over her.'

'Don't be silly.'

'What then? Is she so blind that she can't see that I am the one whose life has been devoted to her?'

'Thea has to make her own decisions, Jason. Besides, you are assuming a lot.'

'What do you mean?'

'As far as I'm aware, they're just friends.'

'Really?'

'I swear.'

'I think I can show that these abductions have only started since he came to the islands.'

'Jason! Enough. You are just being stupid now, and I'm sorry to say, very immature. Why even think of making life so difficult for yourself?'

'Really? Don't you think it's strange that he brings a woman to the island, and two days later, she's dead?'

'Jason, we have supported each other for as long as we've known each other. But this has to stop now. If you don't change your attitude, this agression, I will speak to Thea myself. Recommend you are moved to lighter duties.'

Attard stared at the ageing priest. 'You wouldn't dare.'

'Jason, my son, it is my job to save people from the evils of this world. Sometimes that means saving them from themselves.'

Attard rose slowly from his chair. 'And The Lord said, those who are not with me are against me.' The two men, lifelong friends, looked at each other and knew things were changing in their worlds.

*\*\**

May Hooper had thought, hoped, that Healy would have asked her to dinner, maybe even his bed. But he hadn't. She stepped off the Gozo Ferry. *No matter. I have unfinished business here.*

*\*\**

The drudgery of shopping was something that Claudia Sansome hated. Life with Joseph was an exsistence which, unfortunately, still required food; and it being Malta meant it was the woman who visited a supermarket every fortnight or so.

'Claudia, Claudia.' She heard her name being called but didn't see who it was at first. Mrs Tanti appeared from behind an advertising stand for Caneston Cream—*Do you have thrush?*—which was rather incongruously placed in front of the bird seed section.

Mrs Tanti had been Claudia's neighbour since she had moved into her marital home. She was a kind woman and had done everything she could to consol Claudia afer Thomas' death, but she also loved to gossip.

'Hello, Sylvia. Sorry, but I've got to rush. I'm on duty in an hour.'

'Did you hear about Georgina?' Georgina was Mrs Tanti's none-too-clever daughter.

'No.'

'Well, the stupid girl went for a job interview today. A good job too, in an estate agent's. The man asked her for her date of birth. She replied July eighteenth. The man said what year. Do you know what the stupid girl said?'

'No.'

'Every year! She'll put me in the grave, Claudia, she really will,' said Sylvia as she crossed herself.

'Oh, she might be lucky. You never know. Anyway, I have to go.'

'Oh, I saw Joseph on the ferry. He didn't see me, so we never chatted.'

'Ferry, the Gozo Ferry? When?'

'Wednesday. I know because I only use it on a Wednesday. I go over to see my father in Ta Sannat. Not that he appreciates it, says I talk too much. Ungrateful pig. God forgive me.' Another cross enacted. Sylvia noticed Claudia's forehead furrow. 'Didn't you know? I hope I haven't spoken out of turn!' Mrs Tanti was almost salivating.

'What? Oh, no, I mean yes. I forgot he had to price a job out there. Yes, that's right, Wednesday. He went up on Wednesday. Sorry Sylvia, I must go.'

'*Mela*, see you soon.' Sylvia wished she could have witnessed the next conversation between the Sansomes. She then saw a former work colleague at the cash point. ' Mitzi, have you heard about Mrs Caruana's leg?'


Healy had arrived at Spiteri's house before Francesco, and Spiteri took the opportunity to let him know that May Hooper had flown into Malta on the same flight as the Smarts.

'So?'

'What?'

'Are you going to tell me? Why did you want to know that?'

'Ach, it's just something that's niggling away at the back of my mind. If anything comes of it, I'll let you know. Promise.'

Any objection Spiteri may have had to Healy's stance was pushed aside by the arrival of Father Marandon.

'That smells wonderful, Thea. What is it?' It was Father Marandon who was speaking, but Healy nodded his agreement.

'*Majjal Fil-Forn.*'

'Ah, Thea, you remembered.' Spiteri had cooked this for the old priest a few months earlier, and he had talked about it for days.

'Hope you don't mind me asking, but what is it?' asked Healy.

'Roast pork loin, Matt. Thea rolls it in chopped rosemary, garlic, salt, and pepper. She scores the top and adds peppercorns, cooks it very slowly in the oven, uses the juices to cook potatoes, carrots, sometimes even spinach.'

'Sounds fantastic.'

'Tastes even better, Matt, as you will soon find out. It's a pity you don't drink. The pork goes very well with a nice bottle of red. Do you mind if I ask you if you consider yourself to be an alcoholc?'

'Hard to say, Francesco. I wasn't a heavy drinker in Scotland. But after, well, my downfall shall we say, I packed up and went to Spain. Ended up living in the bars. Lots of Brits do.'

'And Malta?'

'By chance, really. Not quite a pin on a map, more a stained glass, but here I am.'

'And very glad we are too, Matt. Aren't we, Thea?' Spiteri blushed. There was mischief in her friend's eyes.

'Well, there's one person not too happy about it.'

'Ah, Jason? I was going to talk to you about him, Thea. You too, Matt. He came to see me yesterday. He is a troubled young man.'

'I know, Francesco, but what can I do? I would like to maintain a friendship with him, but I am his superior officer. He has to accept that.'

'I don't think he has any problem accepting that, Thea. Quite the opposite.'

'What do you mean?'

'He adores you, idolises you.'

'All becomes clear,' said Matt Healy.

'Exactly.' replied Francesco.

'Shit,' added Spiteri.

'Well, he can't have you.' The words were out of Healy's mouth before he realised. He blushed, Spiteri blushed, and Father Marandon nodded.

'And so it begins.' The priest raised his glass. Healy examined the floor, looking for a hole. Spiteri busied herself in the kitchen, out of view.

'So, Francesco, when did you give up being a dating advisor to become a priest?' asked Healy after recovering at least a modicum of his composure.

'Hard to say, Matt, hard to say. I had a happy enough childhood, got through school, had girlfriends, went to University, but something was missing. I found out it was God.'

'Did you finish University, get a degree?'

'Oh yes, I got a Desmond.'

'A what?'

'A two-two!'

'Ha ha. Good one!'

'That was the answer, Desmond TuTu, a God-like sign.'

'Do you ever regret it?'

'Not really. Of course, there are times when I think another life might have been more fulfilling, but God's work is never done, Matt, never.'

The evening passed, as evenings with friends, old and new, should pass. Healy offered to share a taxi with Francesco. 'No, it's okay, Matt. Thea has something to talk to you about.'

'Right.' Healy was slightly surprised by the priest's reply but wondered if something had come up in one of the investigations.

Healy saw a slightly inebriated Father Francesco off in his taxi and walked back into Spiteri's farm house.

'Francesco says you want to talk.'

'Did he? No, I absolutely don't want to talk.' Spiteri moved forward, put her arms around Healy's neck and her lips to his ear. 'Let's go to bed.'

By the time Healy had fully taken in what was happening, he was locked in the ultimate embrace with a beautiful Maltese woman. Lost in pleasure. *Is this real? Is there really hope for me now, after Susan? Why has this happened? Why?*

Thea Spiteri looked at Healy over the beakfast table. The night had gone exactly as she had hoped—almost. Healy had been passionate, kind, gentle, forceful. They had fallen asleep, drained, at about three in the morning. By three thirty, Healy had been calling out for Susan, beseeching her, 'Why, Susan?' Spiteri knew that the Susan he cried out for was not her, and that Matt Healy cried 'Why' a lot.

# CHAPTER 19

Joseph Sansome was surprised. His wife never usually asked about his whereabouts at any particular time. 'Wednesday night? I told you I was going out.'

'Yes, I know. I'm just asking where you went.'

'Valetta. One of my suppliers was treating some of his customers to a meal.'

'Oh, Okay.' Claudia knew it was another woman and was sure that since she obviously lived on Gozo, she knew who it was. *I'll deal with her.* Claudia had long suspected that Julia Sammut, a former friend of hers and who now lived on Gozo, was the woman involved. She had seen her messages to Joseph on Facebook, messages that seemed to be more suggestive than casual chat to Claudia. *Infidelity I can ignore. With a former friend? No.*

'I'll be away most of the day today, Claudia. I've a lot to do. Are you working today?'

'Yes, a double shift, I'll be late.'

'Okay. See you later.'

*Sooner than you think, Joseph. Sooner than you think.*

Jason Attard had thrown himself into work. He was spending most of his time on Gozo, mainly to get away from Spiteri. But the search for the German child, despite his efforts, had made no inroads into discovering what had happened to Ingrid Lam. Attard was sure the girl was dead, but he was also disconcerted by the forensic findings in the Miriam Calder murder. He had specifically said to the lab assistant that the findings had to be given to him.

Ingrid Lam was not dead. She was cold, hungry, tired... and terrified. She had soiled her pants and was crying at the sight of her own blood, running down her hands from the wire bindings around her wrists. And she wanted to know why her mum hadn't come for her. The steel door to the *girna*, an old shooting hut, she was being kept in creaked open. The light hurt Ingrid's eyes; she couldn't see who it was. She didn't want to see. She just wanted to go home.

'Does your father drive?' The words meant nothing to Ingrid. 'No matter.' The voice came near, placed a cloth over Ingrid's mouth and nose.

All was darkness.

Matt Healy got a taxi home that morning from Spiteri's house, the time passing as he sat in an almost trance-like state. He was now sitting at his kitchen table, trying to work out just how his life had turned around so dramatically. He was living in a beautiful place, he was fit, he was sober... and now he had a lover. *God, how beautiful is Thea. Different to Susan. A chance to move on from Susan, as Susan had done to me.*

He was pulled back from his thoughts by the ringing of his phone.

'Matt, it's Jim.'

'James, my good man, and just what can I do for you, my friend, on this fine day?'

'Fucking hell, you on the booze?'

'No, I am not. Merely the milk of love.'

'Fuck. Don't tell me you've actually pulled?'

'Pulled? Pulled? What age are you, Jim? I have formed a wonderful relationship, if that's what you're asking.'

'Shagged her yet?'

Healy despaired. 'Jim, why have you called?'

'Right. Here's the script. The Greek Police were very uncooperative, basically told us to sod off. They did say that they had considered that the boy had been taken off the island, but nothing really materialised from their efforts. When I asked if the name Hooper had come up in their enquiries, they had no idea what I was talking about.'

'Shit.'

'Wait, some good news. One of the cops in the 1964 case is still around. He's an old man obviously, eighty odds but still got his wits about him. He said you've to phone him.'

'Great, what's his number?'

'Wait, got a cracker for you.' Healy was impatient to get on but knew Frame would press on anyway, so he didn't interrupt him. 'I was in court yesterday, a domestic assault case. The heid banger husband's lawyer says to the wife, who is in the witness box, "What was the first thing your husband said to you this morning?" She answers, "He said, where am I, Cathy?" Lawyer says, "Why did that upset you?" She shouts, "Because my fucking name is Ann!" What a laugh that got. Even the sheriff started laughing. So, what about this burd then? You getting married?'

'Yea, next week.'

'You're joking?'

'You started it. Just give me the number please, Jim.'

'Okay. Oh, by the way, I remember that Hooper woman now. I knew it was something more recent than the sixties.'

'You mean her book?'

'No, no really. She was never off the telly a few years back. The Madeline McCann thing.'

'What do you mean?'

'Well, she was there, wasn't she? Staying in the same complex. Media were falling over themselves, trying to speak to the "abduction specialist on the spot."'

Healy was stunned. He spoke very deliberately. 'Jim, this is important. Find out when Hooper's father died. His name was Gary, I think. Get back to me straight away, Jim.'

Healy gently placed the telephone receiver back in its cradle. *Fucking hell. Surely not?*

\*\*\*

May Hooper would have described herself, at this point, as serene. She had hired a car in Mgarr, driven up through Gharb and San Lawrenz, and was now sitting on a sandstone boulder, looking at a local tourist attraction, the Azure Window. If she had been focused, she would have appreciated the beauty of the setting, but her mind was elsewhere.

At first, she had been angry, then devastated, then philosophical. But now, *yes, serene, definitely serene.* The diagnosis of untreatable cancer had come out of the blue, the six-month time frame almost irrelevant. Her time was up; she had done what she had done. She was tired of the lies. Would she pay in the next life? *Well, I'll soon know.* Hooper had told her agent that she liked Malta and was going to look for a holiday home either there or on Gozo, so she was going to stay on indefinitely. She loved the islands. She felt that she might never leave. She would be right.

\*\*\*

Thea Spiteri had never been in love. She'd never dwelt on the fact, immersed herself in her work, and progressed steadily through the *Pulizija*, despite the pressures of male prejudice and barely disguised female disdain at a Maltese woman her age not having a husband and children. Things were a bit better now, in the new millennium, but Spiteri knew Malta still had a long way to go to catch up with the rest of Europe. However, she didn't doubt that it would... eventually. *Have I made a mistake with Matt? Is he so damaged that there is no way back? Am I prepared to help him, prepared to wait, and prepared to lie beside a man who talks of another woman in his sleep?*

As Spiteri thought about him, Healy paced his kitchen floor. He wondered if he should call Frame back. He pondered over whether the May Hooper scenario that was enveloping his brain wasn't just him fantasising. Just at that point, his mobile rang.

'Jim?'

'No, Matt, it's Francesco. Sorry to disappoint you.'

'No, Francesco, don't be daft. I'm expecting a call from Scotland, thought that was it.'

'Not a woman, I hope!'

'A woman called Jim? No, Francesco!'

'Matt, the reason I'm calling. Thea is obviously very busy. Do you know if there is any progress with this desecrater?'

Healy shook his head. *Fuck Francesco, I've got more important things to think about.* 'Not as far as I know.'

'They've got video, you know. Yet they can't even say for sure if it's a man or a woman!'

'Well, video pics are notoriously poor quality.'

'Is Ms Hooper away back to the UK?'

'No, but I think she may be heading off soon. She stayed on to help with the abduction investigations.'

'And did she help?'

'Well, the kids are still missing, so...'

'Quite. It's all so sad, Matt.'

'I've often wondered about that view. Christians are always banging on about heaven, never-ending happiness, meeting up with your loved ones etc, etc; but when someone dies, it's to be viewed with great sadness. Why? You should be happy that someone you love has gone to a better place.'

'Very true, Matt, very observant. You'll remember we went to the Dingli Cliffs one day. I go there in times of stress or when I need peace to think. I have pondered that same issue many times.'

'And?'

'And I've no idea. I'm not God, merely an employee!'

Healy's house phone rang, so he said goodbye to his friend and grabbed the handset. 'Jim?'

'Sure is. This woman you're....'

'Jim, shut the fuck up. When did the father die?'

'Alright, Mr Grump. Two thousand, tenth March, heart attack. Happy now?'

'Yes. Sorry, Jim, but that is all I needed. I'll be in touch.'

Healy cut the connection and then dialled the retirement home where ex-police superintendant Ian McFadden lived. He was surprised to get straight through to his room.

'Hello.'

'Iain, my name is Matt Healy. I'm calling from Malta.'

'Ah yes, the Hooper case. Frame told me you might call.'

Healy was taken aback at how young the voice at the other end of the line sounded. 'Thank you for letting me.'

'Well, it's a bit of excitement. You don't get a lot of that around here, I can tell you.'

'It's quite simple really, Iain. The murder of the young girl. Did anyone, at the time, think it could have been Hooper's daughter, May, who did the killing?'

There was a long silence on the line. Healy feared McFadden had gone to sleep. Then....

'Jesus Christ, there's a thought. No, that possibility never crossed anyone's mind. Things were different back then, Matt. The notion of a child being a killer, well, it just didn't happen.'

'I understand that, Iain, and I'm not looking to appoint blame. Just tell me this: looking back, everything you remember, is it possible that May Hooper could have killed her friend?'

Another long pause. 'Yes, it's possible, but... God, I don't even want to think about that.'

'Thank you, Iain. You've been a great help.'

'No, thank you. You've given me something to think about, apart from what the dinner might be. I'll get back to you if anything comes to mind. Why are you asking anyway? Do you know something?'

'No, Iain, I don't. I'm working on a hunch. You know what it's like.'

'I do indeed.'

Healy hung up. *It has to be now. Once she's away, that's it.*

Healy clicked on May Hooper's number. 'Hi, May, where are you? Fancy dinner?'

# CHAPTER 20

Thea Spiteri was at her cracking point. The search for the two missing children had, long ago, ground to a halt. There was now very little chance of a conviction against Peter Smart for the murder of Miriam Calder, and little chance of a conviction over the abduction. The deputy commissioner was demanding answers from her, and now she had picked up a message on her voicemail from Matt Healy which merely said, "We need to talk." Healy's voice sounded cold, flat, matter of fact. *I know what's coming now. "Thea, I'm sorry, it was a mistake. Hope we can still be friends." What was I thinking about? The bastard...*

She buzzed through to the outer office and asked Jason Attard to come through. Jason appeared to have calmed down and was back to his normal self. He had hidden on Gozo for a while, keeping out of the way, but Spiteri had decided that the nature of these crimes had gotten to everyone. *Besides, he might be right about Healy.*

Jason, sit down. The commissioner wants a full report on the progress of the two abductions on his desk tomorrow morning. I want to go over things with you.'

'What progress?'

'I know, I know, but I have to produce something.' Just then, Spiteri's phone rang.

'Is that Inspector Spiteri?'

'Yes, who's this?'

'Inspector, my name is Daphne Arrigo. I'm a journalist. I'd like to set up a meeting with you.'

'Concerning what?'

'Noel Borg... and friends.'

Spiteri hesitated. She too was troubled by many of the things that had gone unchallenged in the Borg case, but she knew talking to Arrigo could be dangerous. 'When and where?'

'Are you free tomorrow? I think we should meet somewhere out of the way. How about Mel's in Birkirkara at, say, two p.m?'

'Okay.'

*\*\**

Healy had no difficulty choosing the restaurant. He had noticed before that the restaurants in Hooper's hotel, The Corinthian, weren't busy in the early evening. He booked a table in the corner of L'Aristena for 6.00 p.m, explaining to Hooper that he had a very early start the next day, so didn't want a late night.

'I'm glad you called, Matt. I could do with a little company.'

'And you don't have far to walk back.'

'Yes, that's true.'

'So, you were in Gozo when I called?'

'Yes, it's beautiful there.'

'Terrible about the German girl.'

'Dreadful.'

'Any thoughts on it?'

'Not really.'

'Strange, two abductions so close together, time wise, don't you think?'

'Maybe, maybe not. Who knows how these kinds of people's minds work.' Hooper appeared distracted, picking at her food.

'Well, you do, don't you?'

'Usually after the fact, Matt. What they'll probably do, what their profile might be. No guarantees.'

'But you've had first-hand experience, May. You researched a case, accused your own father.'

'Yes, but like I said, after the deed was done.'

'How was your childhood pal killed, do you think?'

'Lots of possibilities. Strangled, hit over the head, suffocated. I don't like to think about it.'

'No. Then you're saying that you think your father might also have been involved in the Ben Needham case?'

'It's possible. We'll never know.'

'Your dad's dead now, isn't he?'

'Yes. Two thousand.'

'So he wasn't with you when you were staying in Pria da Lux, when Maddie McCann went missing.'

'No, like I said, he died in...' Hooper looked up from her plate, her food barely touched. 'What are you getting at here, Matt?'

'Well, you do seem to be present when a lot of abductions take place, May.'

'A lot? Three. And I was only five years old myself for one of them.'

'Five. And that's just the ones I know about. Two abductions here, May, and you were around for both of them.'

'You're mad.'

'Am I? Remember one of the policemen, back in sixty-four, McFadden was his name.'

'No.'

'I should have said "is his name." He's still very much alive. I spoke to him today. He told me that you were very much in the frame for your little friend's murder. He remembers you: a precocious, bad mannered, spoilt little bitch. Yes, I think that was his description. They just couldn't get the procurator interested. Not back then.'

Healy had expected a scene, Hooper to bawl and shout, storm off. She did neither. She looked out to sea. A tear formed in her left eye, rolled down her cheek.

'I'm dying.'

'What?'

'I'm dying, Matt. Soon. I was glad you called, I wanted company. Even this hasn't changed anything. Maybe even helped.'

'Helped?'

'Matt, can I tell you a story?'

'Okay.'

'I don't know what age I was when my father first abused me. All I can remember is that by the time I reached four years of age, we played Daddy's Game two or three times a week. I neither liked nor disliked it; it was just another game. Then he started playing the same game with some of my friends. Some never came back to play with me, some did. My best friend, Jill Hart, did come back, and my father gave her a doll to thank her. I didn't understand. If this was Daddy's Game, how could he play it with her? When he gave me my dollie, he said it was for "his special girl." So why did Jill get one, too?

'We had days out, too. My dad would take us for a ride on his bus. We went all over, even the countryside sometimes. Dad said that it was best if only one of us went on the days out. He said it was a treat. So, I went on a Monday and a Wednesday; Jill went on a Thursday and Sunday.

'But on *that* day, my day, she still got on the bus, even though she knew it was my day, even though she even saw me.' May Hooper looked out over the bay. 'She shouldn't have done that.'

'What really happened, May?'

'She sat at the front of the bus.' Hooper shook her head. 'Why? She knew it was my day. She even had her horrible doll with her, the one my dad gave her. I was angry. I looked around the back seat. Then I saw it. A hammer in a plastic case, on the wall of the bus: *In case of Emergencies. Break Glass.* Well, this was an emergency. It was a Wednesday, my day. I managed to get the hammer out without making too much noise. I walked down the aisle of the bus. I stood behind Jill. "Why are you on the bus?" I said. Jill never looked around. "Because your dad wanted me to come. He says he likes going on the trips with me more than you."

'"Jill?"

'"What?" she shouted as she turned to look at me.

'I smashed her face with the hammer so many times that her nose fell off.'

Healy sat in stunned silence. He didn't know what to say or do. He mumbled, 'You were just a wee girl yourself, May. You wouldn't have gone to prison or anything. You would have been helped, even back then.'

'My dad came running up the stairs. I'll never forget what he said. He looked at Jill's mangled face and then looked over at me, slumped on the seat opposite. "Don't worry, baby, she was nothing. Daddy will sort everything." Of course, I realised, years later, that he was protecting himself, not me.'

'He was a terrible man, May, but he wasn't a killer. Why did you do the book?'

'He owed me and, believe it or not, I genuinely wanted Jill's body found, returned to her family.'

'So you don't know where the body is?'

'No. Dad drove me home, told me not to say a word to anyone. I never did. Until now.' Hooper looked straight into Healy's eyes. 'You'll never be able to prove any of this, Matt. You know that?'

'Maybe not, May, bit I'm going to try.'

'I'll be dead and gone long before you're even close.'

'Don't you feel any guilt?'

'Not really. I was a damaged child, Matt. You said so yourself.'

'What about redemption?' Healy wasn't religious; he just felt he had to say something.

'Yes, I'll have to seek that.'

'May, what about the others?'

Hooper's brow furrowed. 'Others?'

'The other abductions, the other children you killed?'

'What are you talking about?'

'Come on, May... It's over. Kos, Algarve, Malta, God knows where else. You are always there, May.'

May Hopper lifted her napkin, dabbed the corners of her mouth, and walked away.

'Shit,' said Healy.

\*\*\*

Ingrid Lam wished she was dead. Thought she might be dead. She knew the harbinger would be back. She didn't know when, just that it would be for the last time. She cried again for her mother, but the tape across her mouth stifled all sounds.

\*\*\*

Claudia Sansome watched her husband. She didn't understand. She had followed that morning up to the terminal for the ferry to Gozo. She watched as her husband sat on the terrace of the Mojo Cafe in Victoria. He ordered a coffee, but he also ordered what looked to Claudia, at least, a double brandy. She didn't understand. Joseph never drank spirits. *What's going on? Where's your whore?* Joseph finished his drink and walked over to his car, which was parked in the Arcadia Car Park. He got in and drove off towards the centre of Victoria.

\*\*\*

Father Francesco Marandon was considering retiring. *I have given my life to the church, these islands, God's work. For what? A second child missing, a woman murdered, churches being desecrated. I committed to God's work for my whole life but, ha, yes, the mind is willing but the body is weak!* Father Francesco smiled to himself.

It was 8.00 pm, and he was just about to leave the confessional box when he heard the creak of the door on the other side of the dividing curtain opening. It closed slowly.

'Father, are you there?' said the invisible voice.

'Yes, I am. Can I help you?'

'No one can help me I'm afraid, Father.'

'You don't believe that, child. You would not be here if you did.'

'Can I ask you something, Father?'

'Of course, child.'

'Are you Father Francesco?'

'Why yes!'

'Good. I am a friend, well, former friend I suspect, of Matt Healy. He says you are a good man.'

There was a slight pause. Hooper wondered if perhaps she should not have brought names into the sacred confessional; it had been a lifetime since she had been in one.

'Matt is a good man. I only do my job. Why did you say *former friend?*'

'I left him not long ago after telling him I had killed someone. It was many years ago.'

'Someone?'

'A childhood friend. We were both five years old.'

'You were a child. It was certainly a terrible thing to have done, but you were still an innocent. Is Matt going to report this crime?'

'I don't know, but in any case, I am. I need to put things right. Before...'

'Before?'

'Before I die. I have cancer. Not long to go.'

'I see. I'm sorry to hear that. You have some heavy burdens to carry. When are you going to the police?'

'As soon as I can. I'll check what flights are available from here to Scotland, book the soonest one. I'm not unknown there; I wrote a book about it, you see. About the murder. I accused my father of doing it. I've been involved in trying to help troubled children ever since. I've been called into many abduction investigations. I know lots of names, lots of worse people than me, still walking around. I'll give them to the police, too. With the advances in DNA, who knows, lots of old cases could be solved.'

'And your father?'

'Dead. Many years ago. Will you absolve me, Father?'

'I will.'

'And my penance?'

'You will be meeting a far wiser judge than me shortly. I will let him decide.'

The confessional door creaked back open before gently closing with the smallest draught of wind rippling the confessional curtain. Father Francesco listened but did not hear May Hooper's quiet footsteps as she left the chapel. Before praying, the old priest sat thinking about the terrible burdens life can impose on people, the hardships, the worries, the fears. He wondered if it was life or God that was so unfair.

*** 

Joseph Sansome was concentrating fully on where he was going and the task that lay ahead of him. If he had checked more carefully, he would have recognised his wife's car not too far behind him.

Joseph Sansome drove through Victoria and took a quiet side road heading towards Xlendi. A hundred meters or so along the road, he turned into an even quieter road and stopped about halfway down outside an old, run-down café that obviously hadn't traded for years.

Claudia Sansome pulled up behind a large white van that was parked at the top of the road, leaving just enough space to allow her to watch her husband. Joseph had gotten out of his car, produced a set of keys, and let himself into the abandoned cafe. Claudia couldn't hold back any longer. She got out of her car, walked down to the shop, and stormed inside. With her imagination in overdrive as to what she might discover, Claudia didn't notice the pile of rubble on the floor. She stumbled over it and only managed to stop herself from falling by grabbing onto the old bar counter.

Her husband was standing with a large, white sheet of builder's plans, looking at a sandstone wall that had obviously seen better days. 'What in God's name are you doing here?' he said as he rushed over to help her.

'I... I...'

'What? You followed me? Why?'

'I thought you were having an affair!'

Joseph Sansome appeared stunned for a moment. He then put the plans down and walked over and hugged his wife. 'Never.'

'But, what...'

'I'm thinking of expanding. This restaurant used to be busy until some idiotic British couple took it over and tried to turn it into a wine bar. But, thank God, they never got rid of the original stone oven. That's what I wanted to see for myself. Wood fired pizzas are the best you can get.'

'Oh, Joseph, I'm so sorry. I felt you were acting a bit oddly, what with language classes, out late at night. God, Joseph, I am sorry.'

'It's alright, You're just daft!'

Claudia nodded and laughed. 'What language are you learning anyway?'

'Oh, Spanish. I'm not sure I'll keep it up, though. Very time consuming. Look, I have to stay here. I have people to see etc etc. You go home. I'll see you tonight; rest your ankle.'

Claudia Sansome nodded and walked back to her car. She waved to her husband as she drove off.

Joseph Sansome waited a few moments to check that his wife didn't come back for some reason. He then looked around the street before walking over to the boot of his car.

# CHAPTER 21

May Hooper had been sitting in her car outside the monastery for twenty minutes. She was confused and bewildered. Something was playing on her mind. She shook her head and concentrated on the present. She wasn't thinking of the ignominy and disgrace that would follow her confession to Healy, but that her charity would probably have to close down, as the funding would, inevitably, be withdrawn. Although it was now dark, May Hooper decided to visit the nearest bay, Golden Bay. *One last cocktail by the sea, May.* As she drove her hired Renault, she wondered if Matt Healy would already have phoned Scotland, even told Spiteri. *Maybe I should just end it now. What am I holding on for, a slow lingering death, the scandal?*

Matt Healy had sat in the restaurant for a few minutes after Hooper left before going to his car. He didn't know what to do. Hooper had been right: if she was telling the truth about the cancer, justice would never be done. *Yes, it must be, Matt. You must ensure it.*

It only took May Hooper about fifteen minutes to reach Golden Bay. She parked her car and pondered her next move. *Beach or cliffs? Either way, cocktail first.*

The cocktail had no taste, held no enjoyment for May Hooper. She elected for the beach. *Coward to the end, May. Coward to the end.* Suddenly, she felt a presence behind her. She turned slowly, she smiled. The moon glinted on the knife. May Hooper swung her arms wildly, turned, and attempted to run. The thrust of the blade made sure she would never run, or even walk, again. A car pulled into the car park, its headlights momentarily illuminating the scene. Hooper's assailant panicked, dropped the knife, and ran into the darkness. May Hooper stretched out a hand and dug her fingers into the sand.

***

Thea Spiteri arrived early for her 2.00 p.m. meeting with Daphne Arrigo. She had heard a lot about Arrigo's aggressive style and, for some reason, it made her nervous. Arrigo arrived a few minutes later in a storm of note pads, mobile phones, and apologies for being late. Both women ordered coffee and pastries.

'Thea, I'm going to tell you some of my thoughts about certain things, people. When I'm finished, you can either comment, not comment, go, or stay. Either way, my investigations will continue. However, I realise I can only go so far. I need someone within the *Pulizija* to help me. I've decided to put my trust in you. I saw you at the Borg trial; you looked uneasy at times. If I'm wrong or you don't want to become involved, then fine... I'll find someone else. Okay?'

'So far,' replied Spiteri.

'Right, let's start. Borg was as guilty as sin; we both know that. But he wasn't alone; he's the sacrificial lamb. I'd like to find out exactly who paid Borg the money. It wasn't that low life who ended up in a ditch, I'll tell you that. Next: nobody disputes that there was a load of cash involved in all this, but no one seems to know where it ended up. Next: how come Borg never spent a day in prison? Depression? Christ, Thea, nobody would go to prison if saying you were depressed got you off. Next: how come such a high profile case got, and is still getting, so little coverage, relatively speaking, in the media? There's even one paper championing Borg's case by citing a legal argument of "sub judice"... the only problem with that being that one, "sub judice" isn't a defense, and two, even if it was, then a judge has to specifically rule that there's to be no reporting of a case. Next: how come your boss, Debono, isn't going after anyone else to do with this case? It's just a story of "one guy in jail, that's that. Keep quiet and everyone will go away." Finally: why is nobody investigating Debono himself? As you know, the media has hounded a few commissioners over the years, but Debono seems beyond criticism. Why? Is the reason linked to why Borg seems to be media proof as well? Tell me this, Thea. How many of Nicola Tizian's enterprises has Debono investigated? The double murder you solved in record time. How come only one guy, out of an obvious crime network, was arrested? I'm not criticising you, Thea, but the guy who got life... he's dying of cancer, and his wife and kids are now living in a villa in Corsica.'

'What is it you want from me?'

'Anything. Anything that you think just doesn't feel right. Let me know; I'll do the probing.'

'What the fuck is wrong with all these people? Everyone just seems to be out for themselves.'

'Simple. They don't understand what organisations are.'

'What do you mean?'

'That there are lots of people who join organisations but can't get it into their heads that they should be working for the interests of the organisations; not for their own interests. They believe that the organisation that they work for is a vehicle for satisfying their own personal ambitions and desires and not that they should, in fact, be contributing to what the organisation is trying to achieve. Borg is a classic example.'

Spiteri's mobile rang. She hoped it would be Healy. The screen showed it wasn't. 'Thea Spiteri,' a frazzled Spiteri hissed into her phone. *Where the hell is Matt!*

'Inspector Spiteri? It's Officer Rizzo. Sergeant Attard told me to call you. A body has been reported on the beach at Golden Bay. He told me to tell you it is someone called May Hooper.'

Spiteri disconnected. 'Sorry, Daphne, I need to go. I'll call you.'

Golden Bay is on the other side of Malta from Birkirkara, but with lights flashing, and sirens wailing, Spiteri arrived at the scene in twenty minutes. She was greeted by Jason Attard.

'It's definitely Hooper, Jason?'

'Yes, and there's something you'd better see.'

Spiteri walked over to the body, which was lying in a foetal position on the sand. At the end of an outstretched arm, *Why?* was written in the sand.

'My God.' Spiteri took a moment to compose herself. 'Any witnesses, the weapon, anything?'

'We have a knife.'

'Right, Jason. I'll stay here. Take the knife to forensics now. I'll phone them, get them in. Don't leave till you can tell me if this is the same knife that killed Miriam Calder or not. We can match it to this killing tomorrow.'

Attard frowned, wished that he had made the suggestion. 'Okay.'

Spiteri's mobile shrilled again.

'Hello.'

'Matt, where the hell have you been? I've been calling you since yesterday.' said Spiteri.

'Yes, sorry. There was something I had to do.'

'Something?'

'It's not important.'

Spiteri didn't want to leave the conversation at that but realised she had something more important to talk about. 'Have you heard about May Hooper?'

Healy took time to reply. Spiteri thought he may have been cut off. 'Matt?'

'Yes. How did you hear so quickly?' replied Healy.

'What? What are you talking about?'

'She told me herself. That's what I wanted to talk to you about.'

Spiteri was totally confused. 'Matt, May Hooper is dead. Murdered.'

\*\*\*

The following afternoon, the photos from the murder scene at Golden Beach were displayed all across the long whiteboard positioned on the wall opposite Spiteri's office.

'At least they put a question mark this time,' said Healy.

'Do you think that's relevant, Matt?'

'Who knows? You assuming it's the same killer?'

'Well, it looks that way. I've got Jason camping in the forensics lab just to find out if the knife used here was also used on Miriam Calder.'

'You got a knife, then? Fingerprints?'

'Don't know anything yet. All down to forensics. Matt, come in to the office, will you?'

Healy sat opposite Spiteri. He sensed a change in her.

'Matt, when was the last time you spoke to May Hooper?'

'Why?'

'Matt, come on.'

'Last night. We had an early dinner, about six o'clock. It finished more abruptly than I thought.'

'Oh, why was that?'

'Let's just say the conversation was over.'

'The conversation, or the relationship?'

'What?'

'You heard.'

'I did, but I can't believe you said it.'

'Look, Matt, I'm investigating two murders here. You knew both the women in question, you...'

Healy stood. 'You investigate away. You want to speak to me again, arrest me.'

A white-coated lab assistant, bleary eyed, dishevelled from a long night, approached Jason Attard, who was dozing on a chair. May Hooper's corpse had been delivered during the night, a call from the commissioner adding to the pressure. He shook Attard's shoulder and handed him a beige coloured folder. Attard sat up, quickly opening the folder as he did so. He looked up, stared at the non-descript wall opposite, and slowly shook his head.

As Spiteri's door slammed, her mobile rang.

'Yes, Jason.'

'The knife wounds don't match.'

'Right. Is that good or bad? I'm not sure.'

'The same person could have done it, used two knives. Why not?'

Spiteri hung up. She rubbed her eyes. *Two outstanding abductions, two unsolved murders. One fucked-up relationship. Jesus, things can't get any worse.*

Thea Spiteri would be very wrong about that.

# CHAPTER 22

Malta is divided into two regions for *Pulizija* purposes: Region A covers the South, Region B, the North. Each region is headed by an assistant commissioner and takes in five districts. Each district is headed by a superintendent, with several divisions in each district. Thea Spiteri was an inspector in CID. The murder of May Hooper had prompted the commissioner to call a cases review meeting, and Spiteri was to conduct it. The commissioner himself didn't attend, but he ensured that the deputy commissioner did, along with all officers involved in the investigations.

Spiteri wasn't intimidated by the people attending; she knew she needed help. Spiteri and Attard sat at the front of the room, photos of the three crime scenes displayed behind them. Attard was overjoyed that he was at the forefront of the investigation, and even more so to see Healy wasn't present.

'So, two murders, one abduction, still outstanding. Any ideas? Is there anything we've missed? Anything we should be looking at that we haven't up till now?'

Over the course of the next hour, lots of views were expressed and a lot of ground gone over, but Spiteri felt that nothing new, nothing original, was coming out of the discussions. One of the assistant commissioners concluded the meeting with, 'All of these cases must be solved. We need them solved, their families need them solved, Malta needs them solved. The commissioner himself wants daily updates.'

\*\*\*

After storming out of Spiteri's office, Healy had driven home and phoned Jim Frame.

'Jim, have you heard over there about May Hooper?'

'No. What about her? Don't tell me you've got her pregnant!'

'She's dead. Murdered. As far as I, or anyone else know, I was the last person to see her alive.'

'Christ. What happened?'

'Stabbed, and Jim, the word *Why* written in the sand again, same as Miriam Calder.'

'Same killer?'

'You would think so, but who knows.'

'Bit odd, both victims writing the same thing in the sand. Mind you, Hooper would have known what Calder wrote; maybe it was just a kind of subconscious action, following on from Calder. I don't know. A plea for answers, maybe?'

'Maybe. Christ, Jim, am I ever going to get away from death?'

'Step away. It's not your problem. You did what you could for the wee boy, but that's it. Especially if they're thinking you're involved somehow. Come back over here for a week or two, crash at mine.'

'Thanks, Jim, but no. I don't think that would impress anyone, do you? Anyway, I better go. I'll not mention football!'

'Good move! Keep in touch.'

Matt Healy opened his fridge door: *water, fruit juice, Coke. Fuck it. I need a drink.* Healy grabbed a sweater that had been lying over the back of a chair, threw his car keys into a bowl of fruit. *The Crows Nest it is.*

Thea Spiteri called Jason Attard into her office. 'Jason... Calder and Hooper. How many people on this island met both women?'

'Hard to say for definite, but it can't be many. Why?'

'I just think that although the knife wounds were different, if one person did kill them both, then he must have known them, or at least have met them previously.'

'Well, there's you and me! And Claudia possibly, couple of uniform drivers, Smart, maybe some people at the child protection thing that Hooper spoke at. There's bound to be some more, but how would we know? Father Francesco...'

'No, Francesco never met Calder, but...'

'But?'

'Matt Healy did.'

Attard wanted to press home this unexpected bonus that Spiteri had given him. He decided instead on the devil's advocate role: so many ifs and buts. 'Inspector, it's not necessarily true that the killer must have known the two women.'

'No, I suppose not.' Spiteri hated herself for having the thoughts that she was, but she was a police officer first. She considered calling Healy, then decided against it. *Probably with his girlfriend. God, I'm such a fool.*

\*\*\*

'Hey, Anna, how do you know when a woman is about to say something smart?'

'Don't know,' replied Anna, the blonde-haired barmaid in The Crows Nest bar.

'She starts with "a man once told me."' Healy had been in the pub for three hours. It had taken him less time to forget Thea Spiteri, Susan Dornan, two dead women, and destroy the last six months of his sobriety than he expected. He didn't care. He was glad, he was happy, he was enjoying himself.

'Hey, hey, Joe, come here, you'll like this one. Why do women fake orgasms?'

Joe, the bar's owner, smiled, shrugged his shoulders. Pandering to drunks being part of the job.

'They think men care!' shouted Healy before breaking into a fit of coughing. He stumbled to the toilet. After amusing himself by seeing how many times he could swing his urine stream over and hit the handle of the toilet brush, he turned and caught sight of himself in the toilet mirror. Something in the back of his mind was trying to break into his thoughts. Healy shook his head. *Handsome bastard. That Anna's getting it tonight.*

\*\*\*

Joseph Sansome had not sexually assaulted Ingrid Lam in any way before he killed her. He only wanted justice. Death had come quickly for the child, just as it had for Catherine Sansome, and Joseph was satisfied.

Sansome had then used all his butchery skills to dismember Ingrid's body. It had taken him very little time to carve the small body, so he was pleased that he had fired up the pizza oven before starting. He threw the child's clothes in first and watched them burn. Satisfied with the result, he put the limbs in separately, also ensuring they burned properly. He stayed on the property all day; content that there were no signs of his visit left. *I'll phone the agent tomorrow, tell him I've changed my mind.*

# CHAPTER 23

Michele Grech had been an *orfnilti* for as long as he could remember. At first, he did not know what that was—both his parents only spoke English—but he grew to accept the fact that he was an orphan soon enough. After his parents had been killed in a car crash in Zebbieh, he soon realised that the various nuns and priests that arrived in his life were more interested in telling him that his parents death was all part of God's Plan than showing him the comfort that he sought, and so he decided to live on the streets. Michele Grech was seven years old.

\*\*\*

Mosta is approx five kilometers from St Julian's Bay, and Matt Healy had woken up there looking at a flying lion. He had a vague recollection of leaving The Crow's Nest, sans Anna, the previous night, getting into a taxi, and issuing directions to the driver that seemed sensible at the time. Healy closed his eyes.

*I'm okay. I'm on top of this. A limping apparition in black. Michelle Pfeiffer. Cat Woman. Lady Macbeth. A skulking figure, dressed in black, staring. A*

*Jesuit, Mum? People laughing. People shaking their heads. Other people in the haze, people he somehow knew.*

Jason Attard did not take many nights off from work. Even when off duty, he dedicated himself to doing all he could to help impress Thea Spiteri. He only had one friend, and so, when asked to go to his friend Karmenu's "Boy's Only Night" in Mosta the previous evening , he decided to take a time away from thinking how to tie Matt Healy into the murder of the two Scottish women. Jason was neither a drinker nor a dabbler in social drug taking, but after little food, too many pints of Cisk, and a tablet of something that no chemist prescribed, Sergeant Attard was convinced that he saw his nemesis across the square that, at that moment, he himself was vomiting beside. He wiped his mouth with his sleeve, looked up, and the square was empty.

Malta may be small, but the grapevine is huge. Thea Spiteri had heard that Healy had stumbled out of The Crow's Nest at 2.00 a.m, but she did not know where he had headed. *Do I care? Bastard.* Spiteri agonised over her feelings about Healy. She had two murders and two child abductions to deal with, but Healy kept seeping into her thoughts. *Dear God, please tell me he has nothing to do with any of this.*

Father Francesco had been delighted to receive a phone call from Father Carlo the previous night. One of the curates in the Mosta Parish had been unexpectedly called away. 'Would Francesco be available to say Mass in Santa Maria Assunta?' the following morning. 'Come up tonight, Francesco, some rabbit and wine!'

'Marvellous, Carlo. I have some work to do there anyway. This is perfect."

Healy opened his eyes, the early morning sun temporarily blinding him. The *Pulizija* officer standing over him was firm and clear. "Move!"

Healy staggered to his feet. His bleary eyes focused on the bronze lion on top of the column he had slept beside. He glanced over at the huge church with the impressive dome before turning to the *Pulizija* officer. 'Who are you talking to, ya Maltese cunt?' Matt Healy embraced the darkness again moments later.

***

'Hello, is that Mrs Sansome?' said a voice Claudia didn't recognise.

'Yes, who is this?'

'Hello, this is Jane Wright from Malta University. Can you let your husband know that, unfortunately, the German class is cancelled tonight; the tutor is sick.'

'Don't you mean the Spanish classes?'

'Eh. No I don't think so, let me check. Hold on a minute... No, its definitely the German classes your husband enrolled on.'

'Okay, thank you. I must be getting mixed up.' Claudia Sansome gently replaced the handset. The call had troubled her, but she wasn't exactly sure in what way. The next call would only trouble her even more.

'Hello?' she hoped it was the university calling back to say they had been mistaken.

'Yes, hello. Is Mr Sansome there?'

'No he's not. Sorry. Who's calling?'

'This is Tom Pisani, from Rabat Estate Agents in Gozo. We gave your husband the keys to a property here. We've since had a lot of complaints about the day he was viewing concerning a smell and smoke. I've now inspected the property and it's clear that your husband must have used the pizza oven.'

'Well, he needed to know it was working. It was that feature he was most interested in.'

'Okay, but the ventilation shafts haven't been cleaned for years. He caused a lot of upset for the residents above. It was probably pigeons or cats or God knows what, but the residents could smell burning meat.

They're not happy. And to top it all, he says he doesn't want the property now. Tell him he'll be getting a bill from us for the clean-up.'

Claudia Sansome had barely heard the last sentence; a fear was gripping her mind.

# CHAPTER 24

It was already 10.00 a.m, but Thea Spiteri was still sitting at her desk, depressed and at a loss of where to turn to next. She was under constant pressure from her superiors to get results, and that morning's edition of *The Independent* newspaper was running a front page feature headlined: *Are Our* Pulizija *Asleep* with a secondary headline of: "or merely incompetent." Spiteri pulled an A4 pad over and started writing:

Jamie Smart   Missing?   Dead?   No idea          Father?

Ingrid Lam     Missing?   Dead?   No idea

Miriam Calder                       Dead        No idea          MH?
Why

May Hooper                  Dead     No idea      MH?     Different killers?     Why?

*Christ. I've no idea what I'm doing.*

Spiteri's mobile vibrated on her desk.

'Thea?'

'Yes, Francesco.' Spiteri's weary tone was easily picked up by her old friend.

'Is everything okay?'

'Not really.'

'Why, what is wrong child?'

'I've got no idea how to proceed. Two murders and two children missing, probably murdered, and all I know is that a German driving a Jeep might be involved.'

'Pray for God's help, child.'

'I don't think God is around here much these days, Francesco. Anyway, why are you calling?'

'Oh, it was just to say that there has been another desecration. This time in Mosta. A cat nailed to a cross, and left against a statue of Our Lady. Terrible. But you have bigger things to worry about, I know. I'll let you go.'

Spiteri walked out of her office. 'Where's Jason?' No one seemed to know.

\*\*\*

Jason Attard thought he was dead. Wished he was dead. Somehow, he had managed to get home from Mosta, but getting to his bedroom had proved to be one challenge too many. He lay looking at his hallway ceiling, wondering how it was possible to sleep on cold, hard tiles. He could smell the dried vomit on his shoes and, he assumed from the sticky feeling on his fingers, his hands. He eventually summoned up the courage to sit up; it was then that he noticed that the stickiness on his fingers wasn't vomit. It was blood.

'So you used to be a police officer, Mr Healy?' said the officer at Mosta *Pulizija* station. Healy had been allowed to sleep the day away in a darkened cell.

'Yea. A long time ago now, it seems.'

'You had a lot to drink yesterday?'

'A fair bit.'

'Where are you going now?'

'Back down to St Julians, I suppose.'

'I'll get you a lift.'

'That's good of you. Thanks.'

'When you were lying opposite the church, did you see any activity? Anyone walking about?'

'Sorry, no. Why?'

'Have you heard about the cats being killed? Stuck on church doors.'

'Yes.'

'It happened here, last night.'

'Good. I fucking hate cats.'

'I think I'll get you that lift, Mr Healy. Don't hurry back.'

Healy wandered outside to wait for his lift. He looked at his watch. *Half six, good. The Crows Nest will be open. Wonder if those two sexy barmaids will be working tonight.*

# CHAPTER 25

Jason Attard's was finding it difficult to work out in his mind just what had happened in the last twenty-odd hours of his life.

He had managed to phone into the station that he was unwell before heading to the toilet to wretch into the pan. Attard wasn't surprised that nothing came up; his stomach was empty of everything except pain. He had then stumbled into his bedroom and slept for another four hours. But now, only one question was on his mind: *Where did the blood come from?*

Although he didn't have any sort of answer, Attard knew that it wasn't just a case of a drunken fall. When he had washed the copious amounts of blood away, he realised that none of the blood was his. For the first time in his life, he knew what panic was. Jason gathered up all the clothes he had been wearing the night before and put them in a plastic bag along with the hall rug. He filled a bucket with boiling water and bleach and mopped the hall. He showered. He then called Thea Spiteri's mobile.

'Hi, how are you feeling now? What was it, curry?' his boss asked.

'Possibly. I thought the chicken tasted a bit off.'

'Will you be in tomorrow?'

'Yes, definitely. That was why I was phoning, to let you know. Anything happening?'

'Apart from two murders and two missing kids? No, not a lot.'

'Yea, sorry.'

'I'm glad you're feeling better. See you tomorrow.'

\*\*\*

'Couldnae afford it! Couldnae afford it! Are you kidding me, son?' Matt Healy had managed to corral a young English couple, who were sitting at the end of the Crows Nest's bar.

'England couldnae afford it, you mean. You're fucked without our oil. Fucked, son. Sorry about the swearing, hen.'

'What about when the oil runs out?'

'Runs out! Never mind runs out. The Scots invented most things worthwhile. We'll keep doing that. No danger.'

'Yea, TV and telephones are what you're always going on about, yea?'

'Correct... and hypnosis, chloroform, and the hypodermic syringe.'

'Yea?'

'Yea... you'd have thought it would just have been easier talking to a woman, mind!'

Healy was the centre of attraction and, despite his bluster, the young couple were enjoying the banter. 'You'll still be rubbish at football, mind.' said the lad.

'Rubbish! We invented the game, son. Tell me this? Where do all the best managers come from? Scotland, that's where. Who were the first UK team to conquer Europe? Celtic, that's who. Scottish.'

'But your international team is crap!'

'Compared to who? We're a small country, only five million people, don't forget that. By the way, did you know that all the present England players have insisted that their wives go to Brazil for the World Cup as well?'

'No, why's that?'

'Cause John Terry's no goin! Marisol, a few more drinks if you please! We don't hate the English. Not at all. We just don't want to be governed by them' Matt Healy was going into full-steam-ahead mode for his new-found friends.

'Do you know a lot of English people, Matt?' asked Helen, the pretty, young holiday maker.

'I wouldn't say I know many, but I've met lots.'

'Where?'

'Tourists, visiting Scotland.'

'Nice people, then!'

'Well, the English tourists you meet in Edinburgh tend to be middle class; the English tourists you meet in Glasgow tend to be in hospital, so it's hard to say!'

'We're going for a pizza, Matt. Would you like to come?'

'No thanks, Peter. I have a rule: never eat when the pubs are open. It's been nice talking to you. Come back in tomorrow if you want to hear more about Scotland!'

'Will do, Matt. Thanks for the drinks. Bye.'

Peter and Helen wandered off into the warm night. Healy headed for the toilet. Once again, Matt Healy looked at himself in the toilet mirror. Someone he didn't recognise stared back.

# CHAPTER 26

Thea Spiteri had come into work a little bit later than normal but felt fully refreshed after ten hours' sleep.

She had been slightly shocked when Father Francesco had called her earlier to tell her he had decided to retire, but she agreed with him that it was the right thing to do. The old priest had asked her to let Matt Healy know, that perhaps they could all go to dinner one evening. Spiteri didn't have the heart to tell him that she had not seen or heard from Healy in days, and that he had started drinking again.

A gentle tap on her office door preceded Jason Attard's entry

'How are you feeling, Jason?'

'I'm much better, thank you, Kap.'

'What's all the hilarity out there?' asked Spiteri, pointing at a group of *Pulizija* surrounding a TV screen.

'Oh, it's just the CTV tape from Mosta the other night. The old guy can hardly walk and when he tries to get the cross up the stairs, he slips, the cat falls off, he picks it up, it slips off again... takes him five minutes to get the cross to stay balanced against the statue.'

Spiteri smiled at the mental picture. 'Don't tell Father Francesco any of that. I don't think he'll see the funny side!'

'No, I don't suppose he would.'

Spiteri's land line rang.

'Thea?'

'Yes, Commissioner.'

'You better get yourself up to Mosta straight away. A child has been found, throat cut, been dead about two or three days apparently. Report directly to me.'

The artillery shell landed more than a hundred meters from Matt Healy, but the blast shook his body and the noise woke him more dramatically than any alarm clock. Healy was stiff, sore, and totally disorientated. Another shell exploded, this time a bit further away from where Healy lay. His mind started to race. *Is this real? A dream? Christ, what's happening to me?* Another shell pounded into a concrete outhouse further up the hill. *I need to move.* Healy stumbled to his feet, looked around. He recognised everything. He was in Pembroke, and he realised that he must have fallen asleep in an old boat shed as he attempted to walk home by a route only a drunk man would choose. Unfortunately for Healy, his resting place was in the middle of the gun range in Pembroke that the Maltese Army often used for practice. Suddenly, Healy became aware of whistles, car horns, and sirens. Two minutes later, Matt Healy was under arrest for the second time in two days.

Spiteri and Attard looked down at the broken body of Michele Grech. His body had been stuffed down a drain behind The Chapel of the Assumption. His shorts were at his ankles and his throat had been cut. The smell had led to a city worker investigating. It was him who had called the *Pulizija*. Attard turned, walked over to the nearby flower bed, and vomited. Spiteri was surprised, as Attard had always seemed quite detached, no matter how bad the scene. Attard walked back.

'Sorry.'

'It's okay. Maybe you're still not right after your illness.'

'Yes, maybe.'

Spiteri spent the next two hours at the scene, organising everything that needed to be done with a priority of finding out who the victim was and why no one had reported him missing.

\*\*\*

As Spiteri arrived back at her office, a civilian secretary told her that St Julians Station needed to speak to her.

Once in her office, she called St Julians. *What now?* 'Hello, this is Thea Spiteri.'

'Morning, Inspector. Sorry to bother you, but do you know a Matt Healy?'

*Oh God, no.* 'Yes. What's happened to him? Is he okay?'

'Yes, he's fine. Hung over, nearly blown to pieces, but fine.' Spiteri got a quick rundown on the story.

'Take him home. Tell him if he ever gets sober to call me.'

Spiteri had no time to dwell on what she had just heard; Commissioner Debono was on the phone for the second time that day. 'What are your thoughts?'

'Looks like a possible sex killing. No name yet for the child.'

'Could it be the same person who took the other two children?'

'I suppose it could be, but this child was basically left in the open.'

'Maybe he's getting bolder; they say serial killers do.'

'Serial killers?'

'Well, we've got three missing kids. What would you call the bastard? Keep me informed.' The line went dead.

*Goodbye to you too, Commissioner.*

It took three days to identify the body of little Michele Grech. No one ever claimed his body.

\*\*\*

Joseph Sansome was a contented man. He let himself into his house and could smell the Oregano sauce he loved so much coming from the kitchen.

'It's ready. Go and sit at the table,' shouted Claudia.

Joseph, as always, did as he was told. Claudia laid two plates on the table and sat down opposite her husband.

'How are the Spanish classes going?'

'Yea, okay, but like I said, I'm going to stop going.'

'That's a shame. No other language you fancy, French, Dutch... German.'

Joseph Sansome sensed that there was a problem, but he had made plans.

'Maybe. I enquired about other classes. I think German was one of them actually, but no, I'm not going to bother.'

'What about the pizza place in Gozo, are you still interested?'

'Yes, still thinking about it.'

'Really? That's odd.'

'Why?'

'The estate agent rang. He seemed annoyed that you had used the oven. A lot of complaints from residents.'

'I had to test it! What kind of complaints?'

'Burning flesh type of complaints,' said Claudia, staring directly at her husband.

Joseph Sansome stared back at his wife, and then spoke quietly. 'Germans took our daughter; I took one of theirs.'

Claudia dropped her cutlery and put her hands over her mouth. 'Joseph, what have you done? That is not the way to remember Catherine.'

'It's my way.' Her husband rose from the table, walked around, and kissed his wife on the top of her head. He then walked back out the door.

# CHAPTER 27

'So, do we even know if we are dealing with two murderers, or two abductors, or one murderer, or the bloody Invisible Man?' This time, it was the deputy commissioner who was pressuring Spiteri for answers.

'I just don't know. Sorry.'

'Thea, you have to go with what you've got. The three murders? Well, it seems unlikely that we have gone from no murders for years, apart from Maltese family disputes, to three different murderers all surfacing at the same time, don't you think? I know we've charged Peter Smart with the Calder killing, but set that aside; Smart is obviously out of the picture for the Hooper killing and the kid in Mosta. So you have a second killer.'

'Michele. His name was Michele.'

'Right, Michele. I think you should be focusing on one killer for the Hooper and Calder killings, and one child abductor. I just can't see how the first two murders can be connected to the killing in Mosta. I'm supporting you as best I can, Thea, but you need to find this guy. This has been going on too long.'

'With respect, Dep...' It took a moment for Spiteri to realise the deputy commissioner had hung up.

\*\*\*

Matt Healy sat at his kitchen table, staring at a bottle of Hennessy Brandy. He had been sitting in the same place for two hours. His hands were shaking, his t-shirt was soaked in sweat, and a tear was rolling down his left cheek. He hadn't eaten, as he knew he would just throw up. He had then taken out the brandy and a beer glass. *No brandy balloon for me, not for the hardened drinker.*

Out of the corner of his eye, he noticed a slight movement in a recess on his kitchen wall. A spider was trying to weave its web between one wall and another. It took five minutes and several attempts before the spider succeeded. Healy stood up, put the brandy away, and picked up his phone. Thea Spiteri's phone went straight onto voicemail.

'Thea, its Matt. I've had a Robert the Bruce moment, call me... please.'

\*\*\*

Father Francesco Marandon was sitting in the square outside Verdala Palace. The sun was shining, and he too had a brandy on the table in front of him. A small, local brandy along with a coffee. He was slightly annoyed when his phone rang, and disturbed his reverie.

'Hello.'

'Francesco, it's Matt.'

'Matt, hello. How are you? I was talking to Thea about you only the other day. We're going to arrange a meal one night, celebrate my retirement.'

It took Healy a few seconds to realise that Thea couldn't have told the old priest that he was drinking again, and that Francesco thought he already knew about his retirement.

'Great. Francesco, listen. Can we meet? Today if possible.'

The wise old priest detected there was something wrong but did not ask.

'Yes, of course. Come now. I'll meet you back at the monastery. I'm not far from there now.'

'Thanks, Francesco. I'll be there in half an hour.'

'Fine.'

Healy cut the call. Francesco turned to Jason Attard. 'You'll have guessed that was Matt Healy? He wants to talk.'

'What about?'

'I'll soon know.'

'Call me later. I don't trust him.'


Matt Healy's grooming efforts hadn't worked; he looked rough. 'Are you okay, Matt? You look… well, ill.'

'I'm fine, Francesco, honestly.' A few moments of knowing silence passed between the two men. 'I've been drinking.'

'Ah.'

'I've stopped now. I won't do it again.'

'Life's a long journey, Matt. We all stumble and fall from time to time. Do not reproach yourself. Get up and keep on walking.'

'I ended up hating my mother.'

'Go on.'

'I have a problem with women, Francesco. I'm sure it goes back to my mother. Nothing I did was ever good enough. I was a disappointment to her.'

'Your father?'

'Not around.'

'Many parents unwittingly damage their children with their expectations of them.'

'I don't think unwittingly comes into it in my case, Francesco.'

'And when you grew up? Girlfriends, a wife?'

'Girlfriends? Yes, a few. One in particular. I ended up punching her one night. She was a policewoman. She could have reported me, got me thrown out. She didn't. She just walked away.'

'Do you see yourself as a danger to women?'

'No, but I can't seem to get one to stick with me.'

'Who's Susan?'

'How do you know about her?'

'Thea told me.'

'Shit. Really? Right. Well, Susan was my boss… and my lover. I thought that it was the real thing. I was wrong.'

'Are you still in touch with her?'

'She's dead.'

'Ah.'

'Killed by the guy she dumped me for. I should have seen it coming, saved her.'

'Matt, if you could have, then you would have. It's easy to look back with *What ifs*. It doesn't solve anything. This girl, Susan, she walked some of your journey with you, and you hers. Now other people are walking it with you.'

'Who, for instance?'

'Thea? She's very fond of you, Matt. I can tell.'

'I like her too, but like I said, I can't keep a relationship going. I've already blown that one.'

'No you haven't. It may take time to heal, but if you give it a chance, it will. Believe me.' The old priest hesitated for a moment. 'Matt, are you aware of recent developments? A lot has happened.'

'What developments?'

Father Francesco spent the next fifteen minutes outlining everything that had happened during Healy's time away.

When the old priest had finished, Healy felt even worse than before. The two friends embraced and went their separate ways. In his car, Healy tried Spiteri again.

'Hello, Matt.'

'Thea, I'm so sorry.'

'For?'

'Everything. Can we meet? Not in a restaurant or anything; can you come over to my place? I know you're busy; I've just left Francesco. He told me everything, but please come. I'm so sorry.'

'I'm not sure what time I could be there.'

'It doesn't matter.'

'Alright, I'll see you later.'

'Bring wine.'

'Not funny, Matt. Not funny at all.'


Father Francesco sat mulling over what Matt Healy had just said to him. He knew that the information would be music to Attard's ears. But only if he, Father Marandon, gave it to him. *He's basically a good man. Why try and destroy him?* The old priest wearily reached for his phone.

# CHAPTER 28

Matt Healy paced his living room floor as he waited for Thea Spiteri to arrive. He was dying for a drink. *One? Just one. How can that hurt?* He grabbed his phone, pushed *JF.* 'Jim, it's me, Matt.'

'How ya doin, man? Still shagging away?'

'Not in the mood, Jim, not in the mood at all. There's been another kid killed over here.'

'Shit, sorry. Killed or abducted?'

'Killed, throat slit, possibly abducted first. The body wasn't found for a few days.'

'Are you helping out again?'

A silent pause ensued.

'Matt?'

'Yea, I'm here. I've only just found out... I was back on the booze.'

'Right. How are you feeling?'

'Like shit.'

'Are you still seeing your lady friend? Thea, is it?'

'Ask me again tomorrow. She's coming over tonight. Let's just say she's not impressed.'

'Any progress with the Hooper thing? It's not in the papers at all here now.'

'Nothing, or on Calder.'

'Fuck. Listen, Matt, it's not your problem. Let the Maltese Police get on with it. You've done all you can.'

'We'll see. Anyway, I can see Thea's car coming. I'll need to go. How's that team of yours doing now?'

'You'll never guess what now? Castles. Fucking castles! The guy Green, who was here for about ten minutes, has already fucked off and bought a castle in France. And that Craig bastard, he's getting his castle in Scotland taken aff him for no paying the mortgage! You couldnae make it up, Matt.'

'So he's not exactly whiter than white then?'

'Naw, no exactly... wrong spelling right enough.'

'Wrong spelling! Wrong name, you mean. He should be scarlet, not white.'

'Scarlet?'

'Aye, Scarlet Pimpernel... he was always taking money from mugs and then pissing off!'

'Listen, Healy, ya...'

'Byeeee.' The line went dead with both men laughing.

Jason Attard was in a pensive mood. The information he had gleaned from Father Francesco only added to his belief that Healy could easily be linked to the killing of the two women—although he got the impression that the priest wasn't telling him everything. He knew that Healy had been cleared of any involvement with the killing of females in Scotland while he was involved in those investigations. *Still. It couldn't be that hard to show that every where Healy goes, women die. Show Thea, at least. That was all that mattered.*

\*\*\*

Father Marandon was uneasy. He had given Jason too much information. He was unhappy that the way Jason was using their friendship was not part of their arrangement. He thought that Matt Healy was basically a good man, but a good man with problems. And a temper. And a man who was now seeing his beloved Thea.

'Thea, you're looking nice; thank you for coming,' Healy said with a guilty look on his face.

'Thanks. Can you make me a coffee, Matt? I'm drained.'

'Sure.'

Healy and Spiteri fenced around the main issues for a few minutes before Spiteri said, 'Why did you start drinking again, Matt?'

'Thea, an alcoholic doesn't need a reason, only an excuse. I was upset with you, I felt frustrated about the Hooper thing, and about not finding Jamie... It was all too much. I just gave in.'

'And now?'

'I'm fine.'

'Till the next time?'

'Thea, I could easily sit here and say "There wont be a next time," but there could be. It's never over. I feel like a drink now. I'll feel like a drink in the morning, and tomorrow morning. It never goes away.'

'I'd like to be here for you, Matt. If you'll let me.'

'Let you? There's nothing I want more, Thea.'

Healy almost collapsed into Spiteri's arms as they both fell into an impassioned embrace; both their tongues desperately probing, searching for an escape to another plain. Twenty minutes later, Thea Spiteri emerged from Healy's bathroom wearing only his towelling bath robe. 'I think we both needed that, Matt.'

'I certainly did. Thea, I...'

'No, don't say anything, Matt. Let's just take a day at a time.'

'Okay. Do you want to talk about what's been happening at work?'

'Not everything; some of it is just too sad for words. But you can give me your views on this. We have three murder victims and two child abductions. Do you think we're looking for one killer or two, and are the abductions linked?'

'Two.'

'Why?'

'The same guy killed Calder and Hooper. Slitting a child's throat is not his style. So it's a different guy, but possibly the same guy who took the other two kids.'

'That's what I think too.'

'I know you think it might be me.'

'Ha ha, very funny. I didn't think it was you, but I needed to ask. You used to be a policeman, Matt. You should know that.'

'Yea, I do. Sorry.'

Healy and Spiteri sat in silence for a few minutes.

'We'll never solve these cases, Matt. I just know we won't.'

'You can't say that. Something will turn up, turn the case on its head.'

If Matt Healy had been a clairvoyant, he could not have had better timing. Spiteri's phone rang. She listened in silence, then got up quickly and headed towards the bathroom, then hung up. She glanced over her shoulder as she started picking up her clothes. 'We've found Jamie's body.'

# CHAPTER 29

Thea Spiteri never suggested that Healy go with her, and he never asked. He had an important phone call to make.

'Hello Mary, its Matt Healy, from Malta.'

'You've found him,' said Mary Smart in a calm, matter-of-fact way.

'I can't say for definite, Mary, but yes, I think so. I've only found out this minute. I said I'd call.'

'Thank you, Matt. What will happen now?'

'Well, I don't know for sure. I don't know how the Maltese handle these kinds of things. I'll make sure you are kept informed all the way, especially about bringing Jamie home.'

'I want him to be buried in Malta.'

'What? Why? You're maybe not thinking clearly, Mary. There's plenty of time to think about things.'

'Matt, Jamie was five years old. His father was a bastard. I was out working all the hours God sends, just to make ends meet. Malta was Jamie's first, and now only, holiday. I'd never seen him so excited or happy. He gave me a cuddle every day, said, "Thanks, Mum. You're the best." He never did that here. He didn't know the plastic sandals he was wearing weren't the best, that I'll be paying the Credit Union all year for his shorts and t-shirts. He only knew I was the best mum in the world. And now he's gone, but he doesn't need to come back to this shit hole ever again. He doesn't need to hear some little cunt at school telling him that his sandals are crap, his Dad's an alky, his mother a poxy cleaner. No, Mr Healy, I will come there, bury my Jamie where he will be happy forever. Will you let the authorities know that, please?'

'Yes, of course. Mary, please don't be angry, but are you okay for money? I'll help you if there's a problem.'

'No, thank you. I'll be fine, but thank you for asking. You can do one thing for me, though.'

'Yes, anything.'

'Catch whoever did this to my baby. Catch him and kill him.'

Matt Healy didn't have time to form a cogent answer before Mary Smart hung up.


Jamie Smart's grave site was taped off and surrounded by sombre faces when Thea Spiteri arrived. The body had been disturbed by a farmer's dog that had gotten its master's attention by returning on his command, carrying a plastic sandal.

The small body had been placed inside one of the countless religious monuments scattered all over Malta. This one consisted of a hollow stone mound with a statue of St Bartholomew on the top. It was extremely old.

'What's he the patron saint of, Jason?' said Spiteri, as they both walked towards the opening in the mound.

'Medicine and hospitals, I think.'

'Bit too late for Jamie.'

Spiteri did not consider herself to be an overly emotional woman. Her years in the *Pulizija* had hardened her to most things, but as she first caught site of Jamie Smart's distorted body, she felt like crying.

'What is wrong with these people? Jesus Christ.'

The pathologist and scene of crime officers had almost finished their initial work. The body would be taken to the mortuary at Mater Dei Hospital for a post mortem.

'Any first thoughts, Monique?' asked Spiteri of the on-call pathologist.

'Well, something doesn't look right.'

'What?'

'Well, the poor child's throat has been slit wide open.'

'Right. So?'

'So, why so little blood?'

'He was killed elsewhere? Brought here later?'

'Looks like it.'

'That's the cause of death, I take it?'

'That's the thing; I'd say not. I'd guess strangulation. I'll let you know for sure in a few hours.'

'Okay, thanks, Monique.'

Spiteri and Attard were glad to be back out in the night air. 'So, as if we didn't know, that's now four unsolved murders we've got,' said Spiteri.

'A strong suspect for this one, though: Peter Smart,' responded Jason.

'Strong? You really think so?'

'Don't you?'

'All I know is that I'm drowning.'

'I'm beside you all the way, Thea. We'll get through this.'

Jason Attard's statement had made Spiteri feel strangely uneasy.

'I'll see you in the office at seven tomorrow morning. Night, Jason.'

Spiteri got two phone calls before she reached home. The first was from the deputy commissioner. 'Is it the Scottish boy?'

'It looks like it.'

'Good.'

'What?'

'Oh, come on, Thea, you know what I mean. Forensics are there, I take it? Let's hope they can come up with something. Well done, Thea.'

*Well done! Fucking well done. A child is brutalised. We have no fucking idea by who. Well done! Jesus wept.*

Before Spiteri could silently rant any further, her phone rang again. It was Healy.

'Is it Jamie?'

'Yes.'

'Bad?'

'Bad.'

'Do you want to come back here?'

'No, Matt. I need some sleep and a change of clothes. I've called a review for seven a.m. I'll know more then. I'll catch up with you tomorrow afternoon hopefully. Get your expert view!'

'Okay. One question: was Jamie's throat cut?'

'Yes...' By the time Spiteri's car came out of the tunnel, the connection had gone. *Sleep, Thea, sleep. Speak to Matt tomorrow.*

***

Matt Healy saw that it was Francesco calling.

'Good morning, Francesco.'

'Morning, Matt. I've been trying to get a hold of Thea. Have you spoken to her?'

'Not since last night, no. She's very busy, Francesco.'

'Is it true that the abducted child has been found?'

'Yes, up near Gharghur. Terrible. He had his throat cut.'

'No!'

Healy felt that there was almost venom in the old priest's response.

'Are you alright, Francesco?'

'Yes, sorry, Matt. All these killings have upset me. Besides, the boy was strangled; Jason Attard called me with the news.'

'Right, I must be mistaken.'

'Okay, I must go. We'll meet up soon.'

'Yes, that will be good.' Healy placed his phone gently on the café table. He started to pick at his nails, always a sign that he was deep in thought. *What the fuck was that all about?*

# CHAPTER 30

1988 Malta

Constable Christopher Debono was in hell. He loved doing the job that he'd always wanted to do; his parents were proud of him, and he was married to a lovely woman who adored him. But Chris Debono was in love with another woman, deeply and passionately in love, and she was carrying his baby.

Maria Azzopardi knew that she and Chris could never be together; the shame for both their families would be too much for either of them to bear. Chris Debono and Maria sat and talked for hours on end, looking for a solution. There wasn't any. But despite the situation he found himself in, Chris Debono was an honourable man. He promised to look after Maria and the baby. At that moment in time, he just wasn't sure how.

Almost every day when he finished his shift in the *Pulizija*, he went to a bar well away from his station and looked to see if whisky could show him a solution.

'What's wrong, Chris? You look as if the world is about to end,' said, Debono's best friend, Nicky.

'It already has,' said Debono.

'There's always a solution, Chris. What's wrong?' One of the things Chris loved about Nicky was that, even from their school days, Nicky was a doer, a fixer, a get-you-anything friend. Even so, Debono was reluctant to admit to the problem he had.

'I'm not leaving till you tell me, Chris,' said Nicky, so, over the next half hour, Chris Debono explained his predicament.

'Shit, now I see why you're down. What solution would you like, within reason?'

'We know we can't be together, and Marie knows she can't have the child here. All we can think of is that she goes away, and I help her and see the child as and when I can.'

'How would you feel if I told my father? He might know what to do.'

'He wouldn't say anything to anyone?'

'No.'

'Okay.'

The following day, Nicky provided Chris with a solution.

Nicky's father had arranged for Maria to be taken in by a private hospital in Corsica and four months later, when Maria was worried that her mother suspected something, she was admitted to the hospital. Maria told her parents she had gotten a job in a hotel in Sicily, and Debono said he had been put on a training course in Italy. Debono sat in the hospital with his true love for two days and soothed her brow when the pains of giving birth to their beautiful son, Pietro, proved to be nearly too much. And the man who would one day be *Pulizija* Commissioner Christopher Debono stayed with Maria Azzopardi as she died the day after giving birth to the child she would never know. Debono never knew for sure if the shame and secrecy had drained Maria of her will to live, but the thought haunted him every day thereafter. Two days later, Christopher Debono saw his son for the last time, as a nun carried him out of the room in which his mother had died giving birth to him, and his father had experienced grief like no time before or since.

*\*\**

Sarah Said gave Thea Spitieri's door an almost imperceptible knock and when told, "Come in," she entered almost timidly.

Spiteri was smiling. 'Sarah, sit down. Are you scared of me?'

'No, Kap. I'd like to emulate you, to be honest. Rise as high as I can in the *Pulizija*.'

Spiteri's smile turned to a full laugh. 'Sarah, I wouldn't wish that on my worst enemy! What can I do for you?'

'The killing of the young boy in Mosta, Michele Grech? I've been studying all the video footage, not just the bit showing the cat thing. I think I've found something that may be useful, but maybe not. I don't want to bother you, though, if you are busy.'

'Don't be daft, Sarah. We have nothing on the killer at the moment. Let me see the tape.'

Like most surveillance pictures, the quality was okay for some things, but not for close-up identification. The blurred image showed a young man running on the far side of the square from behind the Chapel, stopping, appearing to stoop over and be sick, start running again, and appearing to throw something into a large rubbish skip belonging to a construction company, who was doing renovation work on the adjacent building.

'I wonder if that skip is still there? If it's been emptied?' asked Spiteri.

'I'm afraid it has been. I called the construction company.'

'Okay. It's still great work, Sarah. Contact the company again. Find out where they dropped the load.'

Said rose to leave.

'Sarah, you'll be my boss soon enough!' said Spiteri.

***

'Do you intend staying on the island, Francesco?' asked Jason Attard.

'I don't know. I may travel, I may not,' replied the old priest wearily.

'Are you content with your life?'

'I did my best, but content? That is hard to say.'

'You have been a good father to me. You have taught me well.'

'Really? We shall see.'

'I'm not stupid, Francesco. I know you don't approve of my ways sometimes, but I have work to do, too; just the same as you.'

'Then God bless you, Jason. I can at least wish you that.'

Jason Attard headed back to the station. He was still peeved with the fact that Spiteri still seemed infatuated with Healy. *Not for long.* As Sarah Said entered the room, he was about to shift from peeved to panicked.

'Hi, Jason.' Said was almost singing.

'What are you so happy about then?'

'The video! Spiteri is "very impressed."'

'What video?'

'The Mosta video.'

'What about it?'

'Haven't you heard? There's an image in it that might well show the killer.'

'What? Where? Show me.'

Attard watched the video in silence. 'You can't tell anything from that!'

'I've to send it to be enhanced. It's amazing what the tech people can do now. I'm quietly confident.'

'I'm going over to the lab just now. I just want to double check something about the Hooper killing. Do you want me to take the disc?'

'Oh, yes. That would be great. Thanks, Jason.'

'No problem.' Jason slid the disc from the machine and headed for the door.

'Jason.'

'What?'

'Don't you be putting your name on that, taking the credit!'

'As if!' Attard smiled, winked, and disappeared through the office door.

***

Since Thea Spiteri had seen Claudia Sansome approaching, Spiteri shouted for the other woman to come straight in. Sansome came in and slumped into the chair opposite Spiteri without being invited. Spiteri looked at her colleague and knew something was seriously wrong.

'Claudia, what is it? What's wrong?'

The reply was almost inaudible. 'The abductions.'

'I know it's terrible. They're affecting us all.'

'You don't understand.'

'What?'

'I know who has done them.'

'What? Who?'

'Joseph.'

'Joseph? Joseph who... your Joseph?'

'Yes. He's admitted it to me. Thea, he's not well... ever since Catherine was taken...'

'Where is he now, do you know?'

'Yes, he's downstairs in my car. I told him to wait there until I'd spoken to you.'

Spiteri was incredulous. 'Claudia, are you sure about all this? You're not just stressed?'

'Go down and see for yourself.'

# CHAPTER 31

Thea Spiteri looked in bewilderment through the one-way mirror that separated the viewing room from Interrogation Room 1. Joseph Sansome appeared to be calm, even happy, and with no signs of stress or nervousness. Spiteri decided to go and have a quick word with Claudia, partly for confirmation of what had already been said and partly to commiserate. *Did she know?*

Claudia Sansome was walking back from the coffee machine when Spiteri went back to her office; she noticed Sansome limping.

'What happened?' asked Spiteri.

'I went over on my ankle the other day in that terrible place in Gozo where... it was okay at the time but it hurts like hell now.'

Spiteri picked up her phone. 'Is Dr Pace still here? I saw him earlier.'

'Yes,' replied a duty officer.

'Okay, good. Send him to my office, will you?'

'Is there anything you can tell me about this, Claudia? Did you know about it? Why did you go to Gozo at all?'

Claudia looked at the ceiling for a few seconds before looking Spiteri in the eye.

'I knew nothing, Thea. I thought he was having an affair. Someone told me she had seen him on the Gozo Ferry. I followed him.'

'We'll need the name of the person who saw him.'

Claudia gave a resigned smile. *Mrs Tanti will think she's died and gone to heaven.*

'Claudia, do you think Joseph took the other boy, Jamie Smart? Killed Michele Grech?'

'No.'

'Why not?'

Claudia stared at the ceiling again. 'I don't know.'

'The forensics team are at your house at the moment, Claudia. Any trace of Jamie there, and Joseph will spend the rest of his life in prison. I can't help you. You know that?' Claudia Sansome merely nodded.

A brusque knock on the office door heralded the arrival of the eccentric Dr Pace. 'Good morning one and all. What seems to be the problem?' A quick explanation and examination then took place.

'The ankle is badly bruised and a couple of nasty cuts, but it's not broken. She just needs to rest it,' said Dr Pace.

'Thank you, Doctor,' replied Spiteri.

Dr Pace then pulled a plastic bag from his case and proceeded to place a luminous green compression bandage over Sansome's ankle. 'Keep this on for a few days. Bye, all.' And he was gone.

Claudia shrugged her shoulders.

'Okay, Claudia. Go home now. I promise I will keep you up to date with everything. I'm putting you on compassionate leave. The forensics people should be finished at your house. Try and get some sleep. Maybe give Father Marandon a call?

'Thank you. Yes I will.' *I need to go out tonight anyway.*

\*\*\*

Interrogation Room 1 seemed cold when Spiteri and Said walked in and sat down.

'Hello, Joseph,' said Spiteri.

'Hi,' replied Joseph Sansome.

*Christ, it's like we were at a party.* 'Did you kill Ingrid Lam?'

'Yes.'

*Nothing, no emotion, pity, nothing.* 'Why?'

'An eye for an eye.'

'Come on, Joseph. Are you saying this is all to do with the death of your daughter? That was an accident.'

'So I didn't feel any loss?'

'I'm not saying that. But you can't kill another child as a sort of tit-for-tat arrangement! What about Ingrid's parents? What about their loss?'

'Good, now at least someone else will understand.'

'You're sick in the head.'

'I'm free, you mean.'

*Bastard.* 'Why did you kill Jamie Smart?'

'Who?'

'And Michele Grech; were they eye for an eye, too?'

'I've no idea what you're talking about.'

'Did you sexually assault Ingrid before you killed her, Joseph?'

'No.' For the first time, Sansome's head was bowed, his eyes not looking at Spiteri.

'Do you prefer little boys, then?' asked Said.

'What? No way! What the fuck is this?'

'Interview over. You're going to the cells. When I get the forensic results, I'll let you know how many murders you're going to be charged with. I'll let Claudia know that you're free, shall I?'

***

'Ta Hagart Temples?' asked Nicola Tizian of Michael Bonnici. 'So what?'

'Nicola, you have to understand. This is not easy. You are talking about building right next to a UNESCO Heritage site. In a place already designated as a buffer zone!'

'A buffer zone? A buffer for what? The ancient fucking past? And dragging this fucking island into the Twenty-first century?'

'I'm not saying it can't be done. I'm trying. Believe me, but it will take time. There are all these conservation idiots to placate.'

'Michael, correct me if I am wrong. I got you the job of... What is it again? Oh yes. Head of Planning and the Simplification of the Administrative Process, did I not?'

'I know, Nicola but...'

'But nothing,' interrupted Tizian. 'I am paying you a lot of money, you little *gurdien* get me that planning consent or I will be taking you off the payroll. Permanently. Do you understand?'

'Yes.'

***

Thea Spiteri knew that the preliminary forensic reports wouldn't be back for hours. She informed her team to go home and be back in at 7.00 a.m. She then called Healy.

'Hi.'

'Hi. Tough day?'

'Well, we've got the killer of the little German girl, maybe of the other two kids as well. I'm just waiting for forensics.'

'That's great.'

'You know Claudia that works here, don't you?'

'To look at, yes, but...'

'It's her husband; she turned him in.'

'Christ. Do you want to come over?'

'I won't tonight, Matt. I'm going home, hot bath, bed... in here at six-thirty a.m.'

'Okay. Maybe see you tomorrow then. Night.'

Spiteri decided to give Francesco a quick call as well.

'Hard day I hear, child.'

'You could say that. How did you know?'

'Claudia called me. I went straight over. Terrible; just terrible.'

'How did she seem to you?'

'Strangely normal, to be honest. Shock, I suppose.'

'Francesco, can I ask you something? It must go no further.'

'Of course, child.'

'Do you think she knew?'

'No, never.'

'Her husband has killed a child, possibly three. How is it possible that she didn't see any signs?'

'Maybe there weren't any signs. What do you mean "possibly three?"'

'The other two dead kids. It could be him.'

'Really, I never considered that.'

'Anyway, Francesco, nice to hear your voice; I'm going home now to sleep forever.'

'Goodnight, child.'

Francesco turned over in his head everything that Thea had said to him. *Is that possible? Could Sansome have killed the three children?*

Spiteri opted for one last, quick call to Claudia. There was no reply. Spiteri switched off the light in her office and headed for the door. She had had a hard day, but the next one would be a lot harder.

# CHAPTER 32

When Spiteri returned to her office the next morning, the Forensic Report from the Sansome home was on her desk. She poured a coffee then started to read the report.

After pouring over the report for ten minutes, Spiteri's sense of depression returned. The Sansomes' flat had traces of all the usual things that would be expected in any household, including some cat's blood, but also a strand of hair belonging to Jamie Smart and a urine stain from the German girl, Lam, mixed with a small amount of Joseph Sansome's semen. A quick scan of his laptop had also revealed thousands of child pornography photographs. *Sansome, you fucking bastard. I'll crucify you for this. Claudia or no Claudia.*

The CID Room was packed by 6.45 a.m. in readiness for Spiteri's instructions. In fact, she would be very brief.

'Everyone, listen please,' Spiteri announced. 'I have the initial forensics report from last night's search of Sansome's house. Jamie Smart's DNA was obtained from the scene. As you know, he is already in custody for the Ingrid Lam killing. He will now be charged with the abduction and murder of Jamie Smart. The cause of death has been confirmed as strangulation, and the child was sexually assaulted. Jamie's throat had also been slit, but, again, it has been confirmed that this was done when he was already dead; was Sansome practising for the Grech killing? Also, we still have the Calder and Hooper killings outstanding.'

'Could it be a case of overkill in Jamie's case?' asked Sarah Said.

'Possibly. Who knows? Hopefully, we'll get some answers from Sansome.'

A civilian support worker caught Spiteri's attention from the adjoining room. Spiteri motioned for her to enter.

'The commissioner wants you to call him, Thea.'

'Okay. Right, any more questions? Okay, let's get on with it.'

Spiteri went into her office, closed the door, and called the commissioner.

'Is it true? You have a cast iron case against Sansome?'

'Yes, pretty much.'

'Pretty much?'

'Well, we still have the issue of the post-death wound.'

'Thea, the man is obviously mad. Charge him with the three child abductions and killings and intending to pervert justice. If I can think of anything else, I'll let you know. This is great news, Thea. Well done. Right, I'm going to release a statement to the press but, and this is vital, I don't want it getting out that this bastard is married to someone in the *Pulizija*.'

'We've been lucky. Not everyone would hand over their husband. Commissioner, don't you think we should wait before charging him for the Grech killing? We don't really have any evidence yet.'

'We will, don't worry. Just follow instructions, Thea.'

'Right.'

'Any progress with the other two murders?'

'No, not really. We're doing everything we can. We need a bit of luck there, too.'

'Okay, keep going. Bye.'

***

Interrogation Room 1 still felt cold to Spiteri, but she didn't intend staying in it too long; hoping Said's presence would help speed things along. Joseph Sansome still sat opposite her with the air of a man without a care in the world.

'Remember when you worked in a slaughterhouse, Joseph?' asked Spiteri.

'Yea.'

'Trained in how to slice flesh, I take it?'

'Yea.'

'Did you enjoy that?'

'Yea. I suppose. It was a job.'

'You liked using the knives, didn't you, Joseph?'

'What are you getting at here?'

'We found Jamie Smart's blood, you know, the boy you'd never heard of. Well, we found his blood in your house.'

Sansome jumped up on to his feet. 'Fucking liars! That's impossible.'

'He was sexually assaulted as well. You sure you don't like little boys, Joseph?' asked Said.

Sansome attempted to grab Said across the table, but the ever present *Pulizija* guard grabbed him. Half an hour later, Joseph Sansome had been charged with three murders and was sitting in the back of a prison van.

Thea Spiteri was sitting at her desk with her head back and eyes closed. She knew she still had two murders to solve, but also that a certain weight was off her shoulders, even though she had some doubts about the Grech case. *What did Debono mean by "We will?" I'll just have ten minutes and then I'll phone Claudia, break the news. Shit.*

The sound of laughter from the outer office woke Spiteri from her nap before her desired ten minutes of peace.

191

'Jason, what are you lot laughing at?'

Attard walked in to Spiteri's office. 'We're just looking at last night's footage of that madman that's sticking dead cats and dogs everywhere.'

'For God's sake, don't tell Francesco you've been laughing at it. I don't think he finds it funny!'

'No, don't worry! The guy's getting madder and madder, incidentally; who the hell wears one luminous green shoe?'

Spiteri slowly placed her head in her hands. She quietly spoke to Attard. 'Jason, go and bring Claudia in. Just tell her I need to go over a couple of old witness statements.'

Attard paused for a moment, realisation slowly dawning. 'Shit. It never even came into my head.'

'Shit indeed, Jason. Shit indeed.'


For someone whose husband had just been charged with three child murders, Claudia Sansome looked remarkably calm.

'Do you know why you're here, Claudia?'

'Yes, about the cats and dogs... and sugar and spice, and all things nice.'

Spiteri was stunned. 'Not Joseph? He's been charged with three murders; three children, Claudia.'

'It's strange; I never thought he cared enough after Catherine died. He's a good man.'

'A good man? Why did you turn him in then?'

'Because I didn't fully understand his pain. I regret it now.'

'You regret it? Claudia, you are a *Pulizija* officer.'

Sansome didn't seem to take in what Spiteri had just said.

'Why did you do it? The cats and the dogs; why?'

'Why not? People have to know about loss.'

'But how does what you have been doing do that?'

'People lose their innocence. Learn there is no God watching over what is theirs.'

'Claudia, listen to me. I'm trying to help. You'll have to be psychiatrically assessed.'

'You think I'm mad.' It was a statement, not a question.

'What I think doesn't matter.'

'I'm going to France tomorrow.'

'What?'

'I'm going to France. Joseph's got an interview in Paris. Have you ever been to Paris, Thea?'

'No, no, I haven't.'

\*\*\*

Father Francesco answered his phone on the second ring. 'Thea, two conversations in two days. I'm honoured!'

'We've caught the cat person.'

'Really, how wonderful. Is he evil or mad, would you guess?'

'Neither. It's Claudia Sansome.'

'No.'

'Francesco, I'm going to try and help her, get her psychiatric help. Do you mind?'

'No, of course not, child. The poor woman. And Joseph, of course. What devastation a child's death has caused.'

'Do you think that is it? The underlying reason.'

'What else, Thea?'

'I can half understand Joseph's thinking, warped as it is, but why attack churches?'

'She probably feels God abandoned her, didn't save her child.'

'Do you think the Church will push for criminal charges?'

'I'll see what I can do. Get her assessed as soon as you can. I can't see the archbishop wanting to keep this sorry time in the headlines.'

'Thanks, Francesco. I will.'

\*\*\*

Spiteri moved quickly. *At the end of the day, she is one of our own.*

Dr Carbonne, a psychiatrist used often by the *Pulizija*, sat opposite Claudia Sansome, studying her body language. Sansome seemed relaxed, even happy.

'So, Claudia, how are you feeling today?'

'Excited.'

'Excited? That's good. Why?'

'My husband and I are flying to New York this afternoon; holiday of a lifetime sort of thing.'

'Really? That sounds wonderful. Claudia, do you know where Joseph is at the moment?'

'Yes, he's buying swimming trunks, for the holiday.'

'I see. Are you a Catholic, Claudia?'

'Oh yes. In the name of the Father... da de da de da.'

Carbonne held up her hand. 'Okay. And Claudia, do you like cats?'

'Yes, I used to have two. They ran away.'

'That's a shame. But you still like them, and dogs?'

'Yes.'

'Claudia, the cats and dogs you nailed to crosses. Did you like them?'

Sansome appeared to not have heard the question.

'Claudia, were the animals already dead when they were nailed to the cross?"

Sansome stared over at Carbonne. Her facial features seemed to change, harden. 'Hard to say. Does it matter?"

'It matters, Claudia. It matters a lot, as a matter of fact.'

Claudia Sansome shrugged, picked at a thread on her skirt.

'Doctor?'

'Yes, Claudia.'

'Will the swimming pools be open in New York, do you know?'

# CHAPTER 33

The prison guard knew Father Francesco from visits to other prisoners. 'Good afternoon, Father.'

'Good afternoon. How is he coping?' Father Francesco said, motioning to the cell containing Joseph Sansome.

'Hard to say. He hasn't said much.'

'I've brought him a little food, and some water. Is that okay?'

'Of course, Father. I think he needs all the friends he can get, but please, Father, take it away when you leave. The prisoners aren't really supposed to be given anything.'

'I know and, yes, I will take anything not eaten with me.'

'I didn't do it, Father.' Joseph Sansome was a beaten man. He and the old priest sat in the cell in Carradino Prison where Sansome had been taken.

'Joseph, I'm afraid the evidence is against you. Your own wife reported you.'

'I don't mean the German girl, I've admitted to that and I'm not sorry. I mean the boys.'

'I'm not here to talk about the charges, Joseph. I'm here to try to help your soul. To begin with, eat something. You must stay strong.'

'I'm not hungry, Father, but thank you for bringing it.'

The old priest could hear Sansome's teeth grating through his words.

'Keep calm, Joseph. I will do all I can. Have some water, at least.'

Sansome drank a little water. He appeared to be studying the label on the bottle. He looked Father Marandon in the eye.

'What will happen to me, Father?'

'I've no idea, Joseph.'

'Will God forgive me?'

Father Francesco looked at the lost soul opposite him. 'The Lord works in mysterious ways, Joseph.'

A light knock on the cell door signalled that the visiting time was up.

'I'll come back very soon, Joseph. I promise. Keep praying.' Father Francesco collected his unwanted offerings, and left.

A half hour later, he called Jason Attard. 'Jason, can you meet me? There is something I can help you with.'

\*\*\*

Commissioner Debono was also mulling over the implications of the arrest of Joseph Sansome when his phone rang.

'Commissioner Debono? It's Assistant Commissioner Peter Martin from Scotland Yard here. I believe we met a couple of years ago at a conference organised by Interpol, in Basle?'

'Yes, Peter, I remember it, and you, very well. Quite a night!'

'Yes, well, lest said about that the better, Commissioner!'

'Yes indeed! So, what can I do for you, Peter?'

Peter Martin spent the next half hour explaining the reason for his call: he had been put in charge of Operation Grange, which was the name given to the investigation that was set up in 2011 to look into the disappearance of Madeline McCann from a holiday resort in Portugal in

2007. Things had moved very slowly since then, but recent evidence had come to light of the probability that Madeline had been the victim of a serial child molester who was operating in the area at that time, and was possibly responsible for up to eighteen assaults. A fresh appeal for information was made in March 2014 and a young girl had come forward to say that in 2005, when she was ten, she was attacked in the same resort as Madeline was taken from. The girl was nineteen now, but had been too ashamed to come forward before. The team now had a description of the attacker.

Peter Martin went on. 'The guy is tanned, dark haired, speaks English with an odd accent to it, has unkempt hair, heavy growth but not a beard, a pot belly, and "smells strange." Chris, we also know the guy moves around a lot.'

'Right, I think I'm ahead of you here, Peter, but how do you know about our bloke here so quickly?'

'We got a call from the Scottish Police. A quick-thinking detective up there, I think his name is Frame, had been keeping an eye on your cases because he's got a friend living in Malta. Anyway, he was told about your guy, checked the description of our suspect... and got in touch.'

'Jesus, what work!'

'Good police work, Chris.'

'So what do you want to do?'

'I've got a criminologist who's been working closely with us here; his name is Roy Cosgrove. Can I send him over to you? He doesn't need to speak to the suspect, just examine the sights. He'll be able to say from that whether he could be our guy. We'll then see where we go from there.'

'Of course, Peter. When do you want him to come over?'

'Tomorrow, but Chris, no publicity and no police involvement apart from one of the investigating officers going around with him. Maybe a driver as well, but that's it.'

'I'll organise it right now. What flight will your man be on?'

'I'll get back to you on that. Thanks, Chris.'

Debono contacted Thea Spiteri as soon as he had hung up on Martin. 'Use your Scottish friend as a driver, Thea. The less *Pulizija* that know about this, the better.'

The arrival of Professor Roy Cosgrove on Malta was low key and, under further instruction from the commissioner himself, no one but Spiteri and Healy had to deal with him or even know he was working on the cases. "Thea, don't tell Cosgrove this, but two people have tried to help on this case already, and they've both been murdered. I do not want a third. So no one knows and you report directly to me. Understood?"

Matt Healy had met Cosgrove on his arrival at Luqa Airport that morning, and on the drive to Valetta had explained what he knew about the abductions.

Cosgrove listened intently then said, 'I know I'm not supposed to get involved with the Miriam Calder and May Hooper killings, but they were friends of mine. Not close friends, but we worked together on quite a few occasions, and both of them being killed here is no coincidence. I'd like a quick look at their crime scenes, too; I want to help there, if I can.'

'Well, Roy, can I just say that the Maltese *Pulizija* are no mugs, but there has just been nothing to work on. There is a guy in prison awaiting trial for Miriam Calder's killing, young Jamie Smart's father, as a matter of fact, but I'm not convinced. Even less so now that another guy has been arrested for Jamie's murder.'

'Were there any signs of sexual motive in Jamie's killing?'

'Yes, apparently so. Remember, I'm not actually "official" here.'

'Who do you think killed Jamie?'

'Well, it's pretty clear now that it was this bastard Sansome that killed all three kids.'

'Who do you think killed Miriam? Do you think the same person killed May?'

'No idea, to be honest. And I can't think of a motive. There are two things that nag away at me, though. The knife that had Calder's blood on it, but was not the one that killed her, was found in Peter Smart's hotel room. What's that all about?'

'And?'

'And, obviously the fact that both Miriam and May wrote "Why" in the sand.'

Healy picked up Spiteri well away from Floriana, made the introductions, and headed to St Julians.

Spiteri, Healy, and Cosgrove stood outside Andrew's Bar in St George's Bay and tried to re-enact the sequence of Jamie Smart's abduction in their heads.

'So, how far away from here was the body eventually found?' asked Cosgrove.

'About five kilometers or so,' replied Spiteri.

'Which means that the abductor must have had transport. The child wasn't killed where he was found, correct?'

'Yes. He had his throat cut post-death.'

'Then there were two abductors or two people involved in the sequence of events, at least. Can you take me to where the body was found now?'

Fifteen minutes later, Cosgrove, Healy and Spiteri were standing outside the still-cordoned-off shrine. In reality, there wasn't much left to see, but Cosgrove spent a lot of time just looking and taking a lot of pictures. 'Okay. So the guy who has been charged with this crime is also the one who's been charged with the other two?'

'Yes.'

'Right. I'd like to go to the second site now, but I understand it's on Gozo.'

Spiteri had anticipated what Cosgrove's requests would be and impressed him—and Healy—by explaining that she'd booked a helicopter and that they would be in Gozo about ten minutes after boarding. The trio flew to Gozo, had a quick look at the abduction site, and were now standing in the abandoned shop in Victoria. Again, there was nothing much to see as far as Spiteri and Healy were concerned, but they were fascinated as Cosgrove went about his work, comparing the crime scene photos Spiteri had provided and the ones he himself had taken at the shrine. The team then stopped off at Mosta, and Cosgrove did his usual meticulous job examining the site and taking photos of the drain where the boy had been found, and the surrounding area. The trio then headed back to Valetta by car.

'Any initial thoughts, Roy?' asked Healy.

'Well, I'd like some quiet time in a room, if that's okay, Thea, and I'll give you my thoughts this evening.'

'Yes, of course. No problem,' said Spiteri.

'Tomorrow, I'd like to see where Miriam and May were killed, if that's okay. I'll then give you my thoughts on that. Then, I'll have to leave, I'm afraid. The investigations in Portugal have reached an important juncture. I need to be there.'

Spiteri was slightly taken aback. 'You're not supposed to know about them!'

'Matt will explain. Time is the issue. Sorry.'

'The McCann case?' asked Healy.

'Yes.'

'What do you think about all these whispers that it was the parents?'

'Well, you can't rule it out, obviously. Most murdered children are killed by a relative, as you know, but in this case, no.'

Healy nodded his head. 'They're the best actors ever if they are involved, I'll tell you that.'

Spiteri, too, nodded.

It was 7.00 p.m. when Cosgrove knocked on Spiteri's office door.

'Roy, take a seat. Would you like a coffee? Matt and I were thinking of dinner if you're interested.'

'Thanks, but no. I'll get back to the hotel if you don't mind. I have a number of calls to make, and in the morning, I want to be at the scene of Miriam Calder's murder at the same time as the killing took place, or as near as we can estimate.'

'Okay. I'll pick you up at seven a.m.' said Healy.

'Thank you, that's perfect.'

'You don't look happy, Roy,' said Healy, motioning towards the pile of notes on Cosgrove's knee.

'I'm afraid I've chosen a line of work where "Happy" doesn't often come into it, Matt.'

'What did you find, Roy?'

'In my view, you have three different child killers and, unfortunately for me, none of them are my man.'

'But Sansome's DNA was found at two of the scenes.'

'I know, and I can't explain that at the moment. That is your job, Thea, but he did not kill Jamie Smart.'

'So are you saying that the person who did kill Jamie also killed Michele Grech in Mosta?'

'No, I'm saying the exact opposite. First things first: the layout where Jamie Smart's body was found is completely different to either sticking a body in an oven or down a drain.

'Secondly, Jamie was strangled; Michele had his throat cut in a frenzied attack. Your perpetrators are different people. Sorry, I know that this is not what you wanted to hear but I can only report what I think.'

'No, Roy, I'm grateful, believe me. We just have to re-group and start again.'

'What about the throat wounds on Smart and Grech?' asked Healy.

'That, I admit, is a dilemma. Cases of wounds inflicted after death do happen, but usually by the killer, and he will have used violence to actually kill the victim as well. And don't forget, the Grech throat wound is what killed; it wasn't a post-death thing.'

'You don't count strangulation as violence?'

'In this context? Frankly, no. Strangling someone is impersonal. The killer is almost detached, the victim not a person, more an object. Slitting someone's throat... that is a different matter.'

Healy and Spiteri gave Cosgrove a lift back to his hotel, then she and Healy sat in silent contemplation.

Finally, Healy spoke. 'Christ knows what he'll come up with tomorrow. What do you think the commissioner will say?'

'As long as Cosgrove's right and we eventually get these people, then we'll both be happy.'

Thea Spiteri would be very wrong about that.


Even at 7.00 a.m., it was warm in St George's Bay. 'It's slightly lighter now than it was when Miriam was killed, and there are more people around now, as all the cafeés, et cetera are opening now, getting ready for the season starting,' said Spiteri to an intense Cosgrove.

'So she was supposed to be meeting you, Matt, but never made it. How did her killer know she'd be here?'

'We don't know that he did. It could have been an opportunist killing,' said Spiteri.

'Where is the hotel that Peter Smart was staying in?'

'Not far, a few hundred meters.'

'Yet, instead of disposing of *the* knife in any one of numerous places on the way there, he takes it and leaves it in his hotel room.'

'People do crazy things under intense pressure, Roy,' interrupted Healy, who felt Cosgrove was being critical of Spiteri's investigation. 'Besides, it wasn't the murder weapon. Don't ask me to explain that, because I've no idea.'

'Mmm. Can we go to the Hooper site now?'

'Sure. It will take about half an hour or so by car,' said Spiteri.

In the car, Cosgrove decided to clear up any misunderstanding. 'Listen Thea, Matt, I'm not here to criticise, only to study, comment, and advise. I know these cases are grim, and I agree with Miriam Calder's assessment about trying to work out the minds of these kinds of people is a load of rubbish. This may sound harsh, but do you want to know something? Victims are the cause of being victims. What do I mean by that? Victims are very young or very old. They are physically, or mentally, weak. They are gay, they are women, they are prostitutes, and they therefore fall into categories that the perpetrators view as worthless. Perpetrators of these kinds of crimes are in a world of their own. Different rules, different motivators, different moralities. Please don't take anything I say the wrong way, it's just my manner. I'm okay at home, according to my eighth wife!' All three of the trio laughed.

'Thank you, Roy,' said Spiteri. Healy nodded in Cosgrove's direction.

Golden Beach was still deserted when the three investigators arrived. 'So, May's body was on the sand. She had put up a fight. Her assailant had dropped a knife, this weapon proved to be the murder weapon, but it wasn't the one that killed Miriam Calder, as well. Is that right?' said Cosgrove.

'That sums it up,' said Spiteri.

'How long was it before May's body was found?'

'Next morning.'

Cosgrove spent a few moments looking around at the surrounding area. 'Okay, I've seen enough. Let's get back.'

\*\*\*

'Is that all, sir?' said the bored-looking cashier to Jason Attard whilst checking her mobile phone.

'Yes, thanks,' replied Attard, holding his purchase: a small bottle of drain cleaning fluid. Normally, he would have been angry at the level of service, but on this occasion, he was happy. *No chance she'll ever remember serving me, even if she was asked now. Never mind in the future.* Attard walked back to his car, which was parked on a quiet side street around the corner from the forensic labs. He placed the Mosta disc over a small drain in the gutter beside his car and dropped four blobs of the drain fluid onto the disc. He then took out a copy of *The Malta Times*, leaned against his car, and checked up on the latest political storm: gay people being allowed to marry. *Wonder what Francesco thinks about this!* After twenty minutes, Jason picked up the disc, cleaned off the remaining fluid, and walked round to the forensics labs.

By chance, Father Francesco was, at that same moment, reading the same story as Jason. Jason Attard would perhaps be surprised if he did know Francesco's views. The old priest turned to a colleague, who was sitting on a bench beside him, in the Dominican Monastery grounds.

'How would you define love, Father John?'

'Well, I would say it is not one emotion. A man can love a woman, certainly, but he can also love his father, his brothers and sisters, his friends, his dog... but the loves are different.'

'And can a man love another man?'

'Yes, of course.'

'And should a man be able to marry this man he loves?'

'In the town hall, perhaps. In God's house, then no.'

'Why not?'

'When you join a club, Francesco, you have to obey the rules. If you do not like the rules, then don't join.'

'But rules can be changed, no?'

'Not God's.'

'Did God ever say that a gay man couldn't give a child a loving home?'

'Not as far as I'm aware.'

'Father John, we are both old men now. Have you ever doubted your faith, fear what will be coming to us both soon enough?'

'Doubted... ha... every day, Francesco... every day! Fear death? No. Why? If what we have believed and taught is true, then why fear death? Isn't eternal happiness something to look forward to? And, if we've been wrong all these years? Well, we'll be dead, so...'

'Oh, you're going to heaven, then!'

'Not right now. Let's go and get a glass of wine; it's the nearest thing to heaven we can get in this life!'

The two old priests wandered back into the cloistered entranceway. Both held many dark secrets in their souls.

\*\*\*

Sarah Said had gotten a little bit flustered when she realised that it was Deputy Commissioner Kevin Galea on the other end of the line.

'Inspector Spiteri is out, I'm afraid.'

'Get her to call me as soon as she gets back, please.' The line went dead before Said could reply. *Charming.* Her next call would upset her far more. 'Sergeant Said?'

'Yes.'

'It's Mary Rose, from the forensics lab.'

'Oh yes, good.'

'Well, I don't know about that. This disc is unsavable. We can't do anything with it, and it's too badly damaged.'

'What do you mean? It plays here okay.'

'Well, I can't comment on that, but it's kaput now. Sorry.'

Said paused. 'Can you send it back over?'

'Yes, I'll do that. Bye.'

Said was deep in thought when the CID room door opened, and Spiteri, Healy, and a third man appeared and headed into Spiteri's office.

'The deputy commissioner's looking for you, Kap.'

'I'm not here,' said Spiteri, closing her office door with a bang. Healy and Cosgrove were already seated when she reached her desk and sank into her leather chair.

'So what you are saying, Roy, is that we are definitely looking for two different killers for Calder and Hooper?' she asked.

'Yes.'

'But wait. They were both stabbed, both wrote the same thing— "Why"—in the sand. Surely there's a link?' asked Healy.

'A link between the victims... yes... The killers... no. Did you show May Hooper photos from Calder's death scene?'

'Yes.'

'And did she study them, take notes?'

'I can't remember exactly, but she definitely looked at them for a while. Yes.'

'Subliminal stimuli.'

'What?' Both Healy and Spiteri spoke at the same time.

'Subliminal stimuli. It's something of a specialism of mine. When someone finds themselves in a stressful situation, they will often say or do something that they didn't consciously make the decision to do. Rather, they will react in the way their unconscious mind tells them to. May Hooper had studied Miriam Calder's crime scene photos. Calder's last, despairing word is written in the sand "Why... is this happening?" "Why... is no one helping me?" Hooper empathises with this. Calder's final action is embedded deep in Hooper's mind. Then, suddenly, she finds herself in the same situation; she reacts in the same way. If the same knife had killed them... well, that is different, but...'

Both Healy and Spiteri sat in silence for a few moments. Cosgrove rose. 'I need to go back to my hotel and pack. Matt, Thea, it's been nice to meet you. I hope my input helps you find these people.'

After Roy Cosgrove had said his goodbyes and left for his hotel, Spiteri and Healy went out into the square for some fresh air. 'What do you make of that, Matt?'

'I think he's wrong. Maybe not about Sansome not killing Jamie; I've always had my doubts about that myself. But how he can say the Calder and Hooper killings aren't linked? I'll never work that one out.'

Spiteri's mobile rang. 'Shit, it's the deputy commissioner. Good afternoon.'

'Didn't you get my message?'

'What message?'

'To call me?'

'No, sorry. Perhaps there's a note on my desk. Can I...'

'Any progress... anywhere... with anything?'

'Sorry, Deputy Commissioner, but, eh, have you spoken to the commissioner?'

'What? No! What are you talking about?'

'The commissioner only wants me to report to him. Sorry.'

'What's going on here?'

'Sorry, I can only repeat: you'll have to speak to the commissioner.'

# CHAPTER 34

Thea Spiteri was tired, weary, and dispirited. She had worked till 11.00 p.m. the previous evening, detailing Professor Roy Cosgrove's views. She hoped to God his views were wrong; otherwise, there were four, maybe five, killers walking free on Malta. On the other hand, she had no evidence to dispute it and Cosgrove was here on the commissioner's say-so. *I wonder if he's read it yet?* She wouldn't have long to find out. Her desk phone rang; it was the commissioner.

'Inspector, can you come and see me, please?'

'Yes, of course. When?'

'Now.'

Spiteri sat in the corridor outside Commissioner Debono's office. She wasn't nervous, but she assumed she would be put under intense pressure over Cosgrove's results. She would be wrong.

'You can go in now, Thea,' said the renownedly efficient secretary to the commissioner.

'Thea, take a seat. I'm not going to waste time here, Inspector. I can't let this situation go on.' Debono held up Spiteri's report. 'What actual progress has been made here? And now, the one bit of progress that has been made, Sansome charged with three murders, you're now saying is wrong!'

'With all due respect, I'm not saying that. The professor is.'

'The professor? Let's talk about that. He was brought in to look at our child abduction cases, to see if there was a link to his own case. Am I right?'

'Yes.'

'Well, the fucking child abduction cases are solved. Done and dusted. Who gives a fuck what Cosgrove thinks?'

Spiteri was taken aback at the way she was being spoken to. She went to speak but was silenced by the commissioner's raised hand. 'Next point, as far as I'm aware, Cosgrove was here to look at the child abductions and murders. What is he looking at the Calder and Hooper cases for?'

'He made a request. He...'

'Don't bother. You had two murders to work on: Hooper and Calder, and yes, I asked you to escort Cosgrove, but not look upon him as the font of all knowledge! I'm sorry, Inspector, but I feel that these investigations need new eyes, a different approach. I'm taking you off them. The new officer in charge will come to your office for a brief handover after this meeting. Thea, take a month's leave. Lie in the sun, go on holiday somewhere, anything... come back refreshed.'

'Sir, I...'

Debono's raised hand again stopped Spiteri in her tracks. 'It's not a debate, Inspector. Go back to your office, do the handover, do not mention Cosgrove to anyone at any time. Go on, leave. That's final.'

Thea Spiteri didn't remember leaving the commissioner's office or arriving in her own. She felt as if her brain had ceased functioning; she couldn't take in what had just happened. When she entered her office, Inspector Dan Micalef was sitting across from her desk. 'Look, Thea,

I'm so sorry about this. None of this was my doing. To be honest, I think it's a bit of a poisoned chalice.'

'Don't worry, Dan. I know you had nothing to do with this. Read this; it's all you need to know. Good luck.' Spiteri handed Micalef the report she had given Debono. 'No, wait a minute.' Spiteri took the report back, ripped the last two pages out that covered Hooper and Calder, and gave it back to Micalef. 'Sorry, Dan. My supermarket list.'

\*\*\*

Sarah Said and Jason Attard glanced firstly at each other and then into Spiteri's office. They both knew the dynamics of the squad had now changed. They turned back to their desks, trying to second guess what had just happened. But Said also had other concerns. She turned to Attard. 'Jason, the forensics lab phoned me yesterday. They said the Mosta disc was damaged. They couldn't do anything with it.'

'Really, why not?'

'They said something had spilled on it, like acid I suppose, damaging the disc.'

'Typical, they're bloody useless at times. Never mind, it was probably nothing anyway, to be honest.'

Said turned back to her files. She was somehow unconvinced, and disturbed, by Attard's glib response.

\*\*\*

Commissioner Chris Debono stood looking out of his office window. Tears of guilt, frustration, and hopelessness, were running down his cheeks. Debono was fifty-four years old, fifty-five in a few months' time, and preparing for his retirement. He was crying because he knew he was a complete hypocrite; a disgrace to his office. Debono knew that his latest unforgivable act had possibly ruined the career of a dedicated officer. *I'll try and retrieve things when she comes back on duty.* He had read Spiteri's report and the rubbish it contained. Debono knew the report was rubbish because Commissioner Chris Debono already knew who killed the two women—and Jamie Smart and Ingrid Lam and Michele Grech—but he could not say. That was the cross he had to bear.

# CHAPTER 35

Matt Healy was pleased but surprised to find Thea Spiteri at his door. 'Hi. I wasn't expecting a personal appearance!' Healy soon saw that Spiteri wasn't in the mood for small talk.

'I've been taken off the cases.'

'What?'

'I've been told to take a month's holiday. When I go back, they'll "have something for me."' Spiteri then spent the next ten minutes explaining her meeting with the commissioner. Healy sat and listened. When Spiteri stopped talking, he waited a few moments.

'Thea, first of all, this is not a suspension. They've just decided that maybe the cases need a fresh approach. It happened in Scotland, too. It's not personal. To be honest, you have looked drained these last few days.'

'Thanks.'

'You know what I mean. Look, what's done is done. Let's go on holiday, drive round Europe a bit, anything.'

'We'll see. I need time to take this all in. In the meantime...' Spiteri rose from the couch, took Healy's hand, and headed for the bedroom. Healy didn't resist.

Father Francesco had been as surprised as Healy at the news of Spiteri's move. 'Have you not had any explanation at all? Hasn't the replacement inspector, Micalef, said anything?' Marandon asked Jason Attard, who was sitting opposite him in the coffee shop where they often met at lunchtimes.

'Nothing.'

'Is it bothering you?'

'No. Why should it?'

The old priest studied Attard's eyes. 'I'm sure you know why, Jason.'

'*Why* seems to be a very popular word on Malta these days, Francesco. Don't you agree?'

The aged cleric urned away from Attard, looked over at the fields spreading out from the village. 'Do not threaten me, Jason. Can I ask you something, though?'

'By all means, wise one.'

Father Marandon ignored the quip. 'Did you kill the boy in Mosta? I know you were there. Karmenu told me about your boys' night out. How drunk you were. Not that that is any excuse.'

Attard banged his fist onto the wooden table. 'How dare you question me, accuse me. Who are you? An old, worn-out man with old, worn-out ideas.'

'Yes, Jason. I am old, and yes, I am worn out. As you know, I've now retired, but I will always know right from wrong. Will you?'

'My heart bleeds.'

'This is the end for us, Jason. Do not contact me ever again. I could have saved you. May God bless your soul.' Marandon got up from the table, stiffly turned and headed towards his car. On the way there, he threw the water bottle, with Joseph Sansome's prints on it, into a rubbish bin.

Both men's heads were filled with thoughts of what to do about each other. David Decelis, on the other hand, studied the body language of both the men he was observing with binoculars from his car. *Interesting, very interesting.* David Decelis had no doubts about what he was going to do.

*\*\*\**

Commissioner Debono had pulled himself out of the morose state that, more and more, he seemed to find himself living in. He knew he had to accept what he could not change or the rest of his life would be lived in torment. He was ready to retire. He had many regrets but felt that, overall, he had done a good job.

His only remaining task was to oversee the clean-up of the Hooper and Calder killings, and he could then let his successor carry the burden of high office. Micalef was a steady officer; Debono was confident he would perform as he was instructed to. It was a pity that Peter Smart was off the hook for the Calder killing, now that Sansome was charged with his son's death, but the magistrate had ordered his release, so that was that.

*\*\*\**

Despite the precise instructions he had been given, Inspector Dan Micalef was uneasy. He was also confused by Commissioner Debono's almost obsessional interest in his work. Micalef knew that Spiteri was a good CID Inspector, and if she was uneasy with the way some of her cases had been closed, as she obviously was from her report, then he too felt uneasy. When he had been called by the commissioner, he had assumed it would be to discuss Spiteri's report. Instead, Debono had made it perfectly clear that all Micalef had to be looking at were the Hooper and Calder killings. 'Nothing more, nothing less, Dan.' Micalef had tried to raise the point that it was possible that these two crimes were linked to others.

'They're not, and that's an end to it. Report any progress in either of the cases back directly to me, and I don't want anything written down until I have seen it first. I retire soon, Dan. I don't want any hitches in my last two cases.'

Micalef was not convinced but knew he had to comply.

*\*\**

'Francesco, how would you like Matt and I to take you out tonight for that retirement dinner we spoke of?' asked Thea Spiteri.

'That would be lovely, Thea. Thank you very much. Where and when?'

'How about seven p.m. in Salvina.'

'Lovely, I'll be there.'

'Would you like me to invite Jason?'

'No. See you at seven.'

Spiteri was glad that Jason was not to be invited along, but surprised at the old priest's brusque response. When she told Healy, she was even more surprised at his response.

'Lover's tiff, do you think?'

'What!'

'Well, I'm sure Attard's gay, and let's face it, it has been known for priests to be.'

'Not a chance. Matt, I'm taken aback that you can even think that.'

'Just saying. Doesn't matter to me either way, but there is definitely something going on with those two.'

'We'll don't *just say*... absolute rubbish. Poor Francesco.'

A few minutes later, Spiteri's phone buzzed. 'Hi Thea. It's Dan Micalef.'

'Hello, Dan.'

'Thea, can I ask you something?'

'Work related?'

'Yes.'

'I don't mind, but there are those that will.'

'I know, that's why I'm calling. When you were working these cases, did you feel that you were being manipulated? You were being forced to accept decisions you didn't agree with?'

Spiteri let out a hollow laugh. 'Dan, I felt that every day. I resisted... and here I am.'

'Is there anything I can do, do you think?'

'Well, keep everything to yourself until you have cast-iron proof. Do not present any theories or conjectures, far less hunches. You can phone me with those. I'll help any way I can.'

'Right, thanks. I knew this whole thing smelt. I just can't understand how the commissioner is forming his opinions. You've presented the facts, very well in my opinion, and he's ignoring them.'

'Well, opinions aren't formed by facts really, Dan, they're formed by people's perception of what the facts are. Sometimes in police work, we form our opinions on what we want the so-called facts to be showing.'

'Perhaps.'

'Dan, you just do your job, keep everything above board. You'll be fine. What's the worst that can happen? You get a month's holiday!'

\*\*\*

Salvina's restaurant was a traditional Maltese eatery. It wasn't busy when the three friends turned up. They chose a table in the corner, all decided on the dish of the day; *Pixxispad Mixwi*, grilled swordfish, and raised their two glasses of wine and one mineral water.

'Here's to a long and wonderful retirement, Francesco!' said Healy.

'Thank you, thank you, but please don't ask me to make a speech!'

'Speech? No. We're going to a karaoke bar next; we want you to sing!' said Spiteri.

'Now I know you are the devil, Thea!'

The three friends took their time with their meals, Father Francesco especially enjoying the oregano sauce that came with the fish. 'What a lovely meal, my friends. Thank you again.'

'So, Francesco, what are you going to do with all this free time?'

'Matt, let me tell you, it's all a bit of an illusion.'

'What is?'

'Retirement! Since I retired, I seem to be busier than ever. Invitations to conferences, pilgrimages. I've even been asked if I would like to retire to the Vatican!'

'Tell me, Francesco. You are obviously highly regarded in the church. You have been all over, mending bridges, fixing problems. Why have you never been made a bishop?' asked Spiteri.

'Oh but I have been asked; many times. It's not for me.'

'Really, I didn't know. Why did you not want it?'

'Too restrictive. It's all politics from then on, too.'

'Restrictive?' asked Matt.

'I like autonomy, Matt. To work directly with people, ordinary people, the lost and the lonely. I shouldn't really say this, but I take my instructions from God, not men.'

After coffee, the three friends left the restaurant. None of them noticed the young man, who had been sitting alone in an opposite corner of the restaurant, passing them in the doorway. David Decelis, too, had enjoyed his grilled swordfish.

Healy and Spiteri said their farewells to Francesco before Spiteri turned to Healy and said, 'Matt, do you mind if I just head home tonight? I'm tired, and I've got a lot on my mind after that call from Micalef.'

'Not at all. In fact, you just head home from here; I'll walk over to Pembroke.'

'Are you sure? I'll come over tomorrow.'

'Of course.'

Healy wandered down past the Dragonnara Hotel and over the hill leading down to St George's Bay.

'Excuse me, sur, would you happen to know of an establishment near by that might sell a spot of Guinness to a weary traveller?' The lone

Irishman leaning against the metal railings looked as if he'd had one or two Guinness too many already, but Healy could tell he was a jovial drunk and not likely to be trouble.

'I'm pretty sure Andrew's Bar down the hill here sells it. Come on, I'll walk you down; I'm going that way anyway.'

'Ah sure. That's terribly kind of you; will you join me?'

'Sadly no. My drinking days are over. But thank you anyway.'

'Is that a Scottish accent I'm picking up there; you're a fellow Celt?'

'It is. I'm from Glasgow, but I live here now. What about you? Whereabouts in Ireland are you from?'

'I, sur, am from the finest county in the land.'

'Which is?'

'County Galway, sur.' The Irishman appeared to start crying before he burst into song. '"If you ever go across the sea to Ireland... you can sit and watch the moon go down on Galway Bay." Ah God, I miss it, sur.'

'When did you leave?'

'Yesterday.'

Healy couldn't help but like the man. 'It's funny. I only know one other Irishman really, and he's from Galway as well.'

'Really? Now, do you happen to know what town, sur? I might know him.'

'I doubt it; he's been here in Malta fifty-odd years off and on. He's from a place called Tuam.'

The Irishman stopped in his tracks. 'Tuam, The Home in Tuam?'

'Yes, I'm sure that's what he said.'

'Then God bless him, sur, he's one of the lucky ones.'

'What do you mean?'

'Don't you know about that place? It's all over the papers; especially now.'

'Not in Malta, Paddy.'

'I can't speak of it. Go home, look it up in the Internet, any Irish paper, even English ones.'

The two men reached the entrance to the bar. 'You sure I can't interest you in a small refreshment now, sur?'

'Honestly, no. Thank you. Have a good night.'

Healy strode off up the hill towards Pembroke, intrigued about what he had just heard. *I must remember to look that stuff up tomorrow. Old Paddy was probably just havering.*

# CHAPTER 36

Thea Spiteri had had a fitful night. She rose early, showered, made some herbal tea, and then sat thinking until she decided it wasn't too early to call Daphne Arrigo.

'Daphne, its Thea Spiteri. I hope it's not too early to call?'

'No, its fine. Anything wrong?'

'No, but I thought that you might like to know that the officer who has replaced me called me last night. He feels that Debono is pushing certain investigations along paths that he wants them to go rather than where the evidence indicates.'

'Really? What cases?'

'Well you know that there have been three child abductions lately?'

'Yes.'

'Well, all the indications are that they were done by two, possibly three, different people. But Debono has put a stop to the investigations and charged one man. Now, this guy definitely did commit one of the abductions, the German girl on Gozo, and he's happy to admit it; proud even. But he is adamant that he had nothing to do with the others.Debono was also very quick to charge someone for the murder of one of the two women who have been murdered, but he has now been released.'

'My interest is in his connections to the Mafia. Anything about that? The abductions of children; I can't see a connection.'

'Other than what you said yourself about not looking for anyone other than the old man in the drug gang murders, then not really. One thing, though: the priest who was supposed to be handing money over to Debono in the Borg case, Father Marandon, I know him very well. A great man, really. Would you like me to ask him for his thoughts?'

'Good idea. Do that, Thea. Let me know what he says.'

Once she had hung up, Spiteri started having reservations about having called Arrigo. She threw some clothes into a bag and headed over to Healy's.

***

Jason Attard felt that the evidence against Joseph Sansome, for the Michele Grech killing, was weak. *A little insurance policy needed, I suggest.*

Steven Mallia was known to the *Pulizija*, but hadn't been in trouble for many years. Mallia was forty-five years old and had lived with his mother in Mosta up until she died two months before from a brain haemorrhage. He now lived alone in the house. He had no friends, no immediate family, and the neighbours stayed well away from him, as he was considered by many of them to be *mignun*: insane. Indeed, some of the older residents of Mosta blessed themselves when they passed him. But Steven Mallia was, in his own way, happier than any of the other residents of Mosta. Steven Mallia had his own laptop with Internet connection, and so he could download as much child pornography as he wanted. He did not need family, friends, or neighbours. He was surprised, therefore, when he heard a knock at the door. He shuffled over and answered the door, his trouser zip still undone.

'Hello, Steven,' said Jason Attard. 'You still playing with yourself, I see.'

'What do you want?'

'Nothing, Steven. Just a friendly visit. Can I come in?'

'No.'

'Thanks,' said Attard as he brushed past Mallia and entered the dingy flat. 'Cleaner's day off?'

'What do you want?'

'How are your kitchen knives, Steven? Nice and clean? I wouldn't imagine so, mind you.'

'What?'

'You can't really ever get blood off completely, you know.'

'You wouldn't be talking to me like this if my mother was still alive, Attard.'

'No, that's true, Steven. She was a better man than you; but she's fucking dead. A bit like that poor boy you killed and stuffed down a drain.'

'I don't know what you're talking about. Get out.'

'Fine, be that way, Steven. Not very hospitable, are you? Can I just use your toilet? Thanks.' Attard went into the toilet, removed a blood-soaked hankie, and pushed it between the pipes behind the toilet bowl. He then flushed the toilet. 'That's me away then, Steven. Thanks for your time. Oh, by the way, you might want to throw a bucket of shite around that toilet, tidy it up a bit.'

'Mr Muscle.'

'What?'

'Mr Muscle. That's what was on your disc.' The forensic lab assistant, Mary Rose, had promised Sarah Said that she would test the disc when she had time and give her a call.

'Well that's a bit careless of you lot, don't you think? You are supposed to be meticulous after all.'

'Hold on, Sarah. As a matter of fact, we are very meticulous, but yes, it is possible that sometimes we make mistakes. But not on this occasion.'

'How do you know that, for sure?'

'Simple. We don't use Mr Muscle cleaner. The stuff didn't get on the disc here; it must have gotten on it before it was handed in.'

'Are you positive?'

'Certain.'

'Right, thanks. And sorry.'

Sarah Said looked over into Spiteri's former office. Micalef was sitting at the desk, studying some files. Said had no idea what to do.

She was about to be told.


Micalef's phone rang. 'Yes, Jason.'

'Inspector, I've received a tip off about the child killing in Mosta. I'm in Mosta now, at the *Pulizija* station. The guy in question is a bit of a weirdo named Steven Mallia. I've looked him up. I know him vaguely, as it happens. He could be our man. He's not been in trouble for a while and is known for using violence, but I know his mother died recently. They were very close; a bit too close, if you get my meaning. That's maybe thrown him over the edge. I don't want to go to his door. As I said, he knows me. I think it would be worth sending Sarah, along with a couple of constables. If it's nothing, then no harm done; if they find anything, I'm sure the commissioner will not be too bothered about procedure.'

'Right. I'll send Said up to Mosta now.'

'Okay. I'll organise a couple of constables this end.'

Attard went through to the canteen and spotted a constable he knew well, Gary Calleja. 'Gary, you're going to be doing a quiet house search shortly with Sarah Said. It's that fucking nutcase Mallia's flat. I can't go since we have a bit of history. Do a good job, check everywhere, cupboards, bins, under mattresses, pipe runs... everywhere.'

'Okay. What are we looking for?'

'Anything at all that could be connected to the killing of Michele Grech. Knife, blood, kid's clothing... anything.'

'Okay.'

David Decelis watched from his car as Father Marandon walked from his car to the coffee shop he had been at previously with Attard. The old priest looked worried.

Decelis' thoughts were right: Francesco Marandon was in the middle of a moral dilemma. He could, perhaps should, have told Thea Spiteri at their meal about Jason Attard. But he felt it was wrong to break a confidence, never mind two.

***

Thea Spiteri arrived at Healy's house in Pembroke, about 10.00 a.m. 'Fancy a run?' asked Healy, only slightly kidding.

'Wouldn't want to show you up, Matt.'

'Aye, right. Walk then? Over to Madliena Tower.'

'Okay.'

The red flags denoting that shooting practice was taking place weren't flapping in the slight breeze. 'You're safe today, Matt,' said Spiteri with a slight nudge into Healy's ribs.

'Talking of which, Inspector Spiteri. The Maltese Army, the bloody Maltese Army! Is that a joke or what? Who do they attack, Monaco?'

'Lichtenstein.'

Healy and Spiteri locked arms as they laughed and made their way down the rock-strewn path leading to the hill that the impressive Madliena Tower stood on. After half an hour, the couple stood at the base of the tower, looking out on the azure sea. 'Ayr ain't like this,' mumbled Healy.

'What?'

'Nothing. Private joke.'

The couple sat on a stone bench that had been part of a gun turret at one time. The sea sparkled, the sun was up but not too hot, a slight breeze making the whole scenario perfect for what Healy had in mind.

# CHAPTER 37

'What, again? This is victimisation. You wouldn't be doing this if my mother was here.' Steven Mallia was confused and upset. Sarah Said and one of the two *Pulizija* constables started searching the flat while the other constable waited with Mallia. After half an hour, the search had produced nothing other than Said feeling nauseous at the notion of someone living in these conditions.

'You like little boys then, Steven.' It was a statement of fact from Said rather than a question.

'Only for breakfast.'

'That's not funny, Mallia. Not in the slightest.'

The taller of the two constables, Polidano, shouted over to Gary Calleja, 'Did you do what Jay Z said and check the pipe runs in the kitchen and toilet?'

'No, I forgot. I'll do it now.' Polidano shook his head.

A few moments later, Calleja called through from the toilet. 'Inspector.'

Said walked through and Calleja showed her the cloth and where he'd found it. The two *Pulizija* walked back through to Mallia. 'What's this, Steven?'

'I don't remember. I must have cut myself... maybe shaving.'

'We'll get it tested. If this is young Michele's blood, it's good night, Steven.'

The three *Pulizija* left the flat and a bewildered Mallia behind them. The two constables were pleased with the outcome, but a couple of things were troubling Said.

***

Healy stood up from the stone bench. He appeared a little distracted. 'Are you okay?' asked Spiteri. Healy nodded. He then bent over and picked up a large piece of the sandstone that was scattered all around the disused gun turret. Spiteri was uncertain what he was going to do. Suddenly, Matt Healy took a step forward, Spiteri stood up; Healy heaved the boulder as far down the cliff side as he could manage. 'Thea, will you marry me?'

'Well, I would say that that is probably one of the strangest marriage proposals ever, Matt.'

'And your answer?'

'Yes.'

Healy took Spiteri in his arms and held her. 'Thank you, Thea.' Healy's eyes focused on a blue fence, that lay about ten meters away, over Spiteri's left shoulder. Healy pointed to it.

'You know something. I've been here lots of times, and I've never noticed that.'

'It is slightly below eye level, depending on where you are standing. It's a fougasse.'

'What's that?'

'It's a kind of gun, an early canon. Come on, it explains on the side.' A weatherbeaten sign on the far side of the railings explained that a fougasse was basically a hole in the ground that was filled with gun powder and then filled up with stones and rubble. If any invaders then landed on the beach below, a fuse was lit, the powder exploded, and the stones and rubble showered down on the people below.

'Bloody hell! Did it work?'

'How would I know! What age do you think I am?'

Then something else caught Healy's eye. 'No way! Look at the name of the guy who designed this back then... Father Francesco Marandon! I wonder if our Francesco knows?'

'Probably. Maybe this is even where he picked his name.'

'What do you mean, picked?'

'Matt, I thought you said you were raised Catholic. Priests, in orders like the Dominicans, often change their names.'

'Well, I kind of knew that, now that you come to mention it. I wonder what his real name is.'

'Do you really want to know?'

'What, do you know it?'

'Yes, of course, it's no big deal. It's not a state secret.'

'What is his real name then?'

Spiteri started laughing. 'Reginald White!'

Healy bent over laughing. 'No way. Reginald White. No bloody wonder he changed it!'

*\*\*\**

Father Marandon took the call from Spiteri just as he was about to leave the coffee stall.

'Are you still retired, Francesco?'

The old priest hesitated, slightly confused. 'Yes, what do you mean though, child?'

'Oh, okay. You won't be able to marry Matt and I then?'

'I most certainly will! Thea, I am so happy for you, and Matt, of course. When is the big day?'

'No idea! We've only just decided. I wanted you to be the first to know and book your services, of course.'

'Fantastic, child. I need to go, I'm beginning to cry.'

'No, I need to ask you something in confidence. Can you speak openly?'

'Yes.'

'Francesco, you obviously know Borg is out of the holiday camp he was in. This  money he said he got you to take to Debono? I know he never gave you any money, but why would he think Debono would be a good person to give the money to in the first place?'

'Well, they were friends.'

'Come on, Francesco. Look, I'm just going to ask you: do you think Debono is corrupt?'

'No I don't.'

'Positive?'

'As anyone can be. Malta is very corrupt, as you know.'

'Okay, thank you, Francesco. Away and cry now!'

David Decelis continued to watch as Father Francesco sat back down and ordered a brandy; he appeared to be crying. *So you can shed a tear. Good to know.*

***

'Sarah, get your jacket.' Inspector Dan Micalef was walking to the door as he spoke.

Said caught up with her boss outside the office just as he was getting into a *Pulizija* car. Said got in the back.

'The blood in Mallia's flat, it's a match to Grech. We'll pick him up, bring him in, but Sarah, no word to anyone at the moment. Don't ask why; just go with me on this.'

Sarah Said didn't reply. She looked out the side window all the way to Mosta, but she never saw anything. Her mind was too full. Two hours later, Micalef, Said, and Mallia were sitting in an interview room in Valetta *Pulizija*. Mallia's computer was with forensics, but Micalef had already been informed that even a cursory search of the laptop had revealed hundreds of child pornography photographs, all featuring young boys. There also seemed to be a snuff movie that had been downloaded, but the forensics people had not been able to open it at that point. 'So, Steven, I'll tell you what is going to happen now,' said Micalef to a dazed-looking Mallia. 'I am not even going to bother interviewing you. No, what I am going to do is tell you what we know, give you one, just one, chance to tell us all about what has been happening in your life—I'm sorry about your mum, incidentally—and then you'll be going to prison till your trial.'

'But...'

'But nothing, Steven. This is the way it's going to be. Right, your laptop is full of child porn, possibly even a snuff movie. You will go to prison for that alone. A cloth, with the blood of Michele Grech on it, has been found in your house. You have a lot of knives in your house, and two open razors. We have taken all of those, and we are confident one of them will also have Michele's blood on it. Even if they don't, you'll be found guilty just on the cloth alone. So here's what I'm offering you: you confess now to killing Michele. I will ensure that the courts are told that you never resisted arrest and were very cooperative with our investigation. That will help you, Steven. You will still go to prison. You deserve to go to prison, but you will get out one day. If you don't take this chance, this one chance, you will still go to prison, but I will make sure you are there for a very long time. Do you understand?'

'Yes.'

'So, what do you want to do?'

'I want my mum.'

'What would your mum have wanted you to do, do you think, Steven?'

'Tell the truth. Be good.'

'So...'

'I killed the boy. He was calling me names.'

Commissioner Debono was delighted at Micalef's news. 'See what I mean, Dan? You are on the job for a few days, you've got the killer. I'll inform the magistrate that we might have to drop the charge against Sansome, but that makes no difference; he's already finished. I'm afraid that Thea Spiteri is just not cut out for the more difficult cases.'

'To be fair, Commissioner, it was a random tip to Attard. If he had gotten it a few weeks ago, Spiteri would have wrapped it up herself.'

'No, you make your own luck, Dan. The Hooper and Calder cases. Any progress there?'

'Not as yet.'

'Okay, but all hands to the pumps, Dan. I'll see you get full credit for the work you are doing.'

The commissioner's words somehow felt hollow to Dan Micalef.

\*\*\*

Steven Mallia sat in his cell under Valetta *Pulizija*, waiting for the van to take him to prison. Being a Friday, he would appear in front of a magistrate on the following Monday. The cell door opened, and Sarah Said stepped in. 'Steven, how are you?'

'Okay.'

'Steven, I want to ask you something. When I came to your door with the two constables, remember?'

'Yes.'

'You said, "What again." What did you mean? I've never been to your house.'

'My mum says all *Pulizija* are the same.'

'Do the *Pulizija* come to your house a lot?'

'They used to.'

'But not now?'

'No.'

'When was the last time they were there?'

'I don't know.'

'Think, Steven. This is very important.'

'Not for a long time. I don't know. My mum would know.'

'Okay, Steven. That's okay.'

Said turned and knocked on the cell door to get out.

'Only to do the toilet.'

Said turned back. 'What?'

'He never hit me or anything. He only really came to do the toilet.'

'Who did, Steven? Who came to use the toilet?'

'The gay one, but he never took any of my photos this time, just used the toilet.'

'What's his name, Steven? Do you know his name?'

'I think it's fake. He doesn't want me to know.' Mallia was smiling.

'But you do know, Steven. Don't you?'

'Yes.'

'What his name, Steven? I need to know his name.'

'Jason.'

Said returned to her desk and called Mosta *Pulizija*. 'Is Constable Polidano there?'

'Yes.'

'Tell him it's Inspector Said. I need a quick word.'

A few moments later, Polidano came on the line. 'Yes.'

'In Mallia's flat, you said something about Jay Z. I take it you weren't referring to the rapper?'

'No. Jason Attard. J for Jason, you follow.'

'I do indeed, Constable, I do indeed.'

# CHAPTER 38

The following morning, Sarah Said sat at her desk, her concentration fully on a sheet of paper in front of her. On the paper was written: *disc, bloody cloth, Mosta search, knife in Calder killing... blood/not knife*. She heard talking outside the room, folded the paper, and put it in her pocket.

Attard and Micalef came into the room, laughing. Both men looked happy.

'Morning, Sarah,' both men said at once.

'Morning.'

'Sarah, can you come into my office, please? Bring your coffee,' said Micalef.

Said reluctantly sat down beside Attard and across the desk from Micalef. Micalef said 'Okay, we have two major cases left to solve. Any theories, views, anything?'

'So, can I assume then that the Michele Grech case is considered closed?'

Attard and Micalef glanced at each other and then at Said.

'Don't you?' asked Attard.

'Well, there a few things I don't understand.'

'Like?' said Micalef.

'Well, there is one bloodied piece of cloth linking him to the crime. That's it.'

'That's it? He's a proven pervert, the cloth, maybe a knife, snuff video on his laptop... and he did confess, or did you miss that bit?'

'It's not enough. How do we know the cloth wasn't planted?'

'Who by?'

Sarah Said paused. 'I don't know. The real killer, maybe? Mallia can hardly walk, never mind run.'

'What's that got to do with anything?' asked Micalef.

'Well, we had footage of a man running from the murder scene...'

'No we didn't,' interrupted Attard. 'We had video of a man, or woman... running from... we don't know... to... we don't know... after having done... we don't know.'

'Where is this disc?' asked Micalef.

'Destroyed accidently by the forensics lab,' said Attard.

'Not according to them,' said Said.

'Well they're not going to admit it, are they!' shouted Attard.

'Right, that's enough. Sarah, did the video have clear proof, or anything at all, that was definitive to the case?'

'No, but...'

'Sorry, Sarah. The case is closed. Any complaints, talk to the commissioner,' said Micalef as Attard barely suppressed a grin.

\*\*\*

Father Francesco was delighted about the news from Spiteri. He was, however, also concerned. He was uncertain just what effect the news would have on Jason Attard. Some part of his senses was also reacting to the fact that he was sure that he was being watched. He had never actually seen anyone but, given his fallout with Jason, he was unsure what his erstwhile friend was capable of these days. He was also concerned by Thea Spiteri's interest in Debono.

\*\*\*

Matt Healy, too, was concerned. The problem for Healy though was that he didn't know what he was concerned about. His life had never been better. He was truly happy for the first time. He thought he had been happy at one time in the past, when he thought he was in love with Susan Dornan. He realised now that that was just a self-destructing infatuation, a challenge to his manhood, a gladiatorial battle he had lost. He sat back on his patio and thought about May Hooper. *Was it better this way? A slow, lingering death from cancer, the disgrace? No, Matt, murder is never the better way. But who, and why?*

Spiteri had gone for a nap after the walk to the tower, but Healy was restless. *The Irishman! I'll look up that stuff.*

Matt Healy spent nearly an hour reading about the place known as The Home, Tuam. He re-read some of the passages and the numbers being quoted two and three times, as he couldn't take in the scale of what was being claimed. His policeman's mind, as it had done with May Hooper, was starting to imagine connections. Connections that he hoped weren't true.

'The Home, Tuam had been a workhouse from the 1840s but had been taken over in 1925 by the Bon Secours Sisters, who had turned it into a Mother and Baby home for "Fallen Women." It had closed in 1961. It was, however, in the headlines in 2014 after the bodies of 800 infants and children had been discovered in the septic tank of the home. The children had been buried without coffins or headstones, or on consecrated ground.'

*So Francesco would have been there when some of this was going on. An unofficial helper.*

'The Home was surrounded by an eight-foot-high wall, which kept prying eyes out and explained to some extent why the locals said they knew nothing of the goings-on behind the facade. A report from a

Health Board Inspection in 1944 had been found which recorded that there were 61 single mothers in residence, and 271 children.'

Healy read on, almost mesmerised with the things that were written on the screen: *800 bodies*. The report described the children as emaciated, potbellied, fragile, and with flesh hanging loosely on limbs. Infant death rates fluctuated between one per fortnight to two a week. The Home Babies were considered to have come about through 'sinful origins' and were considered 'socially radioactive.' The local children did see the Home Babies from time to time, mostly at school, but one local has been quoted as saying, 'For the most part, the children were usually gone by school age... either adopted or dead. Some seemed to stay about through the years; they were some sort of privileged group.'

After having to overcome many obstacles, a local historian has managed to compile a list of 796 forgotten infants and children and was trying to have some sort of memorial erected. 'This site is a mass grave, a children's mass grave. It's a scandal that it isn't acknowledged. Even when there was any sort of press coverage at the time, the children were referred to as inmates and the Catholic authorities described the conditions as "corrective penance."'

Healy switched off his computer and looked out to the sea. *Some sort of privileged group. I was an unofficial helper.* Dear God.


Thea Spiteri was also happy. Happier than she, too, ever thought possible. Her removal from the cases still rankled with her, but she had been given time to focus, re-evaluate how her life was, where she was going. What she really wanted. *Is it too late for children? Would Matt want to be a father?* She was surprised to see Sarah Said's name coming up on her mobile's screen

'Hello, Sarah. Is everything alright?'

'No, I don't think so.'

'Why? What has happened?'

'Can we meet? I don't want to talk on the phone.'

'If you get caught talking to me, Sarah, it might not look good.'

'Things don't look good anyway.'

'Okay, come to Matt Healy's house, in Pembroke. No point in taking any chances. I'll give you the address. Don't write it down though.'

An hour later, Sarah Said had told Thea Spiteri of her suspicions surrounding Jason Attard.

'Sarah, the way you put things does make you think, but I have known Jason a long time. He can be a pain, I agree, but corrupt? No, I don't think so.'

'There's something else.'

'Oh, what?'

'We had a meeting the other morning, Micalef, Jason, and I. I raised some doubts I had about the arrest of Steven Mallia. An hour later, I got a call from the commissioner. "Detective work is team work, Sarah. It's good that you are thorough, but the Grech case is closed now. Help your team solve the other cases. Any further doubts, contact me directly."'

Spiteri was dumbfounded. 'He actually said contact him directly?'

'Yes.'

Spiteri pondered. 'All you can do is focus on your work and try and work with the team.'

Healy had gone for a walk when Said arrived, he and Thea agreeing that Said would probably prefer that. He went over everything that had happened in his life in the last few months. *Maybe there is a God after all.* When he got home, Said was gone and Thea was sitting on the patio with her eyes closed. Healy's footsteps woke her and she smiled. 'Everything okay?' he asked.

'For me, yes. In the *Pulizija*, no, there is something definitely not okay.'

Matt Healy sat down and for the next fifteen minutes listened intently as Thea Spiteri laid out her own, and now Said's, concerns.

'What are you going to do?' he asked.

'I'm not sure. I can't tell who the enemy are and who aren't. Anyway, let's get going.' Healy and Spiteri had decided, like many Maltese do, to spend the weekend in Gozo. It was far quieter, and had a more pleasant climate, due to the Majjistral wind that blows in, unimpeded by any over-development on the island. It was the perfect setting for a newly engaged couple. But the truth was shortly to be revealed to be something completely different..

# CHAPTER 39

David Decelis was, once again, sitting in his hotel room, looking out over St George's Bay. He too was mulling over the things he had to do, how to do them, and when. He had convinced himself before arriving in Malta that killing these people would be no problem to him. But now, seeing them up close, even hearing their voices, he was uncertain. His doubts did not come from any fear of God. God had abandoned him many years ago; he just needed to be sure.

\*\*\*

Jason Attard brought a coffee over and put it on Sarah Said's desk. 'Don't take things personally, Sarah. This job will eat you up if you do.'

'Right,' replied Said.

'I might have something on the Hooper killing.'

'Oh, what?'

'I've been hearing that there's a group of these fucking Sudanese that are over running the island, have been sleeping overnight in those old caves down at Golden Bay.'

'And, so...'

'Well, you know what they're like.'

'No, not really.'

'Bad bastards. Kill you as soon as look at you.'

'Really? And you're basing this view on what, exactly? How many murders have they committed so far?'

'Okay, but Hooper could be the first, maybe even second. They could have done Calder as well. They're mad for white women. Just look at the way they behave down in Paceville. I'm going to go down to that camp tonight.'

'Really? Oh well, you're bound to find something, eh Jason?'

Attard and Said stared at each other for a moment before Attard turned and headed for the door. 'You'll not be so liberal if you're next, eh Sarah?'

***

Deputy Commissioner Galea was a troubled man. He had always gotten on well with Commissioner Debono, and had assumed he would take over when Debono retired at the end of the year. But now, he was not so certain. Debono had become distant, barked instructions at him instead of engaging in calm discussion, was closing cases down with undue haste and, worst of all, he was now keeping him out of the loop as far as the remaining murder investigations were going. Galea was also displeased that Debono had taken Spiteri off the cases without consulting him, and that other officers were being instructed to report straight to the commissioner. Galea had no idea what was going on, but he intended to find out.

***

Healy and Spiteri sat on a bench on the port side of the ferry, Healy having declared that his maritime skills let him know in advance what side the sun would be shining on, on the cross over to Gozo. The sun was on the other side. 'Shade is better for you anyway!' he ventured to an unimpressed Spiteri.

'Thea, what do you know of Francesco's childhood in Ireland?'

239

'Nothing really. Just what he's told me. Why?'

Healy was uncertain what to do, what to say. *What do I know, exactly? Francesco was brought up in a hell hole... And?* A couple of years earlier, Healy had read a book on The Vienna Woods Killer, Jack Unterweger. Unterweger was a psycho who had killed a lot of women, mainly prostitutes, but Healy remembered reading psychiatric reports on Unterweger, published in the book, which laid a lot of his mental problems on his upbringing. *But you don't know Francesco has done anything; he's your friend, Matt, for Christ's sake.* 'No, nothing. I was just wondering.'

'Best man!' Healy suddenly prodded Spiteri with his elbow as the ferry pulled away from the terminal dock at Cirkewwa.

'What about him?' replied Spiteri.

'I'll need one.'

'Obviously!'

'Who, though?'

'Who do you want it to be?'

'I suppose it will have to be Jim Frame... I'll tell him "No speech," though!'

'Phone him now. Get things moving.'

Healy smiled and pulled out his mobile. Frame answered straight away. 'You phoning to tell me you're sitting beside a pool, I'll fucking kill you.'

'Ha, not quite. I'm on a ferry heading for Gozo.'

'Hard life.'

'Yea, and it's about to get harder.'

'Yea, why's that?'

'I'm getting married.'

'Seriously? Are you nuts?'

'Thanks for those kind words, Jim. You won't want to be Best Man then, given your views on marriage?'

'I never said that! Congratulations, Matt. Seriously, I'm chuffed for you. When's the big day?'

'We've not got that far yet. I'll give you plenty of warning.'

'Do that because I'll need plenty of time to prepare my speech.'

'No speech, Jim... Thea and I are adamant about that.'

'Piss off; there will be a speech, alright. How are the cases going over there?'

'Oh, long story. You don't want to know. I'll tell you when we meet up. What's the latest on the football front?'

'Matt, you won't believe it if I tell you. Look up The Daily Retard on the Net, read it for yourself; like I said, you couldn't make it up.'

'Okay, Jim, I'll do that. Speak again soon.'

'Okay, oh and here's a wee tip for when you're married. If Thea keeps coming out of the kitchen to nag you, what have you doing wrong?'

'Enlighten me.'

'Made the chain too long.'

The ferry was just approaching Mgarr, the terminal on Gozo, as Healy came off the phone. 'That didn't take long,' he commented.

'No, twenty-five minutes or so. We better go down and get in the car; people go mad if a car's driver holds things up by not being ready.'

'Right. Staircase D, wasn't it?'

'Yes.'


'Thea!' Spiteri turned to see Professor Sammut from the forensics lab at Mater Dei, coming over to her.

'Hello. A weekend break on Gozo for you, too, then, Paul?' asked Spiteri.

'Yes. I have a house here. I get up as much as I can. I like to get away from *Pulizija* officers!'

'I don't blame you.'

'Yes, I heard about what happened. I'm so sorry, Thea. I just don't understand it. Shower of idiots. Political pressure probably.'

'Thank you, Paul. I just have to get on with it, I suppose.'

'Yes, that's true.'

'Which reminds me; you never sent me your written report on the Hooper killing. Best send it to Micalef now, I suppose.'

'My written report? Yes I did. I had it hand delivered to Attard. He was sleeping in the corridor as I recall.'

'Oh, okay, he must have forgotten to pass me on a copy. Not that it matters much.'

'No? I'd have thought it mattered a lot.'

'Really? Why?'

'Well, the wounds being a match for a start, and the fact that the knife, therefore, was the one that killed both women.'

Spiteri's mind was a mixture of confusion and near panic.

'You said they didn't match.'

'I most certainly did not; I can assure you of that.'

Healy hadn't noticed that Spiteri wasn't behind him on the stairs going down to the car deck, so he was sitting in the car by the time she arrived.

'Matt, there's a roundabout at the top of the hill, on the road out from the ferry. Go round it, come back down and back onto the ferry. We need to get back to Malta.'

# CHAPTER 40

Father Francesco was sitting in his favourite coffee shop, enjoying a coffee and some peppered *ghejniet*, when a young man approached him.

'Father, may I sit with you?'

'Please, sit down, my son.'

'Thank you, Father. Can I get you anything, a brandy perhaps?'

'No, thank you for asking though…'

'David.'

'Well, David, can I help you with anything, or are you just feeling sorry for an old man?'

'There is one thing you might be able to help me with though, Father.'

'What is that?'

'I saw you here the other day, talking to a young man. I thought I recognised him from school, or maybe university.'

'Oh well, that must have been a young friend of mine, Jason Attard.'

'Jason Attard? No, that isn't him. Definitely not. Thank you for your time anyway, Father.'

David Decelis rose to leave. 'One last thing, Father. Should there be retribution against people over their sins of the past... or forgiveness?'

'Certainly forgiveness, but retribution may also be appropriate. It depends on so many things, David. It is never too late to make your peace with God.'

'Thank you, Father.'

'You're welcome. Going so soon? Remember, David, it is never too late.'

'I know that, Father. I do know that.'

***

'Deputy Commissioner, it's Thea Spiteri on the line. Shall I put her through?' asked the receptionist.

Galea pondered for a moment. 'Yes, put her through.'

'Hello, Thea. How are you?'

'I need to see you. Believe me, it's urgent. Vital.'

Galea could feel Spiteri's anxiety down the line. 'Okay, when?'

'Can you go to the station in St Julians? I don't want to be seen in Valetta.'

'I will meet you there at two p.m.'

'Deputy Commissioner, can you get Jason Attard there as well, on some pretext?'

'This better be a valid situation, Thea. You could be doing your career a lot of damage.'

'Two p.m. St Julians.' Spiteri hung up.

'Well?' said Matt Healy as Spiteri walked out onto the patio.

'He's agreed to meet me, and to have Attard there. If they are in this together, though, I'm finished.'

'But just what is "this?"'

'That's just it. I've no bloody idea.'

'Do you want me to come, sit in?'

'No, that would spook the deputy commissioner, probably. I'll call you.'

Jason Attard was sitting in the coffee area in St Julians station with his feet perched on the side of the coffee machine. He knew that the deputy commissioner was in the station, but he wasn't aware he was in an interview room talking to Thea Spiteri. So, when he was told to go through to the room, he was taken by surprise.

'Hello, Kap.' Attard exclaimed with a smile.i

'Sit down, Sergeant,' said Galea.

'Sergeant, can you explain to me how it is that you informed me that the knife used to kill May Hooper was a different knife to the one used to kill Miriam Calder, given that the wounds were identical?'

'No, I didn't.'

'Jason, yes, you did. And you never passed on a copy of the forensic report.'

'Maybe not. It would just have been an oversight, though. Things were hectic. You know that.'

'Didn't you think it strange that, given the same knife was used, that we didn't link the two killings?'

'I… never read the report.'

'What?'

'I never read it. I just told you what the lab people told me. Sorry.'

'What happened to the Mosta disc?'

'I don't know.'

'How come you just happened to go alone to Peter Smart's hotel and find a knife covered in Calder's blood, a knife that strangely wasn't the one that killed Calder?'

'It was good police work. You said so yourself, at the time. Maybe he had two knives.'

Galea interrupted Spiteri. 'Sergeant, you're under suspension. Once I get to the bottom of all this, you may well be arrested. Go home and wait till you hear from me.'

'But…'

'Out, now,' said Galea, pointing at the door.


Matt Healy had been glad that Spiteri didn't want him to go to the interview with Attard. He knew Attard couldn't stand him, and the feeling was mutual. *Wait till the little prick hears that Thea and I are getting married!*

Healy pottered about the house for a while, put the rubbish out, and threw some bread out to some sparrows that were obviously nesting somewhere in his garden. *So, what to do? Walk or TV?* He remembered what Jim Frame had said about looking up the latest football news on the Internet. Healy went inside and Googled *Daily Record Scotland* although to most people in Scotland, the paper was known as the *Daily Retard* on account of its poor journalistic quality. The paper's front page soon appeared on Healy's screen. *CRAIG WHYTE BUSTED*, the headline screamed, a reference to the former owner of Frame's favourite football team being arrested. Healy snorted. *It's a shambles over there right enough.*

Healy was still chuckling away to himself as he headed into the kitchen to make a coffee before he wallowed in the sordid details that were no doubt contained in the rest of the article. As he waited for the kettle to boil, Healy again thought about the dramatic changes in his life and how happy he was. The kettle boiled. Healy liked his coffee strong, so he spooned two teaspoons of Gold Blend into his mug and headed back over to the living room. He took one step into the room before reeling against the door frame. He felt he had been struck by a sledge-hammer. *Fuck no!*

# CHAPTER 41

Healy looked down. He had spilled coffee down his shirt and his trousers, but hadn't felt a burn. His hands were trembling, his forehead damp with sweat. *Think, Matt. This can't be right. You can't be right. Jesus, what about Thea?*

Healy picked up his mobile from beside the laptop. He glanced again at the screen, closed his eyes, and pleaded to an unknown divine power. *Please answer, Thea. Please.*

'Hi, Matt.'

*Thank you, God.* 'Is Attard still there?'

'Just leaving, why?'

'Keep him there! I'm on my way in. Ten minutes.' Healy ran to the bedroom and pulled on a pair of jeans and fresh t-shirt, *Let's Get It On- Marvin Gaye* emblazoned on the front. *Yea, let's fucking do that, Jason.* Healy ran out to his car, raced down the steep hill from Pembroke to St Julians. He was at the *Pulizija* in seven minutes. Spiteri showed him into the room where the deputy commissioner was still sitting.

'Matt, what is it? You're scaring me a bit.'

'Thea, you might not understand or like what I'm going to be saying in here, but please, let me run with it. Back me up when you can. Deputy Galea, I know this is unusual to say the least, but Thea trusts you, and that is good enough for me. You know that there is something seriously wrong in the *Pulizija*. I haven't got all the answers, but I've got some. I'm hoping to get some more from that bastard, Attard—if you'll let me.'

'Okay, let's hear it,' said Galea.

'Let's get Attard back in, We need to hear it from him.'

Galea nodded to Spiteri.

'I'm not talking to him,' shouted Attard as he realised Healy was going to question him. 'He's not even a UK cop, nevermind a Maltese one!'

'Fine. In that case, you are under arrest until I can find a suitable officer to question you. That might take a couple of weeks. Inspector Spiteri, have him transported to Valetta…'

'Alright, alright! Christ. Right, Healy, what is it?'

'Jason, why did you kill Miriam Calder?'

Jason Attard sniggered. 'Don't be stupid, Healy. Is that it? Is that why I've been brought back in here? What a fucking joke. I was on duty when Calder was killed. You can check that, if you can read, that is.'

Healy ignored the antagonism. 'Stupid? Let me see. You attend the Calder crime scene. The area is thoroughly searched. No knife. However, not long later, you produce a knife from the ether. It's got Calder's blood on it, it was found in Peter Smart's hotel room, by you, obviously. You knew it wouldn't match the wound but, hey, the findings of the forensics lab don't seem to bother you, Jason. You can easily fix them.'

'We've already done this gig, Healy. It was shit when they said it, and it's still shit.'

'Well, let's see. The knife in the Calder incident, plus the report on the knife in the Hooper murder, plus the Mosta disc being destroyed, plus the blood-soaked rag in the Grech case; it all adds to one thing.'

'Really, and what's that?'

'You killed Jamie Smart, Jason. And the two women, and probably the poor kid in Mosta, too.'

'You're mad, Healy. Thea, you know I couldn't have killed Calder; I was with you, both of you… in Mono. Remember, Healy… duh.'

'Yes, and left early,' said Spiteri.

Matt Healy nodded his appreciation to Spiteri for backing him. He also suddenly realised what had been bothering him that night.

'Yes, I see it now. There's always been something niggling away at the back of my mind about you, Jason.'said Spiteri ' I know now what it is. You are empty, Jason. You lack empathy. An amoral soul. You'll be charged with these killings. Enjoy the next thirty years, won't you.'

'Wait a minute! This is bullshit; you can't do this! Deputy Commissioner, you can't be going along with this.'

'It wasn't you, then?' said Healy calmly.

'No!'

Healy walked slowly over to Attard, put his hands on the arms of his chair, and leant in to within inches of Attard's face. 'Then who are you protecting, Jason?'

Even though there were three people in the room, no sound could be heard. Attard looked at Healy, then Spiteri, then, finally, at Galea.

Matt Healy looked over to Thea Spiteri and silently mouthed the word "sorry." Thea Spiteri appeared confused at first; then she slowly raised her hand to cover her mouth.

'Just what is your relationship with Father Francesco, Jason?'

'We're friends.'

'Since?'

'He took me under his wing when I was a boy.'

'And where would that have been, Jason? The orphanage, by any chance?'

'Yes.'

Thea Spiteri pointed at Attard. 'Dear God, you were the young boy that acted as a witness against the priest, weren't you? I see it all now.'

'Yes.'

'What was the priest's name again?' asked Spiteri, almost in a whisper.

'Father Ignacio Thomas.'

'Were you lying? Did Father Marandon put you up to it?' asked Healy.

'Yes.'

Spiteri started to cry.

'Where is Father Ignacio now? Do you know? We'll have to contact him, put him out of his misery,' said Galea.

'He's dead, apparently. Not long after being sent back to Italy, he hung himself.'

'Jesus, it just gets better and better. That's God knows how many young boys dead, Jason. Dead, abused, thrown to the wind, worthless rubbish' said Healy.

Spiteri was slowly pulling herself together. 'Why Jason? You're a policeman, a devout Christian, so you say.'

'I didn't kill anyone.'

'What? Oh yes, you did. You killed every kid and the innocent young priest. Think of his torment, his family's torment. Your silence killed them all!' shouted Healy.

'I was only a child myself!' screamed Attard.

'Maybe, but you became a man, joined the police, for Christ's sake. But never spoke out,' whispered Spiteri.

Attard looked over at Spiteri. 'I joined to be close to you, Thea. I love you. I've loved you all these years.'

'Really? Well, don't expect any prison visits from me, Jason. None at all. You disgust me.'

Attard was left under guard in the interview room while Spiteri, Healy, and Galea crossed the road from the station and ordered three coffees in Tony's Bar.

'We can't hold him. We have no proof he's committed any crimes. If we get corroboration on some of the things to do with tampering with evidence, then we can charge him, but…' said Galea.

Healy looked over at Thea Spiteri. Thea Spiteri hadn't touched her coffee, a glint in her eyes showed that tears weren't far away, and she had torn her napkin into tiny pieces. . 'I'm sorry Thea, but I've got even worse news for you.'

Spiteri just stared blankly at Healy. 'Is that possible?'

'It was Francesco who killed Calder and Hooper, and I'm pretty sure it was him who killed Jamie Smart.'

Healy watched as the blood completely drained from Spiteri's face. She began to look around her, as if she was unsure where she was. For a moment, Healy thought she was going to run off.

'But why, Matt?'

'I think he's a paedophile. Calder and Hooper somehow knew him, maybe from past investigations. I don't know. They saw him here, but, more importantly, he saw them. He couldn't take any chances. He killed them.'

'No!' It was Spiteri. 'You're wrong, Matt. Thank God. Francesco never saw or knew about Miriam Calder coming. You're wrong, Matt.'

'Thea, remember that night, the night in Mono? You spoke to Francesco outside the restaurant.'

'Yes, but Miriam Calder wasn't there!'

'Exactly. He asked if "your other guest hadn't arrived yet." It bothered me. How did he know we were waiting for a fourth guest? Attard must have told him. I'm guessing Calder had then arrived, seen

Francesco and you talking on the street, made the excuse of being tired, and gone back to her hotel and phoned me.'

'And Hooper?'

'Something similar. I don't know for sure.'

'How have you worked this out now?' asked Galea.

'Calder and Hooper. They weren't writing "Why" in the sand, they were writing "Whyte."'

# CHAPTER 42

Deputy Commissioner Galea came off his call to Commissioner Debono with an ashen face. He looked over at Spiteri and Healy. 'Under no circumstances have any charges be brought against Attard or Marandon, and no further investigations are to be done into either person. All cases are closed.'

Thea Spiteri and Matt Healy looked at Galea, then at each other. 'I'm almost expecting a punch line here,' said Healy. 'What do you mean *closed*?'

'As I said to you a long time ago, Matt, the church is very powerful in Malta,' said Spiteri.

The three slightly stunned interrogators crossed back over to the St Julians *Pulizija* station.

Jason Attard had just collected his personal belongings. 'My resignation letter is on your desk, Inspector Spiteri. I'm due some leave, so I won't be back. As a matter of fact, I've been thinking of leaving this decrepit island for a while. I have some relatives in Australia; I might join the police force there.'

Spiteri only managed to whisper, 'Don't expect a reference.'

Attard laughed. 'People higher up than you have already told me that they will gladly provide anything I need.'

Attard then decided it was his turn for close contact. He walked up to within a few inches of Matt Healy. 'Oh yes, I hear congratulations are in order. Marriage? Who would have thought? I bet you'll be pleased to see the back of me, eh Matt? But, being an ex-policeman yourself, you should know things are never as they seem.'

Healy smirked. 'What does that mean? Intimidation is it, a threat? Better men than you have tried, Attard. This isn't over, Jason. I'm going to nail you, you perverted little fuck.'

Jason Attard merely smiled, saying, 'Bye all. It's been nice.' as he walked out the station door.

A few moments later, Deputy Commissioner Galea, too, walked towards the door. He turned and looked at Spiteri and Healy, appeared to be about to say something but, instead, merely shook his head and then he, too, walked out the door.

'Let's go home,' said Spiteri quietly. 'Matt, how did Attard know we were getting married, do you think?'

'Obviously, he's spoken to Marandon.'

'They weren't on good terms, as far as I know.'

'Good enough, I bet.' Healy paused. 'That means Francesco knows that we know about him.'

'We can't do anything, Matt.'

'You can't, maybe.' Healy headed towards the door.

'Where are you going, Matt?'

'To hear a confession.'

***

Healy knew that Marandon would already have been called by Attard. And he also felt that he knew Father Francesco Marandon well enough to know where he'd have gone. It took him half an hour and two wrong turns, but eventually he found his way to the Dingli Cliffs. A black figure stood, highlighted by the dazzling blue sea.

Healy parked on a grass verge opposite from where the old priest's silhouette shimmered in the heat. *The Grim Reaper*. Healy walked over to Marandon.

'It wasn't "Why" they were writing in the sand was it, Francesco?' Healy said quietly. 'Or should that be Reginald. Reginald Whyte?'

'They're only names, Matt. Unimportant.'

'Maybe not, but the spelling sometimes can. Whyte with a *y*, for example.'

'Unimportant, Matt. Unimportant.'

'And the answer phone message I got from Miriam Calder… She wasn't saying it was "the" father, she was trying to say "Father Marandon, aka Reginald Whyte."'

'I suppose, but what does it matter, Matt? What's done is done.'

Healy was torn between being incensed and disbelieving at Marandon's manner.

'And May Hooper… that wasn't a question mark… It was an attempt at a *T*, wasn't it? They both recognised you, didn't they, Francesco? I don't know yet for sure where they knew you from, but I'm guessing it was from previous crime scenes. You must have been around when kids went missing. It was all too much of a coincidence. Calder wasn't stupid. She put two and two together.'

'Ah Matt, why did they have to come here? Why now? When the end was so close.'

'The end?'

'I'm an old man, Matt. My work was done.'

'Lucky you, Whyte. Those kids never got that chance. Where are the bodies, Francesco? Give the mothers some peace at least. Surely a man of God would want that?'

Marandon turned to Healy, his face contorted. 'A man of God! What would you know about that? I have devoted my whole life to God, done everything asked of me!'

'You're trying to tell me that killing all those children was *God's work*? You're fucking mad, Whyte.'

'Interesting. It's Whyte when you're angry, Francesco when you want something. Which brings me to a point: what do you want, Matt? Why are you here?'

Healy's mind was becoming more confused by the minute. *It's as if we're having a friendly chat.*

'I'm here for you, Whyte. Firstly, to try and find out why you have done all these terrible things. Then...' the words of the commissioner echoed in Healy's brain.

Marandon laughed. 'Then? Then? Then, nothing, Matt!' Marandon screamed. 'Plans are already in motion for me to leave these islands, to retire in peace. You asked before about my faith? Let me tell you something, Mr Policeman Healy. My church understands. My church knows about perfect love. A love so strong that you send innocents to eternal salvation. What greater love can there be than that?'

'And Hooper and Calder?'

'They chose their paths; I did not seek them out.'

'You're not walking away from this, Whyte.'

Marandon pointed out to sea. 'See that island over there, Matt? Filfla, it's called. Uninhabited. It's a bird sanctuary; no one lives there. Perfect peace.'

Marandon's attitude was becoming more and more bizarre to Healy. He couldn't relate to what was happening.

'At first, when I saw you here, I thought you were maybe going to jump.'

Marandon seemed surprised. 'Jump? Why would I do that?'

'Remorse, regret, grief even.'

'Can't you see! Don't you understand anything I've just told you? My God will judge me, not the likes of you. Come little children unto me.'

Healy looked down, over the cliff edge, at the sea. A small *frejgatina* fishing boat was heading out to sea, the Eye of Osiris acknowledging Healy's presence.

Marandon sat down on a steel bench just behind where Healy was standing in a state of moral turmoil. *Is that it? Can this be how it ends?*

Marandon's quiet voice turned Healy around. 'One thing, though, Matt. I know nothing about the killing of Michele Grech. Barbaric.'

'Francesco, do you think that you are maybe mad? I promise I will try to get you help.'

Marandon appeared puzzled. The old priest then watched some sea birds in the distance. 'You and Thea won't want me to perform your marriage now, I expect. I won't be available anyway.'

'You're right, Whyte, you won't be.'

Matt Healy covered the short distance between himself and Marandon with one stride. He grabbed the old priest's right arm and shoulder and pulled him to his feet. The two men stared into each other's eyes. Conviction burned in Healy's; realisation slowly registered in Marandon's.

Healy swiveled, and in one movement, threw Father Reginald Francesco Marandon Whyte off the Dingli Cliffs.

Healy slumped onto the bench where only seconds before, Marandon had been sitting, talking about his wedding. He didn't know how he felt. It took a few minutes before Healy realised that someone was standing behind him. Healy slowly turned and looked up at the young man standing there.

'Do you mind if I sit down?' asked the young man.

Healy was confused. He couldn't speak, so he merely nodded.

'I saw everything. Don't worry. I could see you were trying to save him.'

Healy studied the young man's face; again no words came.

'I'll give you my card. Just tell the *Pulizija* to call me for a statement anytime I've written my Maltese number on the back.'

Healy glanced at the card *David Decelis*. He looked back up at the man. Again, a nod would need to suffice. David Decelis nodded back, turned, and walked away.

The following day, Marandon's body was recovered, washed up on the rocks near Rdum Dikkiena. A representative from the church claimed the body, and Reginald Whyte was never heard of again.

*** 

'He admitted everything except the Michele Grech killing. He was adamant about me knowing that, then he just jumped,' said Matt Healy to Spiteri and the deputy commissioner.

'Did he say why he did it?' asked Spiteri, who's death like palour remained the same as at Tony's Bar. Healy could tell Spiteri was still finding it hard to take in all that had happened.

'He just said he was doing God's work. I think he was just mad, Thea.'

Spiteri looked hard at Healy's face. 'And he just jumped? Any witnesses to that, do you know?'

Healy had known that this situation would arise, but was unsure what to do about the witness.

'As a matter of fact, there was.' He handed Spiteri the card. 'His local number is on the back.' Spiteri got up and left the room.

'You know the bird sanctuary opposite the Dingli Cliffs?' asked Healy.

'Yes,' replied the Deputy Commissioner.

'I think you should send search parties over there. I have a feeling there are some kids' bodies there.'

Spiteri came back into the room. Healy searched her face. 'Decelis has confirmed everything you said, Matt. Sorry.'

Healy understood what she meant.

Two days later, the bodies of twenty-four unnamed children were recovered from the bird sanctuary of Filfla.

# CHAPTER 43

The 'untimely death of well-loved' priest Father Francesco Marandon appeared on page two of the *Malta Times*. A glowing report of his
many achievements, including his management of the old orphanage on
Malta, was covered in detail. *After a simple ceremony in the Dominican
Monastery, Father Marandon had been buried in the monastery grounds "as he had
requested."*

'Nice,' said Healy. 'Make you vomit.'

Spiteri was still consumed by sorrow and disbelief at what had happened to her life over the past few months. Much of what she held as
absolute truth had proven to be no more than an illusion. She lay with
her head on Healy's chest. 'I'll never be able to take it all in, Matt.
Father Francesco a paedophile and killer, Jason Attard totally corrupt,
Claudia and Joseph Sansome both headed for mental institutions, the
killing in Mosta still unsolved, and the *Pulizija* that I have always
believed in seemingly being run to a personal agenda.'

'I'll tell you worse than all that,' said Healy.

'Oh God, what now?'

'We'll need to find a new priest for the wedding.'

'Ha bloody ha.' Despite herself, Spiteri laughed. Her mobile buzzed, Daphne Arrigo's name coming up on the screen. 'Hello, Daphne.'

'Hi, so that's any chance of nailing Marandon gone. Only adds to my belief that Borg was telling the truth, about some things at least.'

'I know what you mean. He was my friend, my best friend, but now…'

'Do you think Borg would speak to you? He would have nothing to do with me, but he might speak to you.'

'I don't know; I could call his house and ask, I suppose. He'll not know I'm not officially investigating a case.'

'Okay, do that, will you? Let me know how it goes.'

'Okay.' *No time like the present.*

'Hello, the Borg residence.' The person on the other end of the line appeared to have a Philipino accent.

'Hello, this is Inspector Thea Spiteri. I'd like to call in to speak to Mr Borg. Can you ask him for a suitable time, please? Tell him its important *Pulizija* business.' *God loves a trier.* To Spiteri's great surprise, the Philipino voice came back on the line. 'Visit in one hour's time, please. Thank you. Bye.'

Exactly one hour later, Spiteri walked into Borg's sitting room. 'Thank you for seeing me, Mr Borg.' Spiteri was stunned at the appearance of Borg. *Maybe the hospital unit wasn't as soft as it was said to be.* Borg looked drawn and emaciated—and twenty years older. 'I'll not keep you long.'

'I don't have long.'

'What do you mean?'

'Do you think I'll be allowed to live? Look what happened to Marandon.'

Spiteri was stunned at the way the conversation was going. 'Marandon committed suicide, and he was involved in a completely unrelated case to this. I can assure you of that. I wouldn't lie about that. As a matter of fact, Father Francesco was a friend of mine.'

Borg laughed. 'Yes, he was many people's friend, Inspector.'

'So Marandon was involved in some way?'

'Yes, but I don't know how. He seemed to have some sort of hold over Debono. He snapped his fingers, Debono came running.'

'So you're still maintaining that you gave Marandon the money to give to Commissioner Debono?'

'Yes.'

'But why? If the sentence was already agreed, what was Debono to do with the money?'

Borg laughed again. 'The sentence! The money had nothing to do with that case!'

Spiteri was stunned. 'Well, what was it for?'

'For Debono to pass on to certain politicians after taking his own cut, obviously.'

'So that they would do what?'

'Who knows; there are so many favours being done, you lose track.'

'Who supplied the money?'

'I'm sure you already know the answer to that, Inspector. If you don't, ask your boss.'

'Was it Nicola Tizian?'

Borg shrugged his shoulders, turned the palms of his hands upwards in a sign of supplication. 'It is what it is. Please go now. I'm very tired.'

***

Two hours after her meeting with Borg, Commissioner Debono called Spiteri. He apologised for his 'perhaps hasty actions' and asked her to return to work. Spiteri had contemplated never going back at one time, but when the request came in, she knew it's what she really wanted. She also wanted to nail Debono.

'What about Micalef?'

'He's been put onto less strenuous work. I don't think killings suited him.'

'I'm not sure they suit anyone, Commissioner.'

'No, that's true. Anyway, welcome back.'

Spiteri had a spring in her step as she walked back into work. She knew there were still a lot of unanswered questions, not least being who killed Michele Grech, now that the bloody cloth evidence appeared dubious, to say the least. She'd never accepted the Joseph Sansome arrest for it and far less the so-called confession from Steven Calleja. She would not have long to find out.

The phone on Sarah Said's desk rang. 'Sergeant Said.'

'Yes, sergeant, it's Dennis Vella here.'

'Sorry, who?'

'Dennis Vella, from the construction company you phoned. The one that had the lorry in Mosta a while back.'

'Oh, yes, Dennis. Sorry, I get a lot of names. How can I help you?'

'Well, I got a call today from the garage we use to fix our lorries. I wouldn't be bothering you if you had called about that bloody cat person, but since it was a murder, I thought I should call.'

'To tell me what exactly, Dennis?'

'The lorry you were talking about. It broke down on the way back from Mosta. It's been in the garage ever since. You can't get the spare parts, you see. I blame the Labour government, you know. Did you...'

'Dennis, why are you telling me all this?'

'Well, the lorry still has its load from Mosta. That's what you asked about.'

Said quickly established where the lorry was and told Dennis Vella to make sure the load remained where it was. Half an hour later, a rather dusty and disgruntled *Pulizija* officer shouted down to Spiteri and Said from the back of the lorry. 'There's a knife here alright, lying right on the top.'

'Be careful lifting it. Get it straight to forensics. You go with them, Sarah. Make sure there's no Mr Muscle flying around all over the labs.' Spiteri was praying that Francesco Marandon's prints weren't on the knife. Her prayers would be answered.

*** 

'How many guests going to this wedding?' said Healy in a pained tone. 'I'm not a wealthy man!'

'I have to invite all my relatives; it's what we do in Malta.'

'Even the ones living abroad, people you haven't seen in twenty years?'

'Especially them. It gives them an excuse to come back.'

'And you want the reception where?'

'My house.'

'Your house, all these people?'

'We'll put up a marquee. It will be lovely.'

Healy had to admit that the picture of that in his head was indeed lovely.

'How many people are you inviting, Matt?' Spiteri asked.

'One: Jim Frame.'

'Popular guy.'

'Do you like me?'

'Of course.'

'That's all that matters to me.'

Healy got up to answer his house phone. 'Yes, she is. Hold on, Sarah.' He handed Spiteri the phone and stuck out his tongue.

'Juvenile. No, Sarah, not you.'

'I couldn't get you on your mobile, sorry.'

'Don't worry; the signal can be poor in Pembroke. What's up?'

'The blood on the knife is definitely Michele Grech's.'

'And the prints... Marandon's?'

'No. Jason Attard's.'

'I'll meet you at his flat in half an hour. Call out a forensics team and get the street where that bastard lived cordoned off.'

'Fuck!' screamed Spiteri as she slammed the phone back down.

'What is it?'

'The Grech killing, the kid in Mosta?'

'Yea.'

'It was Attard.'

'Why the fuck did that headcase Calleja confess, then?'

'You answered your own question.'

'What?'

'He's a headcase.'

*\*\**

After being in Attard's flat less than fifteen minutes, the forensics team found blood in the hall, which had seeped under the tiles, along with some hair. 'Get it tested. Sarah, get on to Luqa Airport, find out what flight to Australia Attard got on, but more importantly, what city it was flying to.'

Spiteri went out to her car where Healy was waiting. 'There's blood there, and hairs… What a bastard. How did I not see it?'

'You can't think that way, Thea. These people are expert at what they do. I guess this explains the slit on Jamie's neck. Attard will have done it when he disposed of the body for Marandon. Cosgrove did say two people were possibly involved. The bastard was getting some practice in. At least Jamie wouldn't have known anything about it. Poor kid.'

'What a sick world, Matt.'

Sarah Said came up to Healy's car. 'I spoke to the airlines. Attard left the day after he resigned.'

'What city did he fly to?'

'Ottawa.'

'Ottawa, that's in Canada, isn't it? I have relatives there.'

'Yes. He never went to Australia. He went to Canada.'

'I wonder why he went there.'

'Probably just trying to throw us off.'

'I think I know,' said Healy.

Spiteri and Said both looked down at Spiteri's passenger seat.

'Enlighten us,' said Spiteri.

'No extradition treaty. Check. I bet I'm right.'

He was. A call to Commissioner Debono confirmed it. 'I'm not even going to try, Thea. Years of pointless paperwork. We'll have to let it go.' Spiteri felt that Debono did not seem overly concerned about the situation.

That evening, Spiteri called Daphne Arrigo and told her about her meeting with Borg.

'I'm going to go and see Tizian. I'll make up a story about research or whatever, see if I can pick up anything,' said Arrigo.

'Be careful. Tizian is a fox.'

'Don't worry, I'm a seasoned campaigner!'

Arrigo had already made her first mistake and condemned someone to death.

# CHAPTER 44

Thea Spiteri and Matt Healy met Mary Smart at the airport when she flew in for her son's funeral. They were slightly surprised to see Peter Smart with her. He had been released several weeks before and put on a plane, screaming and shouting that he would never be back in Malta.

Matt Healy, and one of the undertakers, carried the white coffin into the church. Peter Smart had claimed to be too upset. Thea Spiteri stood in the second row, immediately behind Jamie's parents. Two or three of the officers who had worked on the case made up the rest of the mourners. There was no one from Scotland.

Despite Mary Smart's position about Healy offering her money if she needed it, Healy had paid for Jamie's Smart's coffin as well as a burial plot. He had told Mary Smart that, under the circumstances, they had been provided free by the Government of Malta. After a brief ceremony, Jamie Smart was laid to rest.

Davis Decelis found out about the funeral by chance, when he had called into the *Pulizija* station to give his statement on the Marandon suicide. As a final mark of respect, and a farewell to the island, he too attended the funeral.

'Can you take us back to the airport, Matt?' asked Mary Smart.

'Yes, but aren't you going to stay, even for a day or so?'

'No, we're going straight home, packing up, and coming out here to live.'

'To be near Jamie,' added a not-too-upset-looking Peter Smart.

'Right, that's great. You'll be able to pick up some cleaning work here alright, Mary. The bars and restaurants are always looking for good staff.'

'Oh, there will be no need for that now, Mr Healy,' said a smiling Peter Smart.

'Really, why's that?'

'Well, we got paid out by the insurance, didn't we? It all worked out well in the end. No hard feelings, eh?' Peter Smart offered Matt Healy his hand. Healy was too dumbfounded to refuse.

Thea Spiteri had seen Healy talking to the Smarts and had decided to leave them alone. She saw him shaking hands and looking awkward. She idled over, not really wishing to talk to the Smarts herself. Healy looked relieved beyond words. 'Ah good, Inspector Spiteri, can you organise for the Smarts to be taken to the airport now? They have a plane to catch.' The pleading in Healy's eyes alerted Spiteri not to say anything other than, 'Yes, of course.'

'What was all that about?' asked Spiteri after the Smarts had left.

'That, my dear, is what we call in Glasgow, "the scum of the earth." I need to get out of here.'

By the time they walked to the back of the church, David Decelis had already gone.


Healy and Spiteri had earmarked the afternoon for heading to Valetta for some wedding planning and shopping.

'Wedding planning! Listen, you turn up, get married, then go away again. What's to plan?' was Healy's view.

'I'm not even going to dignify that with a reply.'

'Right. What are you intending wearing on the momentous day?'

'A kilt, of course!' laughed Matt Healy.

'A kilt. Are you sure?' replied Spiteri.

'Well, what the hell else would a true Scotsman wear on the most important day of his life, woman?'

'I hope my relatives see it that way!'

'Oh, your relatives will see everything; I can assure you of that!'

Spiteri felt a little confused at the obvious great pleasure that Healy took out of his last response but decided to move on. Just then, Healy's mobile rang. 'Oh, yes. Really? Where? Yes, two p.m. I'll be there. I'm in Valetta anyway, as it happens.'

'Sounds mysterious.'

'The bank. Some bugger has been trying to use my card. I've to go to the Banif Security Office in Floriana, at two p.m.'

'Right. Shall we grab some lunch in the meantime?'

'Sounds wonderful.' Healy took Spiteri's hand and they meandered slowly, the way lovers do, till they could agree on somewhere to eat. 'I want *barbuljata*, and that's final,' teased Spiteri.

'So do I,' replied Healy.

'You don't even know what it is!'

'I don't care. If you like it, I like it.'

Half an hour later, Spiteri and Healy sat at a table with two empty plates in front of them, waiting for their coffees to arrive. 'Why didn't you just say *scrambled eggs*!' laughed Healy.

'I like to sound mysterious.'

'Where is this place I've to go, the bank place. Do you know?'

'Not exactly, but you know the *Pulizija* office where you went to get your Good Conduct Certificate, the one you need for your I.D. application?'

'Yea. Beside your headquarters?'

'I think it's beside that. If it's not, go in there and ask; they're bound to know.'

'Right, that's fine. I'll leave in half an hour. What do you want to do now?'

'Can we talk?'

'Isn't that what we're doing?'

'Ha ha. Talk about us. Well, not us actually… children.'

'What about them?'

'Don't be a pig, Matt. Would you like children after we're married?'

'Would you?'

'I think so.'

'Then so would I. Just one thing, though. He'll be Scottish, and that's that.'

'He?'

'Obviously, the Healy sperm is very masculine.'

'Do you mind! Okay, go and find the Banif Offices. I can see you're not sane enough to be a father.'

***

Sarah Said sat at her desk with a feeling of emptiness. In some ways, she was pleased to have been right about Attard, but in another way, she wished she hadn't been. At first, she had liked him, even considered his dating potential, but his apparent lack of feeling eventually put her off. She had double checked about extradition from Canada and had even phoned the Royal Canadian Mounted Police to see if they knew of any loopholes they might use in order to get Attard back. It didn't take long for her to realise that he was history. *Forget it, Sarah. Move on.* The phone on her desk rang just as she was about to pick up a domestic violence file. She was glad of the distraction. 'Sarah Said. How can I help?'

'Hi, Sarah. It's David Decelis here. You took my statement about the Father Marandon suicide.'

'Yes, hello. What can I do for you, David?'

'Oh nothing really. I was just calling to say that I am heading to the airport now. Australia, here I come.'

'Lucky you.'

'So, as I said, you have my home number in Australia, if you need to speak to me. If you want me to come back though, you'll need to pay!'

'You trying to give the commissioner a heart attack? No, like I said, I think you can safely say that whole terrible episode is over. It went on far too long as it is.'

'That is certainly true. Is Matt Healy there by any chance, just to say bye?'

'No sorry, David, he's not. I could patch you through to Thea Spiteri if you like. I'm sure he'll be with her. I don't have his number.'

'Would that be okay, do you think?'

'Sure, why not? Hold on.'

'Hello.'

'Hello, Thea. it's David Decelis here. Is Matt with you? I'm leaving now and just wanted to say goodbye.'

'Oh, David, that is nice of you, but no. He has a meeting at his bank. I've no idea how long he'll be. I'll let him know you called, though.'

'Great, no worries. Bye, then.'

'Bye David. Have a safe flight.'

*\*\**

Joseph Sansome was used to calculating things like length and weight from his various jobs in construction. He had been told by his lawyer that two of the charges against him, the Smart and Grech killings, were likely to be dropped. He was ambivalent about the news, as he had also been told of his wife's arrest and incarceration and knew of the torments she must have been going through.

Sansome had a job in the prison garden. 'You know, sir, I could do a much better job if you could get me a hose,' he said to the prison guard on duty that day.

'I'm sure there's a hose lying at the back of one of the sheds outside. Come with me,' said the inexperienced guard. The young officer opened up the shed and Sansome went in and retrieved the plastic-coated hose. Sansome smiled inwardly. *It's good, strong.* Sansome went about his daily chores with renewed vigour and returned the hose, as clearly instructed to by the guard, that evening. The missing half meter of hosing was not noticed by the guard.

It was 11.00 p.m. The cell and corridor lights were out, and the prison was quiet. Joseph Sansome lay on his bed thinking of his daughter, Catherine. He pictured her smile, her joy at learning how to ride her bike, her belief that he would lead Malta to the Basketball World Championships one day. He thought of Ingrid Lam. *I just want people to feel what I've had to feel. Be me for just a few days.*

Joseph wiped a tear from his eye, got up, and pulled the piece of hosing he had cut from the longer hose that afternoon from under his mattress. He looked at the grill covering the prison bars on his window. He looked at the small table at the end of his bed. He knew instinctively that his calculations were right.

When Joseph Sansome didn't appear for his breakfast, the young guard from the previous day went to his cell and opened the metal door. He knew he should have checked the cell using the peep hole first; he would always regret that he didn't.

The length of hose pipe had stretched with the weight and Joseph Sansome appeared, at first, to be standing under his cell window. The morning sunlight shining through the window partially blinded the warder, and it took him a few seconds to focus properly. Sansome's staring eyes were bulging out of his red, swollen face. His black tongue was lying in what looked like a lopsided parody of a clown's face. The large urine mark on the front of Sansome's prison overalls was beginning to dry in, but the stench was still strong. The urine smell, however, was slight compared to Sansome's bowel contents, which were spreading out from the bottom of each trouser leg.

The young prison *gwardjan* barely made the rubbish bin before vomiting his breakfast into the black plastic bag lining the plastic container.

# CHAPTER 45

Deputy Galea sat opposite Commissioner Debono and wondered if he would be taking the other chair at the end of the year, when Debono retired. Galea had been called into Debono's office about ten minutes before and, for the first time, had seen an old man sitting in front of him.

'Are you feeling alright, Commissioner?'

'Well, everything is relative, Kevin. Wouldn't you say?'

'Indeed.'

'Do you have any dark secrets, Kevin?' Galea was disturbed by the question. *Was he being assessed, accused, what?*

'We all have secrets, I dare say, Chris. I'm not sure I would describe mine as dark.'

'Mine are.' Debono edged his chair round, to let him look out of the window. 'I've given my whole life to this job, Kevin, at a cost to my family and my heart. And now what? I retire soon. To do what? Sit with a family of strangers?

'Are you sure you are feeling alright, Chris?'

'Do you want this job, Kevin?'

'Well, I've hoped that I...'

'Don't take it. Believe me. Take early retirement. Go on permanent sick leave. Anything. Just get out. Travel the world. Fall in love with life again.'

Galea did not respond. He didn't have the words.

\*\*\*

Claudia Sansome heard of her husband's suicide from one of the psychiatric nurses assigned to her ward. 'How did he do it?'

'He hung himself, Claudia. I'm very sorry.'

'Our daughter, Catherine, was killed a while back. Did you know that?'

'Yes, yes I did. It must have been terrible for you both. Maybe Joseph is at peace now. Maybe he's sitting with Catherine, reading her favourite story.'

'Maybe.'

*Infermier* Peltretti rose from the chair beside Sansome. 'I'll leave you alone now, Claudia. If you need me, press the buzzer.'

'I will, and... thank you.'

Peltretti nodded and headed for the door.

'Nurse!'

'Yes.'

'Does this mean we're not going to New York?'

\*\*\*

David Decelis had reached Hamrun on the way to the airport when he remembered he would need to stop, get some money, and put petrol in the car before returning it to the hire company. He had learned from bitter experience in the past that, if you just let the hire company do it and charge your credit card, then they seem to charge for a tanker load even though you'd hired a Clio. Decelis spotted a couple of banks up ahead and pulled in. He went to the first ATM and withdrew 50 euro. He felt something register in his subconscious, but cleared his head with a twist of the neck. He jumped back in his car and pulled into a petrol station a few hundred meters further up the road. The pumps were operated by a man who looked as if he had been in Malta since the time of The Knights of St John.

'Put in forty euro, would you please.'

*I feel lucky.* The old man filled the car and took the money without speaking. Decelis started to move away, then slammed on the brakes. He swiveled the car round and headed back towards the bank. He double parked and ran over to the ATM. He then ran to the one slightly further away; the signs hanging on both of the bank's glass doors read BANK HOLIDAY. Decelis pulled his mobile out of his jacket pocket. *Spiteri's number, please, please be there.* It wasn't. He dialed Sarah Said. *Come on, Sarah. Come on.*

'Hello, Sar…'

'Sarah, it's David Decelis again. I must speak to Spiteri. It's urgent; patch me through.' The tone of Decelis' voice removed any doubt from Said's mind.

'Hello.'

'Thea, it's David Decelis again. Is Matt back yet?'

'No, but I told you I'd tell him you called.'

'What bank is he supposed to be going to?'

'David, Matt and I both appreciated your help with the Marandon thing, but…'

'Thea, the banks are closed today. Where is Mark? What area?' Spiteri could sense the fear in Decelis' voice but couldn't really understand what was going on. She hesitated. 'Look, David, I'm sure it's nothing. I'll call Matt… get him to call you…'

'Thea, what fucking area… I know these people.'

Spiteri began to panic. 'People. What people…'

'Where!'

'Floriana, beside the police station.'

The line went dead.

Matt Healy was fine, if a little exasperated. He'd walked past the Phoenician Hotel, the Education Offices, more embassies than he thought possible, but was relieved that he had now found the *Pulizija* station at least. There was an officer standing on the pavement, surreptitiously cupping a cigarette in his right hand. He nodded as Healy approached.

'Hi, can you show me where the Banif Bank building is around here, please?'

The officer seemed confused. 'I don't think there are any banks around here, sir.'

'Well, it's maybe not a branch. It's the bank's security building, apparently.'

The young officer looked even more confused. 'Hold on, I'll go in and ask. I've not been here that long.'

A few moments later, an older officer appeared. 'I don't know for sure, but I believe that building there, on the corner, the one with all the glass, I'm sure that's something to do with Banif. It's probably there. If not, they must know where it actually is.'

'Right, thanks.'

Healy crossed over the deserted road and headed for the corner the officer had pointed at. A huge hoarding board on the side of the building read *Banif. The Power of Believing*.

*Good. Mind you, that looks like they financed this monstrosity, not that...*

'Excuse me; are you looking for the Banif Security Building?'

Healy turned. *Thank God for that.* His forehead wrinkled in puzzlement.

Unknown to each other, both Spiteri and Decelis would be turning into the same street in Floriana in about two minutes. Neither of them was looking at the road. Spiteri was racing to the *Pulizija* station. She had no idea why she was so stressed, but she was praying that Healy was there, his Scottish accent baffling the officers when he asked    for directions. Decelis had already passed the station, seen a young policeman outside smoking. *All seems quiet. I'll go around one more time.*

\*\*\*

Matt Healy was dead before his body hit the ground. He did not hear the words, 'Remember, Matt, I told you things are never as they seem.' In his last few seconds of life, as the blood gushed from the gaping slash in his neck, Matt Healy thought of Thea Spiteri, of the son he never had. He thought of Francesco Marandon, he thought of Jamie Smart. He thought of Susan Dornan.

Jason Attard's pleasure at the sight of Healy's lifeless body was interrupted by the sound of two cars screeching around the corner to his left. He wasn't too concerned. He knew the layout well. *A quick dash across the narrow park that lined the square, lose myself in the cloistered walkways in front of the Portes Des Bombes archway that guards the entrance to the City Gate of Valetta.*

But Jason Attard had made a miscalculation. Jason Attard had not taken into account twenty-five years of longing for revenge. David Decelis caught up with Attard before he even reached the gardens. He was momentarily distracted by an agonising, terrifying scream that erupted from somewhere behind him, but he grabbed Attard by the hair as he tried to turn to face his adversary. The two men rolled down the small embankment, landing full force against a metal parking post. Decelis was momentarily winded but kept a hold of the arm that Attard was using to try and sweep the knife across Decelis' throat. Decelis heaved his knee upwards with all the force he could muster. He heard Attard wince, felt him lose power. Decelis twisted his neck round and then launched his forehead into Attard's face. He heard Attard's cries over the sound of his nose fracturing and exploding in a gush of crimson. Decelis twisted, managed to roll on top of Attard. He heard the sirens of an ambulance pull up nearby. Suddenly, Decelis felt no movement below him. He looked down through his blood-soaked fingers, and saw the  knife they had bought fought so frantically for, sticking out of Attard's bloodied throat.

# CHAPTER 46

Daphne Arrigo did not have a contact number for Nicola Tizian, but she knew where to find him most days around lunchtime. The front seating area of The Black Bear was busy, as Arrigo weaved her way towards the bar where Nicola Tizian was sitting alone, reading a copy of *The Independent*.

'Sorry to bother you, Mr Tizian. My name is…'

'I know who you are.'

'Really? I'm flattered, I think.'

Tizian studied Arrigo's face, then smiled. 'What can I do for you, Daphne?'

'I'm doing some research on whether the standard of tourist visiting Malta is…'

'Stop. Let's move over to the quieter area at the back.' Arrigo and Tizian sat in a booth but at opposite ends of the square table. 'What do you really want, Ms Arrigo?'

'You'll be aware that Noel Borg has been released?'

'Yes. Have you been speaking to him?'

'No, but obviously his release has resurrected issues brought up in his trial.'

'Such as?'

'Well, what happened to the money that was paid to Borg... and who paid it.'

'I know it's a mystery. A good investigative reporter like you, Daphne, may be able to get to the bottom of it one day. I hope so.'

'Why do you think Borg said the money was bound for Commissioner Debono?'

'No idea, really. Maybe to help persuade the *Pulizija* not to be too insistent on a long sentence.'

'The money had nothing to do with the drug trial, apparently.'

'No? In that case, I have no idea. I don't wish to be rude, Daphne, but I have an appointment. But perhaps we can have dinner some night?'

'Perhaps.' Arrigo felt slightly thrilled at the idea somehow.

Tizian stood, shook hands with Arrigo, and walked back to the bar. Arrigo left the way she had arrived.

Tizian summoned the barman over. 'Give me the red mobile out of the locked drawer,' he said while handing the young man a key. The barman got the key and handed Tizian the Pay-as-You-Go mobile. Tizian tapped in the code for Corsica: 00 33 495... followed by an untraceable local number. The connection was made, but no greeting made. Tizian merely said, 'Send Spirito over.'

\*\*\*

Two days had passed since the murder of Matt Healy and the death of Jason Attard. Thea Spiteri had driven to her own house after she left the hospital. Matt Healy's death had been confirmed at 3.00 p.m. *The time our wedding was scheduled for.* She had refused medication and counseling. She hadn't taken calls from either the commissioner or the deputy commissioner. She had taken a call from a Father Pozo of the

Dominican Monastery, who offered to visit. 'Come to my door, and I swear I will shoot you,' was all she said before putting the phone down.

Spiteri went to Healy's house in Pembroke. She tidied up, put the rubbish out, and packed any of her belongs that she could see lying around. She then took Healy's phone out of her purse. She pressed *Contacts* for Jim Frame's name.

'Alright, Mr Smooth. This you phoning to get some shagging tips?'

'Jim, it's Thea. Matt's fiancé.'

'Shit, Sorry, Thea… I just thought…'

'Matt's dead, Jim. He was murdered by a fugitive who bore a grudge.'

The silence on the line was eerily long, but Spiteri knew Frame was still there. She thought she heard a sob but wasn't sure.

'Jim, where do you think Matt would prefer to be buried? Here or Scotland?' Frame's silence continued.

Eventually, the voice of a man whose life had just changed forever came back to her. 'He has no one here, Thea. Well, me, but you know what I mean. I'd never known him so content and happy, Thea, than when he was with you. Bury him there. Let me know when. I'll be there.'

'I will, Jim. Thank you. Oh, Jim, Matt was talking about you yesterday, about the wedding and things. He told me you were the best bawbag he ever knew. What does baw…'

Spiteri definitely heard sobs then before Frame hung up.

\*\*\*

David Decelis was sitting up in bed in Mater Dei Hospital when Sarah Said came in.

'How are you feeling, David?'

'I never knew I was cut, that I was bleeding. But anyway, I'm fine.'

'You know about Matt, I take it?'

'Yes.'

'David, there are some loose ends we need to tie up.'

'I know. Let me know when Thea feels she can sit for an hour. I'm ready any time.'

'Okay.' Said smiled. 'Anything else I can do for you?'

'Yes, I want the commissioner at the meeting.'

'What? I'm not sure I can swing that.'

Decelis smiled. 'I've faith in you.'


A week passed in a blur. Davis Decelis had been discharged from hospital and had had dinner with Sarah Said. Matt Healy had been buried, Jason Attard had been buried, and Jim Frame had gotten thrown out of The Crow's Nest bar for calling a guy from the Isle of Man 'a Manx Midget.' Thea Spiteri had gotten the message from David Decelis. She said she would call.

# CHAPTER 47

The call from Thea Spiteri to Sarah Said came on the Friday evening. 'Sarah, set up the meeting with David. This Monday, ten a.m., my office. Make sure the deputy commissioner is informed, and the commissioner, of course. You can attend, Sarah. I'm sure David would like that. Oh, and Sarah, let everyone know that that is me returning to work, as of Monday. I want all active case files on my desk by midday.'

Everyone was impressed by Thea Spiteri's demeanor when she strode into work at 9.50 a.m. on the following Monday. She was wearing an obviously new suit, her hair had been cut considerably shorter, she had make-up on, and she smiled to everyone around. 'Can I just have everyone's attention for a moment? As you all know, I'm returning to work today after a traumatic time in my life. But life goes on. I intend to continue doing my job here to the best of my ability unless I am told otherwise. I don't want any sullen faces or knowing looks. I just want crimes solved. Thank you all.'

Spiteri then walked into her office, closing the door behind her.

'Impressive, Thea' said the deputy commissioner. 'But you don't have…'

'Yes, I do. That is the point. Detective work is what I do, so, yes, I do have to. David, how are you feeling?'

'I'm fine.'

'Are you ready?'

'Yes.'

'Go then. Let's start with your name.'

'Okay, my name is David…'

'Stop!' It was Spiteri. 'No it's not. I called the number on your card. It's a pet store in Melbourne. They'd never heard of you. So, who are you, exactly?'

'My name is… Jason Attard.'

Everyone in Spiteri's office looked at each other. 'Do you mean you were related to him?' Spiteri finally asked.

'No, I am him, but I was also known as Kelp Boy, The Dog Boy or, sometimes, just You.'

'But…'said Galea.

'Let me tell you the whole story, and then you'll understand. I am Jason Attard. I was sexually abused and then murdered by Francesco Marandon. He buried me with the help of another boy in a shallow grave out near Tal Ibrag. Don't ask me how or why; it must have been an old pipe or rabbit hole, maybe just an air pocket in the mud, whatever… but there was air getting into the grave. I survived.'

'You were an orphan at Marandon's orphanage. You were the other missing child, the one that was never found,' said Spiteri.

Decelis laughed. 'The other missing child! You mean one of the many missing children?'

'Dear God,' said the commissioner.

'God had nothing to do with that place, Commissioner. I can assure you of that. I lay there till morning in my own grave; I was too scared to move.'

'What age were you?' asked Spiteri.

'Five or six. I'm not sure. Anyway, I survived. I lived by stealing food, fruit from orchards, eggs from farms, drinking water from animal troughs. One night, I was so tired and had a fever that I overslept in a barn. The next morning, John Decelis, and his wife Elisa took me in. They saved my life. They changed my view of adults. They showed me the meaning of kindness, of love. They had no children of their own. They were desperate for a family and to start a new life, like many Maltese, in Australia. They got me papers somehow, and we immigrated to Australia. The Decelises gave me a good and happy life, but I never forgot Marandon. Both my parents passed away last year. I knew it was time to come back.'

'Why, what did you hope to do?'

'I wasn't sure. First of all, I wanted to see if Marandon was still alive. Then, I read in the papers here that one of the investigating officers was one Jason Attard. Then I knew. I followed them, watched them meeting up. I still didn't know what to do. I followed Marandon to the cliffs that day, saw Matt throwing the bastard off...'

'What?' interrupted Spiteri.

'Eh, well, you know what I mean.'

'No, I don't. Are you saying that Matt Healy threw Francesco Marandon off the cliff? He didn't commit suicide?'

'Well, it all happened very quickly, I...'

'No, David, tell me the truth. I need to know. Did Matt Healy lie to me?'

'I'm not sure I'd use the word *lie*.'

'Don't you? I would.'

A few moments of silence passed before Spiteri continued, 'And Attard... our Attard.'

'I don't know. I heard that Matt had rumbled him. I was sure he'd go to prison. When he didn't and I found out he was in Canada, I decided to leave things be, go home.'

Spiteri's office was deathly quiet for several minutes. Sarah Said was silently crying. The commissioner and deputy commissioner looked stunned. David Decelis was fidgeting with his bandages. Thea Spiteri spoke to no one in particular. 'So who was our Jason Attard?'

'Do we want to know?' asked the deputy commissioner.

'I think I know. Not his name, but who he was,' said David Decelis.

'Who?'

'I think he would have been the boy that helped Marandon bury me. He was like a disciple of his from the start; a cruel little bastard, even then.'

'All the papers from the orphanage were taken away when it closed. We'll never get access. We'll never know who he was.'

'No need for papers. I know who he was.'

Everyone in the room stared at Commissioner Debono. 'His name is, was, Pietro... Pietro Debono. He was my son. I handed him over to an orphanage when he was born. His mother had died in childbirth, I was married to someone else, I couldn't cope... I gave him away. Like a child discards an old toy. Once I started making my way in the *Pulizija*, Marandon approached me. He told me Pietro was damaged, but that he would protect him if I protected both of them. What could I do? I was trapped, I agreed. This is the outcome.'

# EPILOGUE

Commissioner Debono was to be allowed to retire quietly. Neither the Maltese government nor the *Pulizija* wanted the publicity and scandal. He was to hand over to Deputy Commissioner Galea immediately and go on gardening leave by the end of that week. But, soon-to-be MMP Debono had some things to deal with before he went.

'Commissioner, I have Nicola Tizian on the line for you.'

'Fine, put him through. Nicky, how are you?'

'Chris, I'm sorry to hear about your son. What about you? Will you be safe?'

'Funny, I was just mulling that over when you rang.'

'If there is anything I can do, let me know. Oh, by the way, the planning consent came through; thanks for that. Did you manage to take your consultancy fee off Borg's money or did that sniffling little cunt in planning snaffle the lot?'

'Yes, I took the usual. Is that okay?'

'Sure.'

'What about Borg?'

'Someone is visiting him tonight. He'd obviously spoken to Arrigo.'

'Thanks Nicky. See you soon. Bye.'

***

When Tan, the Philipino maid employed by the Borgs, entered the bedroom at 8.00 a.m. as usual with tea and fruit, she thought it was strange that the curtains were pulled closed. She placed her tray on Mrs Borg's vanity unit stool and pulled open the curtains. Then she screamed.

Spiteri and Said looked down at the bloody mass that had once been two human beings. Mrs Borg was still recognizable, as she had been lucky enough to only receive a bullet to the head. Noel Borg's face looked more like a watermelon that had been crushed under a car's wheels. Closer examination showed that Borg's testicles and penis had been cut off. His tongue had been cut out, and the penis and testicles rammed in. The *Pulizija* never found the tongue. There were no prints or DNA. 'It's like a spirit was in the room,' said Spiteri.

***

It was 3.00 p.m. on the tenth of October 2014, and Thea Spiteri looked just as a bride should do on her wedding day. The hot Maltese summer had yielded to a cooler autumn. The Grigal winds were beginning to taper off, the flaps of the marquee outside Spiteri's farm house seeming to move in unison with the birdsong. Jim Frame was sitting in the front row, looking extremely imposing in his full plaid outfit. 'None of that poncy velvet and cravats for me.'

Some in Spiteri's family circle had hoped for a touch of *il-gilwa* in the ceremony, but Spiteri had decided to draw the line at agreeing to some *Ghana*—folk—music to accompany her walk from the house to the marquee, where the ceremony was taking place. She had even laid on a surprise for Matt; an *iz-zaqq* player was going to play traditional Maltese bagpipes as they left the reception for their honeymoon.

Spiteri turned away from a last minute check in the mirror. She looked over at Sarah Said, who just smiled, nodded, and wiped a tear from her eye. Some Ghana started to play and Thea Spiteri walked over to the start of the red carpet that ran down the middle of the marquee. She looked straight ahead. *Concentrate, Thea.* Matt Healy was standing with his back to her, apparently in deep conversation with the priest. Spiteri thanked her God for this day and walked down to the front, passing through smiling groups of guests. She drew level with Matt, looked over to her left to see the face of the man she adored. Matt and the priest seemed to not have noticed her arrival at first, but then they too looked over. There was no sign of adoration on the faces of Francesco Marandon and Jason Attard.

Spiteri screamed and sat up on her bed. Her hair was wet with perspiration, her shoulders shaking, her eyes darting around the room. It took a few seconds for Spiteri's mind to clear. *And so it continues.*

THE END

# ABOUT THE AUTHOR

Paul Lee was privately educated in Glasgow…...but lived. The Maltese Orphans is his second novel, and is set on the Maltese Islands, where he now lives.

His first novel, "Defending Joe" entered the Amazon Top 50 Crime List 3 months after publication; and has had success in Europe, Canada and Australia.

Follow Paul on: www.paulvincentlee.com

Which also contains Paul's Blog: "It's Murder in Malta"

And on: Twitter @LeeAuthor and Paul's FB page – Paul Vincent Lee

Paul can also be contacted by e mail at:

author@paulvincentlee.com

where you can also join his e mailing list.

For Personal Appearance Requests: please contact:

personalappearance@paulvincentlee.com

## If you liked The Maltese Orphans:

Hi, trying to earn a living as an independent writer is tough.....believe me, I know! The reason I've gotten this far is simple.....it's YOU....the reader. If you enjoyed **"The Maltese Orphans"**, please take a few seconds to put a Review on: amazon.co.uk or on your own local, Amazon site.

A couple of lines can be all it takes to make a big difference.

Thank you.

Paul.

*Keep in touch:*

Contact me anytime! By email: author@paulvincentlee.com or on Twitter @LeeAuthor or through my Website: paulvincentlee.com

You can also sign up on my Website if you would like to be emailed about future releases, including the next in The Thea Spiteri Series, due out in 2015.

Paul Vincent Lee is also the author of the Amazon Top 50 Crime Listings novel: "Defending Joe": still available on Kindle.

Lightning Source UK Ltd.
Milton Keynes UK
UKOW06f2226310716

279570UK00006B/40/P

9 780957 239920